Note for Librarians: A cataloguing record for this book is available from Library and Archives Canada at www.collectionscanada.ca/amicus/index-e.html
ISBN 1-4251-1439-3

Printed in Victoria, BC, Canada. Printed on paper with minimum 30% recycled fibre.
Trafford's print shop runs on "green energy" from solar, wind and other environmentally-friendly power sources.

TRAFFORD
PUBLISHING™
Offices in Canada, USA, Ireland and UK

Book sales for North America and international:
Trafford Publishing, 6E–2333 Government St.,
Victoria, BC V8T 4P4 CANADA
phone 250 383 6864 (toll-free 1 888 232 4444)
fax 250 383 6804; email to orders@trafford.com
Book sales in Europe:
Trafford Publishing (UK) Limited, 9 Park End Street, 2nd Floor
Oxford, UK OX1 1HH UNITED KINGDOM
phone +44 (0)1865 722 113 (local rate 0845 230 9601)
facsimile +44 (0)1865 722 868; info.uk@trafford.com
Order online at:
trafford.com/06-3198

10 9 8 7 6 5 4 3 2

Poetry is the highest form of writing —

VETO

Ed Griffin

The Age of Nations is past.
The task before us now,
if we would not perish,
is to build the earth.

Teilard de Chardin

To Carol
Johnson
a poet

Ed Griffin

October 2007

Chapter 1

Appointment Schedule for the Secretary-General
Monday, September 25

10:30 AM –Abdullah Roble Dirie, Somali Ambassador to
    the United Nations,
11:00 AM– Muhammad Faisal Djalil, Minister of Foreign
    Affairs, Indonesia
12:30 PM – Luncheon, The National Council on U.S.-Arab
    Relations
2:30 PM – Thomas E. Brennan, U.S.A. Ambassador to the
    UN

Pilar Marti stood to greet her first appointment on her first day
as Secretary-General of the UN. She took a deep breath and reminded
herself that the newly appointed Somali Ambassador to the UN was
a softball start.

The man approached her desk with a tentative step. She studied
his inexpensive Arab dress, his slight frame and his gray hair.
Abdullah Roble Dirie. The background sheet gave his age as forty-
five, already past the life expectancy of a man in Somalia.

"I'm very pleased, Your Excellency," he said, extending his hand.

She smiled and shook his hand. "Madame Secretary," she
corrected softly and pointed to a chair.

"I'm very sorry, Madame." He sat down and pulled papers,
folders and envelopes from his briefcase, some of which slid to the
floor.

While he retrieved his things, she sat down and waited for the small talk to begin. All her life she'd paid attention to casual words and passing conversations. They revealed things about the speaker, things she could use. It didn't matter if Abdullah only represented poverty-stricken Somalia. Someday she might need his vote.

Abdullah sat up straight and stared at her. "Madame, we need water."

Then – nothing more. No small talk, no request for sanctions against Ethiopia, no UN resolution to condemn Ethiopia's damming of the Jubba and Shabelle rivers, no grandiose desalinization projects, no conservation experts and no peace-keepers to control thirst-maddened crowds.

Just water.

She studied him for a moment. Stark, simple, direct – like his sparse country. The man had no diplomatic background. He owned a teashop in Mogadishu until the shaky national government convinced him to represent the country at the UN.

He shifted on the edge of his chair. A more seasoned diplomat would have listed Arab and African states who supported his request for water and would have teased her with tales of potential oil riches deep in the Somali earth, untapped because of the civil strife.

"Yes, I understand," she said. "Water." She congratulated herself silently – she had listened, not talked; she had affirmed the need, not promised the solution. But something was wrong. This new job demanded more.

"I've brought you some pictures, Madame." He took a brown envelope from his lap and spread a half dozen photos on her desk.

My goodness, she thought, *he has no idea how things are done.* She had already seen the drought on TV – a record, even for a sun-baked country like Somalia. A half million people had died. But she could not let the UN get involved in Somalia again after the disaster in 1993, when the UN's mission ended in a bloody shoot-out between American Rangers and Somali warlord, Aidid.

As she stood to look at the pictures, she caught sight of her navy blue suit in the framed mirror on her wall. "Very business chic," the sales woman had told her on Saturday. Yes, yes, business chic, but would it help reverse the media jabber that a woman running the UN meant the organization had bottomed out on the power scale?

Or as a Chicago tabloid put it, "The UN has gone from a sexy, six-foot senior to a detached, five-foot-six, fifty-two year old queen bee."

If only the gods had given her the looks of her romantic Cuban exile father rather than those of her dour English-Canadian mother. But it was not to be.

She looked at the photographs: a man kneeling on the scorched earth, his eyes heavenward, his hand on a shriveled sorghum plant, a dead goat behind him; a mother sitting under a withered eucalyptus tree, her two children in her lap, their lips parched and swollen. The woman had placed her body against the assailant sun and shadows covered the faces of the children, emphasizing their lifeless appearance.

Abdullah had placed this picture by itself in such a way that the woman's eyes stared right at Pilar, big sad eyes, on the verge of despair. More pictures – emaciated children, dead animals and shriveled banana trees, but still the woman under the eucalyptus tree stared at Pilar. "Water. Please, water," the woman seemed to cry.

Pilar shook her head to break the fixation and stepped back around the desk to her seat. She had to keep her distance. Over her twenty-four years in the UN, she had learned to analyze problems dispassionately. The world was full of sad stories and if a person paid attention to every one of them, madness would result. Besides, she had to weigh the political implications of everything she did – give water to Somalia and Sudan would demand the same. And the supplier country – whose turn was it?

But still that photo on her desk – even upside-down the woman's eyes found her. She turned slightly to get the woman's image out of her field of vision. No need to scold herself for this action, she reassured herself. A person had to pay attention to the big picture. And her way had proven successful. Two weeks previous, after a record struggle between the Americans, the Chinese and the Russians, she had been chosen as Secretary-General.

"I'm sorry, Abdullah, there's not much the UN can do. Any action would be vetoed by the Americans. That picture of an American pilot's dead body being dragged through the streets of Mogadishu – well, they won't forget that."

"We just need water." The man was pleading with her. How interesting. Before the meeting she feared that a Muslim man would walk in, see a woman as Secretary General, and walk out.

"Have you tried the NGOs?"

"The what?"

This poor man had no background at all. "The Non-Governmental Organizations. Things like Oxfam, Doctors Without Borders, the Red Cross and the Red Crescent."

"Yes. They are doing what they can. Can you come to Somalia, Madame, and call the world's attention to this problem? We have a saying, *The small camel follows the big camel's steps.* Others will follow your example."

The simplicity of the man touched her, but she had a lot to do this morning. She had to pick her way through a political mine field and choose her cabinet. Already she had a cobra as her second-in-command. The Americans and the Chinese gave the Deputy Secretary-General post to her main opponent. The Americans won the Secretary-General post so the Chinese secured the deputy's position. According to tradition, the Americans and the Chinese followed UN custom and called on a citizen of a client state, Pilar as a Canadian and Quan Mai Ngo as a Vietnamese. Even thinking of the man caused her stomach to knot.

She stood to indicate the interview was over. "Thank you for coming, Ambassador. I will visit your country as soon as I can."

"You must come soon, Madam."

Must? Getting ready for her afternoon meeting with the new American ambassador – that was *must* enough for today. Working successfully with him was a requisite for a second term.

Finding water for Somalia? The NGOs could take care of that.

"I'll call CARE for you," she said and gently put her right hand on his elbow, guiding him to the door. She kept her left hand by her side to hide her little finger, the top cut off on her father's table saw forty-two years ago – a lesson learned to follow the rules.

Abdullah stopped and faced her. "No, please, you come, Madame. We need leadership at the UN."

She kept light pressure on his arm, moving him toward the door. It wasn't leadership the UN needed, but money. "Thank you for coming," she said as he left.

She stepped toward her desk but stopped as she saw the framed map she had hung on the wall the day before. "Oh, Mom," she said softly. Her mother heard of her daughter's appointment as Secretary-General of the United Nations on a Thursday. On Friday she was killed in a head-on collision on British Columbia's Sea-to-Sky highway.

That was a week ago.

Pilar touched the glass cover of the map. The coast of British Columbia with her mother's notes inked in – archeological sites. How strange for her to come back from the funeral with only this memento. It was a map from her mother's youth when her mother was passionately interested in theories of first nation migration from Asia. It wasn't even her mother's life work. The sociology department offered her scholarships and later a teaching position and she let her interest in archeology die.

Pilar traced her finger down the coast, remembering how her mother explained that the oceans were lower then. Pilar was only five at the time, but because of her mother's enthusiasm the ancient peoples lived and marched down the coast in her mind. It was the best of her mother.

Her finger stopped at the Queen Charlotte Islands where her mother had made several notes. Yes, this map belonged here, in this office. The map recorded the heroic journey of the first settlers to North America, while the office of the Secretary-General, her office, worked to keep the whole human race moving forward on its journey through space and time.

Pilar lifted her finger from the map. She shivered. She knew why she had picked this map – this was her passionate mother, not the prim, bureaucratic sociology professor. And – the knot in her stomach tightened – had she hung it on her wall for a memento or for a message to herself?

She returned to her desk, wiped her eyes and reached for her water bottle. The coldness of the water shocked her tongue. Reality. Back to work. As she took another sip, her eye caught the picture of the Somali woman under the eucalyptus tree. That desperate, begging stare.

"Here," she said, holding out her water bottle. That's all the woman wanted – water. Why couldn't she get her out of her mind? She had reached the pinnacle of her career, the Secretary-General of the UN, yet her mind focused on this ordinary Somali woman.

She only had a few minutes before the foreign minister came in and she had to study the background paper. Oil. That's what he wanted to talk about. And after him, the Saudis wanted to talk to her at the luncheon – about oil.

The Somali woman wanted water but Pilar's day was centered on oil.

* * *

Promptly at 2:30 Thomas E. Brennan, newly appointed American ambassador to the UN, swung open her door until it hit the doorstop with a thud. "Howdy, little lady. Tom Brennan here."

He strode toward her, not with the tight steps of a diplomat, but with the easy lope of a construction boss on an oilrig, which she knew to be his early background.

She took his extended hand, but then glanced more closely at his face. His mean, narrow eyes belied his friendly cowboy manner. They were the eyes of a man that could hit a dog and drive on. She suppressed a sudden gasp for air, shook his hand quickly and motioned toward her new leather office chairs which she had arranged around a teak coffee table. Maybe she was just nervous, she cautioned herself, and he might be, too. He was new on the job as well.

Brennan stopped at her desk and stared at the pictures, picking up the one of the woman under the tree. "Africa?" he asked.

"Yes. Somalia."

"Got to stay away from that place," he said and dropped the picture on her desk. He sauntered over to a leather chair and sat his big body down, twacking the leather as he did so. "Nice chair, little lady."

"Madame Secretary, that's the correct title. Nice of you to come by, Ambassador."

"Call me Tom."

"Can I pour you some coffee?"

"Sure. Cream and sugar."

She poured coffee from her silver decanter, debating whether she'd been firm enough about her title. Best to let it slide for the moment.

"Got a paper here for you. A name for your Minister of the Environment. The United States wants this man. It's a sensitive position. Oil, you know."

He pulled the paper from his suit coat and offered it to her, but she had his cup and saucer in her right hand. She had to take the paper with her left hand.

"What happened to your finger, little lady?"

"Madame Secretary."

"Your finger? Don't look to be nothin' dangerous around this UN building." He spread his left arm toward the floors below. "Every time I come in here, seems like everybody's asleep."

In all her twenty-four years at the UN, no one had ever commented on her missing finger.

She sat down opposite him. "I'll certainly consider your candidate, Mr. Ambassador."

"Consider him? This is the man we want."

Silence, her best response. She knew he was learning on the job. The rumor was that he wanted to step up to Secretary of State when the incumbent Secretary retired next year. She assumed the White House had put him at the UN to see how well he controlled events, a sort of training ground for international diplomacy.

She wondered if he knew how far he was from the center of power in America.

"I mean, you understand the United States backed your candidacy for a *reason*."

There it was. She was bought and paid for. Resist, and no second term. Damn him.

He gestured over to her desk. "What's with the Somali pictures?"

What should she tell him? "The ambassador must have forgotten them," or "He wants me to go there." A diplomatic lie or the truth?

Throughout her career she had worked with people like Brennan. The UN was full of them – political hacks appointed by their governments. Her strategy had been to stay with them and maneuver them into a position where they lived up to their job. When she was in the finance department, her assistant, new to the western world, spent his time touring New York. She praised his accounting skills, she got her colleagues to compliment him and she brought in tourists from his country to applaud his 'financial wizardry.'

The man got back to his ledgers.

So with Brennan.

"The ambassador was in this morning." She sipped her coffee. "He asked me to go there and call attention to the drought and famine. Let me show you those pictures, Tom." She stood to go to her desk. "It's a terrible drought."

"But you're not going?"

"What do *you* think about the situation, Tom? You're the key at the UN, the American ambassador."

He hesitated for a moment and she took a step toward the desk.

"Wait, now. I know it's a serious situation, but you shouldn't go."

"Why, Tom?" What *was* his reason? She hadn't even considered going, but now…

"Ah, now, it would just be a mistake." He dumped another spoon of sugar into his coffee and muttered, "A mistake."

She started back toward him with the pictures.

He held up his hand. "Whoa, there. I know there are lots of people suffering and women get all bothered and sympathetic about situations like that, but Congress has a foreign aid bill in front of them to help and at the right time, they'll pass it."

"Oh?" She raised her eyebrows. "And when is the right time?"

"I've got a special interest in Somalia. Done some studying about it. Our State Department is just as worried about the situation as you are. People dying, starving, no water – it's a perfect setup for the Islamic crazies."

"Why not work through the UN?"

"All due respect now, but the UN doesn't have a very good record at driving out the bad guys. You guys just give 'em water and walk away. The US Government's got a plan."

Just as the commentators always said, the US used the UN when it wanted to and ignored it at other times. The UN was just one tool among many.

Brennan glanced at his watch. "Gotta run, little lady. Sure was nice talking to you." He clinked his coffee cup on the table and stood up.

She rose and stepped in front of him, blocking his way out. "Mr. Ambassador, I think we need to clarify one thing. My name is not *Little Lady*. From now on, I insist that you call me *Madame Secretary*."

She saw anger flit across his eyes, but then he apologized. "Shucks, I'm sorry, Madame. You know, it's just down home Texas style. My wife tells me the same thing. It was only two weeks ago that the Senate confirmed me, so I'm learning on the job just like you. We all try to do what our predecessors did. Mine looked after US interests, your predecessors were smooth diplomats. Sure, they had to take a stand against us now and then, but most things came out our way. All we have to do is replay the past."

"Thank you, Sir." Maybe things would work out. But replaying the past was a poor strategy for the future.

He took a few steps toward the door. "I'm sure you've heard how we stood up for you in the Security Council. You've got some powerful enemies out there."

"I appreciate your support."

"My staff has me studying the past, and, you know, those Secretary-Generals that try to be leaders and change things, well, they don't do well. But if the Secretary-General gets along with our office, well, it's like a beautiful sunset on the range. I'm sure you get my meaning."

"Yes, Mr. Ambassador, as long you remember that when the sun is setting in Texas, it's coming up on another hot, dry day in Somalia."

He motioned to tip a hat that wasn't there and said as he left, "It's been a pleasure, Madame."

That last *Madame* reassured her. Maybe it would work. But his comments about going along with the American office reminded her that the old saying was still true: the big powers wanted her and her predecessors to be more *Secretary* than *General*. No leaders allowed.

She returned to her desk and checked her schedule. Her head throbbed with the tension of her meeting with Brennan. No more appointments, but with the UN in session, she should attend committee meetings. Still. . . She dialed her new chief of security, Alex Richardson. "Can you come in, Alex?"

A minute later he entered, a man with deep ebony skin and gray sideburns. When she hired him, she valued his honest, intelligent eyes as much as his extensive background as a Cleveland policeman and detective.

"Alex, I'm sorry. Do we have chauffeur service at this time?" Budget cuts had limited her service and she had forgotten the cut-off time.

"For another hour," he said.

"I'll be going home."

"Yes, Madame?"

"The picture?"

"Yes, Madame?"

"The picture?"

"I'll get the chauffeur."

Alex picked up the picture. "Oh. This poor woman."

She nodded. "Somalia."

He stared at the picture for a long moment and then looked up at her. What were his eyes saying?

"Alex?" she asked after a pause.

He looked down at the picture again. "I don't know, Madame. When I was a beat cop in Cleveland, I had a real bad area. Rats jumping in the cribs of babies, drugs, shootings, muggings. I convinced the councilman from the area to spend a few days sitting on a folding chair on the worst corner. Things got better from then on, not paradise, but better."

She smiled. An honest, direct man.

"I'll get the chauffeur now, Madame."

Alex left. She walked over to the window and stared at New York, thirty-eight floors below. What was this job she had striven sohard to get? Was she just a functionary, a person who shook hands and made harmless statements? Or was she a woman of power who could help another woman get some water?

Chapter 2

Appointment Schedule for the Secretary-General
Tuesday, September 26

10:00 AM – Meeting of the Security Council
12:30 PM – Luncheon with the International Oceanoographic
            Commission
2:00 PM – Meeting of the Security Council

Pilar listened to her aides as the elevator descended. "Terrorists in the Middle East ...," The Israelis have moved into...", "Argentina is almost bankrupt. It's the worst..." She needed this information for the upcoming Security Council meeting, but yesterday's problem of the woman without water still troubled her.

When she got off the elevator, she walked to the antechamber of the Security Council and checked for the ladies' room. There was one restroom only, clearly marked with the universal male symbol. An aide led her to a ladies' room a little distance away.

As she stood in front of the mirror in the washroom, she reflected on the lack of a facility for women near the Security Council. *What a symbol of my alien status*, she thought. She fussed with her hair a moment and then studied herself. *Step forward with confidence. First woman. In control. Knowledgeable. Diplomat. On top of all issues.* Yes, that's who she was. She took a deep breath, opened the restroom door and walked back to the antechamber, enjoying the sound of her heels clacking on the floor.

In the antechamber she spotted Brennan standing by the door to the Council. The man looked like a diplomat, a UN Ambassador, even a Secretary of State – neatly-trimmed gray temples and an Armani suit with its carefully gauged shoulders, a different suit than yesterday.

"Madame, I've been waiting for you."

"Mr. Ambassador?" She noticed two pins in his lapel: the usual US flag and a small oil well pin. She wondered why he would emphasize his oil connections with the current administration, where the president was a lawyer. Brennan would have fit better in one of the Bush White Houses.

"I just wanted to apologize. I think we got off on the wrong foot."

Maybe she'd misjudged him. "I appreciate that, Mr. Ambassador."

He took her hand. "Tom. Please call me *Tom*."

His voice resonated with sincerity, but those eyes – they scrutinized her with a shifty, advantage-seeking look.

She smiled. "Okay, *Tom*. And mine is *Pilar*."

He let go of her hand. "I was thinkin' about how you were worried about Somalia and shucks… I mean, that's wonderful that our top official pays attention to things like that. That's your job. Why don't you bring it up today?"

Was it a trap? She didn't have a concrete plan to submit.

"We've got a full agenda, Tom."

"Yes, I noticed. The India-Pakistan thing is coming up." His eyes widened and his face beamed with a self-satisfied grin.

The negotiations between India and Pakistan? Why was he so excited? Oh, yes. UN staff had researched the formula for a peace committee about Kashmir and they had decided to feed the formula to him so he could present it to the two leaders. That way it would have the appearance of coming from the US.

The staff had done such a good job, he thought the ideas were his own.

He leaned toward her and lowered his voice. "Wouldn't hurt if the right people heard about this. You know, the Kashmir thing." He wore some sort of expensive cologne that smelled as sweet as his tone.

Did he think she was a phone call away from the US president? She had no illusions about what the US government thought of the UN. Secretary-General and Ambassador to the UN were minor functionaries in Washington's view of the world.

"They'll hear what they want to hear, Tom."

"Yes. And I didn't mean to push so hard on that name I gave you yesterday, the Minister for the Environment."

Was this new Tom Brennan substance or style? Maybe a little probe would tell her.

"Back to Somalia, Tom. I just don't have enough information yet to present a plan to the Council. That's why I'm considering a quick trip there."

The smile left his face. "Now, Little...Madame Secretary, that would be a mistake. It's hardly even a country. The government doesn't control the north; it doesn't even control the capital city. Warlords fight over territory. They send armed men out in jeeps. They call them *technicals*. You won't be safe there."

So it was style, not substance. His staff had probably given him some advice about using honey words with female diplomats.

She'd show them.

An aide tapped her on the shoulder. "It's time for the Council, Madame Secretary."

"I'll be right there," she answered, then turned back to Brennan. "I appreciate your concern, Tom, but there's no need to worry. I'll be perfectly safe. My new bodyguard is an ex-Cleveland police detective, Alex Richardson. He's up on the Somali situation and whom to trust."

Actually she'd never discussed going to Somalia with Alex, but he struck her as a musician who could drum the local music ten minutes after he landed in a place.

"Ah, well now, Pilar.." a warning tone replaced the diplomatic resonance, "...Somalia is a *hands-off* country right now."

"Hands-off?" She almost laughed out loud. *Hands-off* like a cookie jar?

"That dead soldier being dragged through the streets. You know, *Black Hawk Down.*"

What was going on? What was the real reason for his opposition? Did he get his foreign policy from a Hollywood movie like *Black Hawk Down*? She assumed he was smarter than that.

She took a small step toward him and lowered her voice. "I just want to call attention to the problems, Tom – the drought, a half million deaths. The Secretary-General *should* visit such a place."

"Of course I agree with you, Pilar, but, you know, the UN is in session and my government is very concerned with the budget. You have to ride herd on it."

The picture of the UN as a herd and herself as a cowgirl flashed through her mind. Very amusing. "I'm talking about a quick weekend trip, Tom."

A quick visit to Somalia was an exaggeration. She knew she couldn't get in and out of the country quickly. Nothing worked there. Airports were always being taken over and roads were blocked by one tribe after another.

Tight jaw-clenching replaced the diplomatic smile. "Like I said, it's *hands-off.*"

The aide came by again. "It's time, Madame."

"We better get in there," Brennan said. He straightened his tie.

"Wait, Tom. Explain it to me. Why is the American government against a simple humanitarian visit?"

His brow furrowed. "The Chinese are trying to move their people into power here at the UN."

"I'm sorry, Tom. I don't understand the connection with Somalia."

"We – you and I – have to stay united."

He moved to enter the Council chamber. "I was on a talk show last week with an old friend of yours, Stuart Taylor."

She filed in with him. *Okay, change the subject,* she thought. *But why the hands-off?* "Yes, Stuart. Haven't seen him in a long time."

"We were both asked about your appointment. That was the *only* thing we agreed on."

She laughed. They approached his seat. "Nice talking with you, Tom."

"Yes. You know, I'm trying – good relations and all that. Not the Boutros-Boutros Ghali thing."

She left his seat, paced to her own chair, yanked it out and sat down. Damn him. The hammer again. Despite fourteen votes for Secretary Ghali in the Security Council, Bill Clinton and the Americans cast a solitary veto against his second term, similar to what the Soviets did to the first Secretary-General, Trygve Lie, in 1951.

* * *

Following the morning and afternoon sessions of the Security Council, Pilar stood at her office window. The September sun still rode above the city in the west and far below her most of the tourists had left the UN garden. A walk would restore her drained energy, but her deputy, Quan Mai Ngo, the assistant Secretary-General, had asked to see her.

She checked her watch. 4:50 PM, a few minutes to go before he arrived. Both sessions of the Security Council had gone well. By following the careful protocol of her very careful predecessor, she smoothed conflicts and moved issues to resolution. Tom Brennan received kudos for his work in Kashmir and beamed at the praise.

But soon Mr. Quan. She'd been avoiding him. Brennan in the morning, Quan in the afternoon – a formula for a headache.

She slogged back to her desk where the poor Somali woman with the dying children still haunted her. She picked up the picture and put it under some papers to be filed, but then she took it out again and leaned it against her *In* basket.

Should she go? She knew she was in *crisis response* mode as opposed to *rational management*. "Tsk," she breathed out. "Just like a politician."

She checked her schedule for the weekend:

Friday, September 29 – three appointments
Saturday, September 30 – personal day

Sunday, October 1– call Mom.

Oh, dear God. Long ago she had written that note to call her mother. Sunday was the anniversary of her dad's death and now her mother was gone.

She sat back and closed her eyes. October 1. Her mother used to cut a single red rose and put it in a vase on the mantle beneath the big picture of her father with *his* mother and father, his brothers and sisters and his extended Cuban-American family. Pilar loved that picture – her grandfather who told her stories of a beautiful island in the Caribbean, her grandmother who played Cuban rumba music on her tape deck, her wild, playful cousins and, most of all, her father with his quiet, loving eyes.

In her mind she pictured her mother wearing a fashionable light blue pantsuit, standing by the mantle. "Should I go to Somalia, Mom?"

Pilar heard the answer in her mind, the same answer her mother always gave her: "Stick with the institution, Pilar. Play it safe." That was the family motto. In her teen years, she wanted to attend an experimental, theme-based high school. Her mother told her that colleges were impressed with grades, not esoteric learning.

Her secretary buzzed. "Mr. Quan is here."

"Show him in, please."

Quan was a short man, an inch or two shorter than her 5'6". He insisted on his first name being used as a last name. "Ngo is too hard to say for Westerners," he was fond of saying, "and Quan means soldier in Vietnamese."

Even though he had been in the UN his entire career just as she had been, their paths had never crossed – until recently. It was Asia's turn to have a Secretary-General, but the Americans had promised expensive programs to win votes for their choice – her.

Three weeks ago a staff person in the US delegate's office called her. The gist of his call was that if she wanted the job of Secretary-General, she had to provide them with reasons why Quan shouldn't get the position. "If you want the job, you'll do the work," he said.

Pilar did find the stories the US delegation wanted: when Quan managed the UN's Development Program there were several failures, expensive failures. What she didn't mention was that most Development officers had program disasters, some more spectacular than Quan's. Another charge was that he had filled the Development office with several Vietnamese, some of them named Ngo, the same as his last name. What she didn't say was that thousands of Vietnamese shared this last name and she herself had filled the Human Resources Office with a lot of hard-nosed, budget-conscious North Americans.

Of course, Quan returned the favor and spread stories about her – how she ruthlessly slashed programs that weren't self-sustaining and how she supplanted her boss in the budget department when he had a nervous breakdown. The tabloids quoted a high-ranking UN official as saying, "Pilar Marti is a hard-hearted, bureaucratic bean-counter."

But this afternoon Quan was all smiles. "Good afternoon, Madame."

"Mr. Quan. Come in. Sit down." She pointed to her new office chairs, arranged around the coffee table. He stopped at her desk and stared at the picture of the woman. "Somalia?" he asked.

"Yes. Have you seen that picture before?"

"No, but I've read about the situation. Tragic." He picked up the picture and padded over to a leather chair. As he passed her, she picked up the scent of a man's cologne. She was not an expert on scents for men, but she had noticed at the UN that men wore more fragrances than women. *Quan is not much of a soldier*, she thought.

"Tragic," Quan repeated, pointing to the picture in his hand, "the UN needs to take action here. Do you have a plan?"

She gave him a hard look. Somalia was a quagmire and he was maneuvering to have her walk into it. Nothing doing.

She sat down opposite him. "I want to talk to you about the Middle East, Mr. Quan. Would you like some coffee?" she asked, picking up the silver decanter on the coffee table.

"Do you have tea?" he asked.

"Certainly." She returned to her desk and buzzed her secretary, picking up a folder on her way back.

She sat down opposite him again. He was in his early fifties as she was and he wore that painted-on, diplomatic smile common to most of her colleagues. God, how she hoped she didn't have that smile.

He turned the picture toward her and held it up. "You can't let this continue on your watch, Madame."

She opened the folder in her hand. "Only someone with long diplomatic experience can handle the conflicts between Israel and her neighbors, Mr. Quan."

"Yes, of course, but this Somali situation is urgent."

"Yes, it is, and I'm looking into it." He put the picture down on the coffee table. Again, the woman's eyes stared right at her. She looked away and studied her folder.

Her secretary entered with a pot of tea for Quan. She thanked the young man, poured the tea and, still standing, handed a paper from her folder to Quan in a manner calculated to indicate a superior giving an assignment to her employee. "I've prepared a press release appointing you to a special effort to bring peace to the Middle East. Here's a copy." It was a bold move, assigning him to an almost impossible task, getting him out of the way in the process.

He responded in whiny tone. "I came in here to discuss our administration."

"Our administration?"

"That's how China wants me to think about it."

"Let me assure you, it's not *our* administration. Now back to the Middle East, I...."

"What about Somalia?" He gave her one of those diplomatic, phony smiles. "I admire your courage, Madame. We – the UN – failed badly there in the nineties. It would be a great gesture for you to go there, to restore the country's belief in the UN. I can look after things for you while you're away."

I'll bet. "The Middle East, Mr. Quan. I want you to focus on that. As to your other responsibilities..." Damn. She had let her voice rise. It came out as a question. How very Canadian. It was because she had been in Vancouver last week for her mother's funeral.

"I'm prepared to manage the Secretariat, Madame, so you can concentrate on world affairs. That's what my job description calls for."

That *was* the job description of the deputy, but Quan would use the office to subvert her. The office of the Secretariat was where power was. Better to put him on those other high-sounding, but meaningless, parts of the job description.

"I want you to provide leadership in the economic and social sphere, and to strengthen the UN as a center for development policy."

"Of course, of course. And managing the office?"

"I'll take care of that," she said firmly.

"The Chinese were expecting something different."

The Chinese could think what they wanted. She did not intend to relinquish control of her own office.

She stood. "I think that's all, Mr. Quan. Thank you for coming. It will be a pleasure working with you. Good day now." She shook his hand and stood aside to clear his way to the door. He took quick little steps to the door and turned around. "When will you be holding your first cabinet meeting?"

"Soon, Mr. Quan." She hadn't even appointed her cabinet yet.

"And what fundamentals should I insist on with Israel and the Arab Nations?"

Another trap. Solve the very problem she'd assigned to him. She stepped behind her desk and waved her hand toward the piles of paper on her desk. "I believe in delegation, Mr. Quan. Let's trust *your* expertise. Good day now."

He opened the door and turned to her again. A look of genuine worry replaced the entrapping smile. "You know the Americans haven't paid their full assessment yet. We're going to be in trouble."

Was he sincere? At the moment he seemed like a little boy looking to his mother for reassurance. The UN was his life's work, just as it was hers. Without American money the whole thing would collapse.

"Nothing new about that, Mr. Quan. Somehow, we muddle on."

Finally he left. She lifted the woman's picture off the coffee table and placed it back on her desk, standing upright against the In basket. "For God's sake, woman," she muttered, "leave me alone."

Chapter 3

Security log
Alex Richardson
September 26

7:30 PM – Took Madame to Caterina's restaurant on East 53rd. I
sat at a front table observing everyone who
entered. She met with Stuart Taylor and dined with
him.
10:30 PM– Returned to Sutton Place

If anybody could help Pilar understand the US position on
Somalia, Stuart Taylor could. Stuart had worked for the last
Democratic White House as a foreign policy analyst. She hadn't
even thought of him until Brennan mentioned his name.

Pilar waited for him to join her at a back table in Caterina's, a
family owned Hungarian and Italian – and everything else –
restaurant. She used to come here when she worked in the UN
Management office. She appreciated the cleanliness and the modest
prices and she especially loved the occasional gypsy music.

When Stuart came in, Alex got up to greet him. She knew it was
more an inspection, than a greeting, but Alex quickly turned and
pointed Stuart to her table.

What an interesting man he was – not Stuart, but Alex. As Alex
drove her to the restaurant – she had no chauffeur in the evenings –
she told him of her Somali dilemma.

He was silent for a minute, then turned his head slightly toward the back of the limo. "I guess it's a political decision, Madame. But it has something to do with place."

"Place?"

"When I was a detective, I spent as much time as possible in Hough and Glenville, poor areas of the city and a minimum amount of time at police headquarters. I used to do my paperwork in an all-night coffee shop. As a result people got to know me and trust me. I heard about things before anyone else did. It helped me be an effective cop."

"I don't understand."

He looked at her through the rear view mirror. "It was a sense of place."

That made her think and it was still on her mind as she rose to greet Stuart.

Just as she always remembered him, Stuart wore his usual white shirt and bow tie. His face was still that of a scrubbed cherub, but the cherub was aging. He even had a *scrubbed*, soapy aroma about him.

She ran into him every few years, the last time being at a White House function.

"Congratulations, Pilar – I mean *Madame-Secretary*. What's it been – just two weeks now?"

He sat down opposite her. His hair had thinned and his shirt pocket overflowed with notes to himself, as it had twenty-four years before when they lived in a third-floor walk-up in Manhattan. His job then was to untangle neighborhood problems for the mayor of New York, while she finished her doctorate at Columbia. Their relationship ended when she took a position with the UN in Geneva, Switzerland – despite his angry opposition.

"You look great, Stuart. What are you doing these days?"

"I'm just sitting around watching the Republicans do all the things they accused the Democrats of."

Pilar laughed.

"Oh, I'm sorry about your mother. I didn't know she was sick."

"She wasn't. It was an auto accident. She liked you a lot, you know, Stuart."

"Yes, I remember."

"She was not happy with me….many times." Pilar was thinking about the fierce argument she and her mother had when she broke up with Stuart. "You're giving up a man with a good job to go by yourself to Europe? You're giving up family… and children?"

Stuart cleaned his knife with his napkin. "Oh? I thought you two got along well."

"We did in later years, but I remember once in high school a handsome young Punjabi boy asked me out. My mother put up so much opposition, I gave in. And the crazy thing was that she herself had married the son of Cuban refugees when she went to college in the US."

"Well, it's been proven that when parents approve of the marriage, there's more chance for success."

Pilar looked at him carefully. Was that a veiled reference to her choosing a job over him? She couldn't tell. He had never married and he tended toward bitterness sometimes.

The waiter approached them. She ordered a salad and a glass of white wine, he, a breast of chicken and red wine.

"I ran into Dharmesh," he said. "He got his doctorate with you, didn't he?"

She nodded.

"I met him at a White House function. He asked me what I did and I told him I supervised twenty employees who advised the President on foreign affairs. 'And what about you?' I asked. 'Oh, I supervise a hundred sixty five million employees as the head of India's railways,' he said."

She laughed. She wanted to find out immediately what he knew about Brennan and Somalia, but she had to wait for the right moment. And she had to pump him for information rather than outright ask him. After all, the Secretary-General of the UN had to appear knowledgeable.

The waiter served their meals and they chatted, recalling old times and people from their younger days. After dinner and a second glass of wine, Stuart settled back in his chair. "So let me tell you the answer to your question."

"I didn't ask it yet."

"On the phone you said you had a foreign policy question. Any question about the UN can always be answered one way – get rid of the veto. It corrupts the whole thing."

She smiled. Certainly this wasn't the view he took when he worked in the White House. He was probably just enjoying being free to think and say what he wanted now that he no longer worked for the government.

"I mean, why should the five winners of World War II be able to veto any action the others agree on? The organization is flawed from the very beginning."

He knew the answer as well as she. Russia, China, France, Britain and the US would never have agreed to the UN unless they could control it.

She kept silent. After a minute he looked at her sideways. "A rant?" he asked.

"A rant," she confirmed.

"Well, it's true. I have more UN rants. Want to hear them?"

She held up her hand to stop him. "I want to ask you about Brennan."

"Brennan?" He paused for a minute. "Rich oil man raises a lot of money to help the new president get elected and as a reward gets appointed to a harmless post as ambassador to the UN. However the story turns into a tragedy when the oil man starts thinking he could become Secretary of State. But surely you know all that."

"Yes."

"Then the question?"

"Somalia?"

Stuart expelled air through his lips in frustration. "Oil," he said.

"What do you mean?"

"One word questions get one word answers. Besides, it's the right answer. Every question about the Middle East or the Horn of Africa can be answered with that one word. It explains everything."

She would have to tell him the whole story. How strange, she thought, that when she was coming up through the ranks of the UN, she demanded information from people and got it. Autocratic, bossy, she never gave in to anybody. But now that she was the leader, it seemed she was always giving in. The politician had replaced the despot.

Like now. She told Stuart the whole story of the Somali ambassador and Brennan's statement that Somalia was a *hands-off* country.

"*Hands-off.* I love it. Everybody's *hands-off* except his. Brennan and his oil buddies are panting at the gates of Somalia, waiting for things to settle down after twenty years of strife. Uranium, tantalum, but the big one is oil. Something about a big vein of oil running under the Gulf of Aden from Yemen to Somalia. And you can bet the CIA is involved, too. They are probably backing some warlord and they don't want you going over there, solving problems. Their man has to be the problem solver. He'll take over the country and invite the oil men in."

"Too cynical, Stuart."

"Too true."

He played with his wineglass, his eyes down.

"What if I went?" she asked.

He shook his head, still playing with his glass. "It's a collapsed state, Pilar. You know that." He looked up, staring at her. She knew he was trying to figure out what she was going to do. After a moment he said, "Why don't you co-opt Brennan? Invite him to go with you. He can become the hero of the Somali people. Hint that he can check up on his warlord."

"That's a good idea."

"And if he goes, there will be an army of CIA with you."

"I suppose he would want that."

"So? Are you going?" he asked.

She dodged. "I have to think about it. But why don't you go with me? You seem to know the situation."

"Me? With the UN? You've got to be kidding."

She ignored the tone of his comments and changed the subject to old friends until it was time to go. She walked him up to Alex's table and then they parted.

After he was gone, she glanced down at Alex's table. He was putting a piece of paper inside a book.

"What's the book, Alex?"

He showed her the cover: *History of the Somali People.* She saw that the paper had writing on it.

"And the paper?" she asked.

"I'm sorry, Madame. I know it's not my place, but I was so moved by these wonderful people that I just started writing a little thing in case you decide to go."

"May I read it, Alex?"

"Yes, Ma'am," he said.

Pilar took the paper and read it on the way back to her official residence.

> The West says that the sons of the prophet do not respect women.
> But many of your countries have had women rulers long before the nations of the West.
>
> You honor women, in the home and in your history.
> Fatimah, the daughter of the prophet, was kind to the poor.
> Often she gave all her food to those in need, even if she herself remained hungry.
>
> She had fine manners and gentle speech.
> She had no craving for the ornaments of the rich.
> She lived simply.
>
> She inherited from her father an eloquence that was rooted in wisdom.
> When she spoke, people were moved to tears.
> She had the sincerity to stir the emotions of people and to fill their hearts with praise for God.

It is with great joy that the United Nations announces the visit of a woman who honors Fatimah.
She is the Secretary-General of the UN and she comes like Fatimah did to help the poor.

Her name is Pilar Marti. She belongs not to any one country, but to the world.

She comes to pray with you and to share your pain.
She is gentle and wise as was Fatimah.

Please welcome her.

After the short drive to her mansion on Sutton Place, Alex got out and held the door for her. "Alex, this paper is wonderful," she said. "It's exactly the right approach. May I keep it?"

"Certainly, Madame."

She felt a sudden urge to put her hand on his arm in order to thank him more warmly, but she resisted. It was a rule with her – never touch the opposite sex in a work environment. It just confused things. As her mother used to singsong, "No touchy-feel-ly at the uni-versi-ty."

It was doubly important that she keep her distance because Alex was staying in the coach house as a security measure.

While he parked the limo, she stood in the driveway and breathed the cool night air. In front of her lay the four bedroom, three bathroom mansion that she lived in all alone. The studio alone was bigger than her former apartment.

She put her hands on her hips and murmured, "A sense of place."

When Alex exited the garage, she called to him. "Hold your weekend open, Alex."

Chapter 4

Appointment Schedule for the Secretary-General
Wednesday, September 27

10:00 AM – Meeting of the General Assembly
12:00 PM – Luncheon speech to the International Law
                Association
 3:00 PM – Thomas E. Brennan, Ambassador to the UN, U.S.A
                All other appointments are internal.

At 2:45 PM Pilar waited in her office for the worst part of the day – Brennan.

The morning had been a success – the General Assembly had endorsed her – Brennan's – India-Pakistan peace committee. And the International Lawyers received her luncheon speech very well. She traced the history of international cooperation, how it began long before the League of Nations, the UN's predecessor. "History is a continuum," she said. "The idea of international cooperation has been around a long time and it's getting stronger every year. In the seventeenth and eighteenth centuries the great powers got together after wars to discuss security issues. In 1899 and 1907 nations came together at the Hague Peace Conference to promote peace. In the nineteenth century governments created international commissions to regulate river transportation, telegraph communication and postal customs."

The League of Nations, the foundation of the UN – this history she got from a book, but the conclusion came from her. "The world is changing, getting smaller. I call on you, men and women of international law, to create the future. Build a world where people resolve conflicts at the negotiating table and not on the battlefield.

"Someone once gave me a quote from the French scientist-theologian, Teilard de Chardin:

> The Age of Nations is past.
> The task before us now,
> if we would not perish,
> is to build the earth."

The lawyers gave her a standing ovation after that little poem. People standing, clapping, some even cheering for her – for a second she had trouble breathing. Happiness filled her heart, her chest and her head. Her face broke into a beaming smile. Never in her life – or in the life of anyone she knew at the UN – had there been a standing ovation. It wasn't part of UN culture.

After the meeting the lawyers commented on her powerful conclusion – and the conclusion wasn't even part of her original text. In fact it was not advisable terminology for a Secretary-General to use, for it declared that the age of nations was past. Anything that even hinted of world government stirred the American right-wing.

Promptly at three Brennan arrived. Headache time. The rational part of her mind reassured her that she was just keeping him informed, maybe even involving him, but her feelings said she was begging permission to go to Somalia. She hated the thought of appealing for his support.

"Tom, thank you for coming by," she said as brightly as she could. "I wanted to update you on the Somali situation. Do you have time for a coffee?"

"No, no, Lit—Madame— Pilar. The wife and I have a dinner party to attend. What's this about the age of nations being over? The United States of America isn't over."

She said those words less than an hour ago and he had them already. Long ago in high school her classmates shoved her into her locker, secured the door and walked away. The panicky feeling she had then revisited her now.

"You had to have been there, Tom. Read the whole speech." Of course, when he read it, it would be even worse, but that was later.

Brennan sat down in front of her desk and Pilar sat behind it. The picture of the Somali woman still stood by her *In* basket. She turned it toward him. "Tom, I want to go to Somalia and call attention to the drought and I want you to come with me. I need someone with your connections. I want to come up with answers you can support, answers we can actually accomplish. The Somali people …."

"I'm with you, Pilar. You're doin' the right thing." He crossed his legs and leaned back in the chair, perfectly relaxed.

Her hand still rested on the picture. She let go of it and breathed out. What was going on? This was too easy.

"Trouble is," he continued, "I've got to go down to Washington. President wants to see me." She saw his chest expand slightly. "But I think you should go and I've asked our key man from the State Department to accompany you. The guy from the Somali desk. And I think Quan should go with you. That boy – that man – knows the UN. Of course, you'll need a translator and your security and some extra—"

She raised her hand to stop him. "Alex can protect me. He won't want a big entourage."

"Sure, sure he can protect you. But there are some mighty dangerous warlords over there. By the way, did you have a chance to talk to anyone about that India-Pakistan thing?"

She ignored his request for a good word. All of a sudden it was okay to go to Somalia. No more *hands-off*. Why?

She pictured him in his office, State Department types around him, figuring out how to handle the new Secretary-General. Sure, that was it. They were going to let her be humanitarian. But surround her with so much staff that she couldn't do anything, or if she actually *did* something, Washington would know about it right away. Keep her busy with good works as long as she stayed away from the power centers.

"And Quan? I suppose you want him to come along so we keep the Chinese informed."

"Bull's eye. I told them —I mean you are smart."

"Them?"

"And the fellow from the State Department," he said, ignoring her question, "...fella's name is Yusuf. Hell of a guy. Expert on Somalia. From there, actually. He'll go with you and stand in for me. He'll steer you in the right direction. Translator's name is..." he pulled a paper from his jacket "...Asha. From there also. And you won't have to worry about security. There'll be several CIA types along."

Didn't he listen? She didn't want an army. Alex would object. And how come he had this all figured out, that she was going? Alex a spy? No. Just plain *no*, he wasn't. He was too straight up. Stuart? The man was bitter over their failed relationship, but that was a long time ago.

The only explanation was that they had put her neatly in a box, the humanitarian Secretary-General and they guessed what she was going to do

Before she could say a word, he stood up. "Gotta run. The little lady—my Mrs., I mean—she doesn't like me to be late. That Quan is a great little fellow, even though he's from communist Vietnam. He cares about the UN, he wants everything to be stable. That's what the world needs, stability. We have to balance the pleas of these poor countries against the need for stability. Keep the peace, that's the job of the UN."

She stood, her whole body shaking with anger. This was so convoluted. Go to Somalia with her worst opponent who was being backed by the country that put her in power. Go there with Yusuf, a State Department spy and a UN translator who was, no doubt, a CIA employee, along with a gaggle of CIA white men in dark suits.

"Mr. Brennan, I..."

He had already reached the door. "Oh, don't thank me. Washington helped and they approved everything."

He opened the door and then turned back, "Don't forget, Pilar. Please mention that India-Pakistan peace initiative to the right people."

He left. She balled her two hands into fists and pushed against her desk. The Somali woman in the picture stared at her and reminded her that leaders used their anger to get things done.

Chapter 5

Appointment Schedule for the Secretary-General
Monday, October 2

10:30 AM – Press Conference, South Mogadishu Hospital,
Somalia

The Secretary-General visits Hell. Pilar bounced along in the
back of a '94 Chevy Van through the torn up streets of Mogadishu,
Somalia. To take her mind off the ride, she made up headlines. The
car jounced past a group of Somali men in front of a tea shop and
she imagined the headline they would see: *UN Army Invades –
Again.* Her entourage was a lead jeep with four rifle-carrying UN
soldiers, the old van she rode in with UN stickers on its sides, a
small van for reporters, a decoy limo and two cars of CIA types,
minus their usual suit coats in this heat.

"Almost there, Madame," Alex called from the front.

"Oh, dear, this van is just terrible," Quan complained from the
seat next to Alex.

Behind Pilar, in the back by himself, sat Yusuf, Yusuf Ibrahim
Abubakar. No question why he sat alone, Pilar thought. Something
cold and deadly lurked in the back of the man's eyes. He sat erect as
a pole, a thin frame, his skin a deep black – deeper than Alex's skin.
Yusuf seemed to her almost robot-like, a killing machine that
someone had forgotten to camouflage. According to Alex, Yusuf

worked for the CIA, not the State Department as Brennan had told her.

Next to her, in the middle seat, sat the UN translator, Asha, a Somali native. Asha Amina Hassan. The two of them sat, not on a spring filled van seat, but on steel-tube kitchen chairs strapped to the floor. Pilar felt every rut and hole. Yusuf had the same accommodation, but his wasn't strapped down.

Asha had flown with them from New York. She appeared to be in her early thirties or maybe late twenties. She had a perfect oval face, lustrous black hair and skin that women in the west would do anything for. A beautiful woman in any culture.

"Ouch," Asha exclaimed at a particularly bad bump. She touched Pilar's hand and smiled, "Just two more blocks."

Pilar nodded. Thank God for this Somali woman who had lent her a *guntiino*, a white cotton dress similar to an Indian sari. Pilar knew she would have roasted in the suit she'd brought with her. Even with the *guntiino*, she was hot.

Asha had unusual eyes, Pilar thought. Fire burned in her eyes, but, at least for the moment, the fire was under control. What did the flame burn for? And how unusual to meet someone who worked for the UN and burned with any kind of intensity.

"Here's the final copy of your statement, Madame," Quan said, handing a paper to her. "And a copy for the State Department. Please pass this back to Yusuf."

She turned and handed him the copy. "Here, Yusuf," she said. He took it from her, staring at her as if she were a chair or a vacuum cleaner.

"Yes," was all he said.

She turned back and read the statement quickly. "United Nations…record drought…many private agencies helping…must have stability and order." It was nothing new. A public relations event only. No new programs, no new money. "…need for a strong, democratic government to stop the violence …"

It was the same message told to Somalia in the early 90's. That wasn't what she wanted to say.

She folded the paper in half and put it in her lap. Endure a time-consuming trip by car from Nairobi, smell human excrement through a long night in the Araba hotel, listen to Quan's constant chiding and have every step impeded by an army of CIA men – all for a bland, say-nothing statement? *Quan Issues Statement, Says Nothing.*

Quan, the subject of her headline, turned again toward the back of the van. "I want to apologize to everyone about that hotel. I didn't sleep at all. I'm doing my best to find another hotel for tonight. Maybe the Jubba. These sudden trips...."

"There, up ahead – the hospital," Alex interrupted.

"Oh my God," Quan exclaimed. "Look."

Chunks of adobe and charred beams lay where a wing of the hospital had been. Power poles and wires rested across the rubble as light smoke rose from the ruins. Frantic workers erected a tent-like structure, while medical people attended to patients lying on cots in the open air.

"Our press conference," Quan lamented.

The UN vehicles parked along the road and Alex opened the side door of the van. "Let's help," Asha said and rushed toward the hospital.

Pilar followed her, ignoring Quan's direction that she should stay in the van. Asha and Pilar walked into the part of the building still standing. A thick, acrid, burnt smell assaulted Pilar as she groped her way into the darkened building. A European doctor handed them an elderly female patient. "You take her outside. Find cot. Come back. More."

She and Asha did what the doctor ordered. She learned that a clan had fired a rocket at the headquarters of another clan, but had obviously missed.

Two more trips and hallway lights sputtered on along with the noise of a generator vibrating next to a wall of the building. On Pilar's next swing outside, she caught a glimpse of Quan scurrying about, getting folding chairs, setting up a sort of press gallery outside the temporary hospital tent.

When the doctor said, "No more patients," Pilar and Asha went outside. Quan was talking on his satellite phone and he raced over to Pilar when the call ended. "The media are going to play up the missile attack. I had to modify your speech. Washington and Beijing just okayed it." He handed her a paper

Washington and Beijing *okayed it*? She glanced at the paper. "…lawbreakers must be stopped…hurting facilities that help the Somali people… need for a strong central government." Just words, words that would mean little to the people lying out in the open on the cots.

Asha asked to see it and Pilar gave it to her. "No mention of countries that sell rockets to the clans," she said when she finished reading. Though her tone was even, Pilar saw the angry fire in her eyes.

"We don't want to say *that*," Quan reprimanded Asha, but then he turned to Pilar. "So, we'll get started in a few minutes?"

"We'll see," Pilar said. This whole thing was insane – pushed here and there, made to say things she didn't feel.

"We'll see?" Quan repeated. "But, Madame, that's the whole reason we came here, for a press conference. You have to…"

She cut him off. "What do you have planned, Mr. Quan?"

"First, I have a farmer who will talk about the drought. Next you and Asha will take a tour of the hospital – the part that's still standing – and then you will come back out here by the tent and read the statement I gave you and answer questions from the press. The text of your speech is very important. It —"

"Thank you, Mr. Quan."

"I'm just going to check with the doctors to make sure they're ready."

"Fine, Mr. Quan."

Alex approached as soon as Quan left. "Excuse me, Asha. Can I speak to Madame a moment?"

Asha stepped over to the tent and talked to some of the people on the cots.

"I get the feeling," Alex said, "that this trip is not turning out as you expected."

"That's an understatement. I wanted to see what was possible here, if we could work with or around some of these warlords."

"That's what I thought. I have an idea. Right after your statement to the press..." Alex stopped. Quan was returning. "Be ready, you and Asha."

"Is Asha okay?" Pilar asked.

"I checked her out," Alex replied. "She's not CIA, just a translator. We need her."

"All set, Madame," Quan said. "What were you two talking about?"

Pilar ignored him and took a seat at the back of the press conference. Alex left and Quan called Asha to the front. "I need you to translate for the farmer."

Pilar listened to the man. He explained that he grew maize in the Juba valley and most years he did well, selling enough to feed his family and even save a little money. "I used to get additional water from the Juba," he said, "but now it's just a trickle. You see my family behind me. They are malnourished. I'm so ashamed."

Pilar paid attention to how Asha translated. She was no ordinary UN translator who spoke the words without emotion, robot-like. Asha put expression into her English words. "I'm so ashamed," sounded like she really was.

The farmer told of an earlier drought where America provided food and water, but because of the warlords, the help never reached him. "Somalia needs a strong arm to rule," he concluded, and Pilar knew why the farmer had been selected.

Next Quan hurried Pilar to the front and led her and Asha and the media to the wing of the hospital that had not been damaged, the children's ward. She and Asha talked to doctors, nurses and the children, the cameras following them through. The media focused on the emaciated children in their beds. Pilar stopped in front of one teenage girl missing an arm and a leg. "Greetings to you," Pilar said. Asha translated. The girl spoke in rapid Somali. "I lost my dog," Asha translated, "and I went to look for it just outside the village. The dog ran over a hill and I followed it and I stepped on something and that's the last I remember."

Pilar saw the pain in Asha's eyes as she translated. Pilar turned her face away and tears came to her eyes. For some reason her missing finger hurt her and she reflected on how much more this little girl had lost. A nagging thought at the back of her mind made her wonder what country's name would be stamped on the mine.

Quan hurried them away from the little girl and out to the hospital tent. They walked through the tent and Pilar noticed how the people twisted and turned in the heat and how the flies circled around them. Pilar picked up a cloth and poured water into it and used it to cool the forehead of an older woman. Asha did the same to an older man.

"We don't have time for that now," Quan whispered to Pilar as he tried to stop her from soothing another patient. "It's time to read your statement."

Pilar continued applying a wet cloth to a few more patients and then stepped outside and stood in front of the press. On the makeshift podium she spread out the speech Quan had given her and stared at the preachy words. She looked at the dozen or so journalists and camera techs. The noonday sun beat down on her. "I'm angry," she said, folding Quan's statement up. "I'm angry at the clan who destroyed part of this hospital. I saw a little girl inside who stepped on a land mine. I'm angry at the Somali who placed that land mine so near a village. I'm angry at the countries who sold rockets and mines to Somalia – I include my own country, Canada, and my neighbor, the United States, the biggest seller of weapons to the third world. And I'm angry at a world that would let these children…" she pointed back to the hospital "…become so emaciated from hunger."

For a moment the media sat in stunned silence. Then a reporter stood. "Bruce Carlton, United Press. So what are you planning to do?"

"Food and water, Mr. Carlton. We can't let these people die."

"Sure," Carlton continued, "you send in supplies and some warlords grab them and then in comes the American army."

"I don't think that will happen again."

Another reporter stood. "Pierre Vincent Richard, Madame, Le Monde. I hear rumors that America is backing the warlord Hassan Abdullah."

"I don't listen to rumors, Mr. Richard."

"Some people say that the Americans want the situation to get so desperate that no one will care that the Americans send bullets along with the bread. The Americans want Hassan to take over and then invite American oil and mining interests into Somalia. That's the rumor we have."

"That's very cynical, Mr. Richard. The American people are very generous and they don't want to see people dying."

"But what if it's true?"

"I've come to Somalia to find other answers, answers that…"

Shots rang out and a small explosion vibrated through the air. Everyone dove for cover, Pilar and Asha under a table by the podium. Alex roared up in a jeep and fired a submachine gun in the air. Smoke rose from behind the hospital where Alex had popped a grenade and a smoke bomb into a portable ammo locker.

Pilar heard Alex's voice. "Madame. Asha. Quickly."

Pilar and Asha crawled out from under the table and hurried toward the jeep. Alex fired into the air again when a reporter stuck his head up from behind an oil drum.

"The Secretary-General's being kidnapped," someone shouted.

"No, it's her security guard," someone else said.

"Hang on," Alex yelled and the jeep roared away.

Chapter 6

Security log
Alex Richardson
Monday, October 2

Noon – Took Madame and the translator, Asha, to the office of
    Hassan Abdullah. From there we visited three more
    important warlords. Returned to the Araba Hotel after
    dark.

No seat belts. Pilar expected that, but after a few minutes in the
jeep she knew the shock absorbers were played out as well. She and
Asha bounced through the pot-holed streets, Alex in the front. She
thought the open jeep would relieve the sweltering heat of the city,
but the hot air streaming by added to her discomfort. Mogadishu
was only a degree or two north of the equator and the temperature
felt like the high nineties.

Alex shouted over the noise that they would visit Hassan
Abdullah first, the warlord favored by the Americans.

They drove past white stone rubble that had once been attractive
Italian homes. Many streets had neighborhood junk yards where
burnt cars, rusty oil drums, old clothes and garbage decayed together.
On some streets, rusty tin sheets connected piles of rubble and Pilar
saw families living inside. In front of one house a dead dog rotted

in the sun. Next to the wall of a ruined building, flies buzzed over a pile of excrement.

Pilar could hardly breathe with the mixture of smells, all of them foul. This was a city without services, a flashback to plague-ridden, foul-smelling, medieval Europe. She remembered the winter stink of fields near her home in Vancouver, Canada when she was growing up. Farmers fertilized their fields with fish remains, but that was done so crops would grow and there would be life in the fields in spring.

The smell of Mogadishu was one of death, not life.

Through alleys, dirt paths and pitted streets, Alex drove a convoluted route to avoid crowds. At one intersection he pointed a few blocks down the street. "This is Hawlwadig Road where hundreds of Somalis and eighteen Americans were killed." As they approached the Pakistani Stadium, Alex stopped, pulled a small round package from under his seat, took out a flag and put it on the jeep. "We are going into Hassan Abdullah's territory."

Pilar marveled at where this amazing man had come up with a set of local flags.

A man standing on a street corner glared at them and waved his automatic rifle as they passed. Doubt nagged at Pilar's brain. What was she doing, off on this adventure, away from her contingent of guards and the CIA men? What would happen if she were shot? What if someone saw her and that person had a son or a husband or someone whom had been shot by UN troops? The murder of world leaders often caused wars to start.

She leaned forward toward Alex to express her fears and noticed a shiny, black machine gun under his seat. A picture flashed through her mind of her and Asha lying on the ground, bullets whizzing over their heads.

She sat back in her seat and felt sick to her stomach. Asha looked at her. "Are you okay, Madame?" she asked.

"Okay," Pilar answered. It was hard to explain with the noise of the jeep.

Asha took her hand and held it for a second, but a jeep-bounce sent them both grabbing for support.

On October 21 Road, a group of armed Somalis stopped them at a checkpoint. Asha spoke firmly with them and Pilar heard Asha and the men say her own name. One of the men made a call on his cell phone and they were allowed through. A few minutes later, Alex stopped the jeep in front of a white building surrounded by a razor wire fence. Somali gunmen patrolled outside the house and a cage held four snarling dogs.

Alex got out and attempted to talk to the gunmen, but he came back to the jeep to get Asha's help. The two of them returned to the knot of guards and the discussion soon grew heated. Alex kept pointing back to her and Asha grew very impassioned. Finally Alex came back to her.

"What is it?"

"They didn't expect you. Early this morning Yusuf called Hassan and said you wouldn't have time to visit. Now they've called Yusuf and told him you're here. Yusuf and Quan are on the way. They've been looking for you."

Pilar felt a surge of hot anger. "Who does this Yusuf think he is? I didn't authorize him to say one thing about this visit."

"Let's go in before they get here," Asha said.

"Can't," Alex replied. "They're waiting until Yusuf gets here."

Alex took some water bottles from his pack and gave one to her and one to Asha. Pilar took a couple of swallows and sat back in the jeep. The water tasted warm and flat. This was a crazy situation. Quan and Yusuf were pursuing her, trying to control her. For years she had known the complaint of the poor countries that Northern rich countries, especially the US, had taken over the machinery of the UN. For years she had ignored this criticism. The UN was the UN. But now it seemed the poor countries were right and she was the piece of machinery the Northern countries were trying to control.

The day grew hotter. Alex took a swig of his water. "Last night," he said, "I was reading about Ambassador Mohamad Sahnoun, the former Algerian foreign minister."

"And?" Pilar asked.

"Before the Americans came," Alex continued, "the UN assigned him to see what could be done in Somalia. Rather than attack and defeat the clans and the warlords as the Americans did, he suggested that the UN work *with* the clans, build them up and train their armed young men as a police force. He felt that the clan system had worked successfully for generations in Somalia, until the Soviets and then the Americans flooded the country with weapons."

"Interesting," Pilar said, "I heard about that."

"But the Americans overruled Sahnoun and then their marines landed. You know what happened next."

A UN van pulled up, Quan in the front, Yusuf driving and the four CIA agents in the back, all of them armed with machine guns. To walk in and meet Hassan with all this firepower behind her would be a bad mistake.

"Madame," Alex began, pointing to the van. "I…"

"I know," she said. She recognized the sameness of their thoughts and reached out to touch his hand, but immediately withdrew it. *Don't touch* was her rule.

Quan was scolding her as he got out of the van. "…and danger, you have no idea what armed militia you went through. Even with these men…" he gestured to the CIA men "it's hardly safe. And the leader of the UN has to be in communication with the bureaucracy at…"

She watched Yusuf approach the knot of armed Somali men. He, too, carried a black machine gun. He said a few words and then returned to her. Cold, emotionless, he spoke. "We will accompany you in now, Madame."

"No you won't," she replied. "Alex will accompany me."

"These men do not know Alex."

"Then you come, too, but only you."

Without reply Yusuf turned and walked toward the compound. She motioned Alex and Asha to come.

Once inside the gate, Pilar paused and took a deep breath. She straightened her shoulders and stepped up to the door of the house. She was the leader of the UN and had to look the part. Above the doorway an AK-47 was mounted on a board. Someone had scratched marks on the butt as if counting kills. Alex opened the door and she entered a large front room with no furniture. In the next room Pilar saw armed Somali men squatting on the floor against one wall. Tentatively she entered that room and saw a Somali man in a business suit sitting at a desk. She looked for a sign of warmth as he stood to greet her, but no hint of friendship crossed his face. "Madame Secretary, I am Hassan Abdullah. I welcome you to Mogadishu," he spoke politely and in perfect English. "I am honored you come to visit me. I am a friend of the United Nations."

Pilar was unsure of the correct procedure for a woman visitor but she shook his hand anyway. He had a manly grip, but perfunctory. She introduced Alex and Asha. He shook Alex's hand, leered at Asha and embraced Yusuf who held his weapon away from the embrace. "We are of the same clan," Hassan explained.

Hassan nodded to one of the men along the wall. The man went into a back room and came back with a chair. As he came closer to Pilar, she caught a burnt smell on him. Was it gunpowder? She sat down and despaired that she could find a non-military solution to helping this country.

The man went back and returned with a chair for Asha.

"I apologize for the guards," Hassan said. "Our city is not a safe one."

Pilar looked up and studied his face, trying to determine what sort of man he was. He stood behind his desk, looking down at her. Lines fanned out from his eyes, as if he'd been squinting at the harsh Somali sun – or at what foreigners told him. On his desk she noticed a family picture. She hesitated a moment, then reached over and picked it up. His eyes widened and his mouth opened as if no one dared touch his desk. In the picture a beautiful woman in a flowing purple robe sat on his left. On his right sat an attractive teenage girl, while a younger girl sat next to her mother. A girl of about five sat on her mother's lap.

"Your daughters are very beautiful," Pilar said. "You're very blessed." She handed the picture back to him.

"Yes," he said, smiling for the first time. "The oldest is Fatuma, after the daughter of the prophet, the middle one is Sahra or 'flower,' and the baby is Safi for 'pure.'" He sat down and seemed to relax.

She waited a minute, then spoke earnestly. "Hassan, I come to appeal to you. I am going back to New York to ask the UN to send emergency relief to Somalia, no strings attached."

"Of course, Madame." The eyes squinted.

"I swear it to you."

"You mean well, but a lot of Somalis died in 1993 when America sent troops so the UN could give us aid."

"It will be different this time."

He nodded his head up and down as if he'd heard her, but didn't believe her. He gestured around at the men sitting against the walls. "Here's the answer to Somalia, the power of the gun. The US has promised me a big shipment of—"

"No." She was so emphatic her chair bounced on the unadorned plywood floor. The men around the room stirred and she heard a mechanical click, as if a safety had just come off. "No," she repeated, quietly this time. Why was she speaking out so boldly – and in this environment? All her life, she had *listened*. That was the secret to getting ahead. *Listen and say nothing.*

Hassan stared at her, an angry look on his face. "Madame?" Silence in the room. She heard Asha breath in. She glanced at Yusuf – rigid, motionless, holding his weapon at his side. Alex stood next to her, his hand inside his shirt.

She spoke up again. "Sir, I implore you. First the Italians and the British raped this wonderful country. Then under Siad Barre the Soviets came. Some would say the UN is just as guilty, trying to force a western style government on you. We did wrong back in '93 – we used too much firepower. But I beg you for an end to fighting. I offer UN aid."

"Yes, Madame, but I do not see the difference in your aid this time."

"Ambassador Mohamad Sahnoun, he had the right idea," Pilar said. Thank God for Alex.

"Yes, he had a good idea," Hassan said, "but you see how far that went."

Pilar stood to emphasize her words. She spoke distinctly, with emphasis. "I will not use the military. I will appeal to every leader, to every warlord, to let the help get to the people."

"And if you fail? If someone appropriates the food and water as last time?"

"I am going to ask them not to interfere."

"And if they do?"

She began to sweat. Honesty. All she could do was tell the truth. "I want to get the technicals …" she glanced at the men along the wall "…trained as police as quickly as possible. We have little time. The people need help now."

"I am sorry, Madame. The UN had its chance. This time will be different. The Americans are helping us directly. They are going to give us the weapons so we can bring order to this country."

"Pardon me, Hassan Abdullah, but it was the Americans who were in command of UN forces when all the people were killed."

He waved her comments away. "Those are squabbles from the past." His face changed to a sardonic smile. "Hollywood makes movies of those past times, *Black Hawk Down*."

Asha jumped up. "I've had enough," she said, her voice rising. "You trust America when they make a movie about eighteen American soldiers and they say nothing about one thousand Somalis who died the same day. You warlords are ruining this country. My father and mother, my little sister, were all killed by this stupid fighting between clans. Your bandits, Hassan, accidentally shot my little sister and the Hawiye clan shot my parents because they found a letter in our house from me on UN stationery. Damn you all."

Pilar tried to make herself smaller in her chair. What would Hassan do at this outburst? And from a Somali woman? Everything Pilar knew about Somali society indicated that women were to be quiet.

But Asha wasn't through. She stepped in front of Yusuf and glared into his eyes. "Give me your weapon," she said, her voice quiet and serious, like a mother talking her child away from a deadly snake. She put out her hand and when he made no motion, she reached down and calmly took his submachine gun.

Pilar heard the click of a safety coming off a weapon. Would she hear a burst of fire next? But only silence. Asha placed Yusuf's weapon at her feet and moved slowly toward the first man along the wall. Pilar saw the fear on her face, but also the resolution. Asha put out her hand in front of the man, demanding his weapon. The man looked at Hassan, then at Asha, then back to Hassan.

"What are you doing, woman?" Hassan spat out. Then he switched to Somali: "*Intaadan falin ka fiirso.*"

Asha turned to Pilar. "He tells me to *Think before I do.*"

Asha addressed Hassan. "*Waa duni la kala ilbsaday, aan nala ogaysiin.*" She glanced back at Pilar and Alex. "It's another Somali proverb. *The country is sold without our knowledge.*"

Yusuf looked at Asha with disdain. "*Naag ha kaga jirto guri ama god.*"

"He gives us a Somali proverb, *Your woman should be in the house or in the grave.*"

Ignoring Yusuf's insult, Asha turned her attention back to Hassan. "I ask you, Hassan Abdullah, to give up your guns. Let the word go forth that you have done so. All the clans will hear of this."

Asha again reached for the weapon of the first of Hassan's men along the wall. Pilar saw Hassan shrug his shoulders and gesture to the man to surrender.

Asha collected all the guns in the room and put them at Pilar's feet. Alex pulled his own handgun from under his shirt and threw it on the pile.

Pilar and Hassan stared at each other while this went on. Finally Hassan squinted at Pilar and said, "Is this how you plan to disarm Somalia, gun by gun, leader by leader?"

"No more children must die," she said and she started to pick up the weapons. Asha helped her, as did Alex. Yusuf stood aside and did nothing. Pilar noticed he and Hassan exchange glances.

One of the guards spoke up. "We have many more weapons and the US will give us what we need."

Pilar looked at the man and spoke quietly. "Somalia should be for the Somalis."

Hassan nodded in agreement. "Yes, in times past we would stand under a tree and negotiate, just us Somalis. Now things are different. But how do I know you can deliver, Madame Secretary-General? You must get your promises past the Security Council, where the US has the veto."

Yes, good question, a little voice inside her said. "You will just have to trust me, Hassan," she replied.

"And why should I?"

"Because I give you my word."

"The words of Westerners are as the sands of the desert. There is no truth in them."

She repeated her words, her face set hard. "I give you my word."

A *click, click, click* sounded somewhere on Yusuf. He reached inside his shirt and the noise stopped. Pilar knew he had taped this whole conversation. The CIA and the State Department and Brennan would know exactly what she had said. He had no right to tape her without permission.

"Give me that tape," she said quietly to Yusuf.

She got the answer she expected. "What tape?"

Tape or no tape she had to do her job; she'd deal with it later. Her arms hurt with the four heavy submachine guns she carried.. She stepped toward the door, but turned back to Hassan. "I want to thank you for your cooperation in disarming. I intend to approach the others and ask them for the same thing."

She turned and left, struggling with the load of weapons. Outside Quan sat in the UN van, talking on the satellite phone. When he saw them, he put the phone down, got out of the van and ran toward them, taking some of the weapons from Pilar. "Oh my goodness, what's this all about? Our job isn't to collect guns. What are we to do with them? What does this mean?"

Pilar felt the outside heat. It was mid-afternoon and very hot. "Put them in the van, Mr. Quan, and take them back to our hotel. Give them to the UN office here in Mogadishu."

"We can all do that together," Quan said.

Pilar, Alex and Asha put their stack of weapons in the UN van and then Pilar pulled Alex aside. "I'd like to visit a few more warlords, the big ones. Do you know where they are?"

"I marked a map early this morning. It's in the jeep."

"Can you get through the roadblocks?"

Alex nodded back toward the UN van with Yusuf, Quan and the CIA men. "Not with them," he said.

"Okay," Pilar replied. She returned to the van and spoke to Quan. "With all those weapons you'll have to go around the roadblocks. We'll meet you back at the hotel. Let's go, Alex, Asha."

"Just one second, Madame," Alex said. "Yusuf, could you step up ahead on the road with me? I want to ask you some security information."

Pilar watched the two of them walk a few paces in front of the vehicles. Alex stopped and turned suddenly, tripping Yusuf and knocking him off his feet. As Alex reached down to help him up, Pilar saw him rip open Yusuf's shirt and pull the tape recorder out.

Alex came back and got in the jeep. "Good to go, Madame." He handed her the tape recorder.

Quan ran over to the jeep. "Where are you going?"

Chapter 7

Appointment Schedule for the Secretary-General
Tuesday, October 3

11:00 AM – Press Conference, Farjano, (Spring of Heaven)
Jowhar, Somalia

Pilar shone the flashlight into her room in the Araba Hotel. The hour was late and, just as last night, the power had gone off. She needed time to reflect on her day and time to sleep, but most of all she needed a bath. Layer upon layer of Mogadishu dirt and her own sweat caked her skin.

The furniture in the room consisted of a canopy bed, an old dresser, an oil drum with a water jug on top, and a green plastic chair. Pilar smiled wearily as she remembered Asha's comment about the room. "Not bad for Mogadishu," the younger woman had said. "But a canopy bed and an oil drum – they just don't mix."

As the beam of her light played around the room, she caught the glare of glass shards on the bed. She moved the light up. Sure enough – the window near the bed was broken and the light revealed a bullet hole in the ceiling.

Had someone broken in? No, her suitcase sat on the chair, still locked. She sighed. It was just another stray bullet in a town with no law and order.

Pilar took off her sari-like guntiino and washed herself, using a cloth and the water from the jug on top of the oil drum. She put on comfortable slacks and a top and sat by the window with a bottle of water to play back the day in her mind.

The warlords were not the evil men the media made them out to be. They wanted to feed and protect their clans, much like the TV version of a mafia don. So any attempt to help Somalia had to respect clans and tribes or it was doomed.

Someone knocked at her door and she answered it. Quan. He stepped into her room without being invited. "All afternoon and evening. Where were you? Who did you visit?"

"Alex and Asha and I—"

"I made appointments for you with Somali officials and people from agencies. They were very upset. And we needed Asha today. I can't do my job if you don't tell me what you're doing."

A hint of a smile crossed Pilar's lips. Quan sounded like her mother, but he was worse. "We'll talk tomorrow," she said, blocking his way further into the room and pointing back to the door.

"Who did you see today? Khalid Omar? Mohammed Adam?"

"Tomorrow. It's late. I'm tired."

"I had to assure people at the press conference that you weren't kidnapped."

"Thank you."

"I told them your security man spirited you away as a safety measure."

"Thank you. Now goodnight, Mr. Quan."

He left and she returned to her chair by the window. Khalid Omar and Mohammed Adam and the third warlord, Samatar Geeddi, all received her warmly and listened attentively, but, like Hassan, promised nothing. Of the four, Hassan seemed to care the most for his people. Perhaps the Americans had chosen wisely.

And Yusuf recording her. The nerve of the man. He would have a lot to report to Brennan including how Alex got the tape back.

Yes, Brennan would hear a lot. And it wouldn't be good for her second term prospects. She closed her eyes and imagined Yusuf's report: *She refused her approved text at the press conference and she launched into a diatribe about the weapons industry. Her security man put on a little show and took her and the translator to meet with warlords. She confiscated weapons (which she is not supposed to do by UN charter. That's the role of the peacekeepers.) Her security man mugged me for the tape I made. Finally she showed up late at night after more unauthorized visits.*

Maybe she was just tired and thinking negative thoughts.

She dragged herself over to the bed, shook the glass shards off the covers, collapsed on the bed and fell asleep within a minute.

*   *   *

The next morning the UN entourage prepared to drive the ninety kilometers to the small town of Jowhar where they would tour the UN-developed water system. Quan and Yusuf had acquired two air-conditioned SUVs for the trip. "You and Asha better come with me in one SUV," Quan said. "Yusuf and the CIA men will be in the other."

"Alex will drive us in his jeep. Thanks anyway, Mr. Quan. Where did you get the SUVs?"

"Ah...Yusuf."

"And he got them from?"

"I...I don't know."

Pilar assumed they came from Hassan. In any case, a bumpy, hot ride with Alex in the jeep was better than ninety kilometers of reprimands from Quan.

As she and Asha approached Alex's jeep, she saw him fiddling with a cover for the jeep.

"Protect you against all the dust," he said.

"But hot," Asha added.

"Not exactly," Alex replied. "I acquired an air conditioner last night. A mechanic and I installed it."

"You're amazing," Pilar laughed and the three of them set out. Alex gave her a copy of the United Press story from yesterday. The headline read: *Strike Two? The UN Tries Again.* The story blamed the UN for the Somali disaster of 1993, a usual American response.

Further the reporter stated that Pilar didn't know where the strings of power were in Somalia. This also sounded like a Pentagon response: *How could a woman accomplish what the American army couldn't?*

When would reporters dig for the truth, think for themselves and not just accept government press releases?

Earlier in the morning Alex had connected her laptop to the Internet and she checked the French papers. They had it right – that the Americans called the shots in 1993 and it was they who decided to make a military operation out of a humanitarian one. "Madame Secretary has drive and compassion," the French reporter said. "She visited the warlords and talked to them in person. She will not accept the old way of doing things."

As they drove along, Asha told her about the Somali people, how proud they were and how they fought the British in the first part of the twentieth century. "We had a great leader who almost beat them," she said. "They called him the Mad Mullah."

"I have read about him, Sayyid was his name, right?"

"Yes, and he rallied his troops with something we Somalis love – poetry."

"Poetry?"

"We are a very verbal people, Ma'am. We love words and we love to spar with words. Our language was only written down in the last century."

"I hear the love of language in your speech, Asha. Is that true for all Somalis?"

Asha pointed to the SUVs in front of them. "Some Somalis emigrate and forget their ancestral values. They adopt only the worst of their new country."

Pilar assumed she meant Yusuf.

The potholes increased, the air conditioner failed and conversation became impossible, but Pilar reflected on how the proud Somalis would never accept an arrogant person or an arrogant country.

In Jowhar, Pilar inspected the water system. When warring clans destroyed the pipelines and water pumps, the inhabitants drew water from a polluted river. In 1996 the UN, through its subsidiary UNICEF and with the financial aid of the European Union, rehabilitated the system. But UNICEF did more than repair pipes – it set up a council of the warring clans to administer the system. The Farjano (Spring of Heaven) Water Council now managed the entire operation. The company was showing a modest profit and, more important, the inhabitants were drinking clean water.

This is what the UN is all about, Pilar thought as she toured a sample house that now had a clean water tap. Forget the politics. Small projects like this were the greatness of the UN.

"What do you think?" she asked Asha as they left the house.

"Impressive, Madame, impressive. But compare that house to one in North America."

"You are only supposed to translate," Quan said. "Nothing more."

"I asked her," Pilar responded. Asha was direct and honest. Yes, she was often critical of the West, but she had the fire of youth in her. As for Quan, he was getting on her nerves. She had to find him a job that would keep him out of the way – something in the basement of the UN, working on… interstellar diplomatic relations.

"What did you think, Alex?" Pilar asked.

"I drank some," Alex responded. "It was very good water."

"Mr. Quan," Pilar ordered, "Be sure to send a note to the European Union and thank them for their generous help. And please prepare a press release about Farjano, stressing the contribution of the European Union."

She really wanted to say that other countries – especially the United States – should do what the Europeans had done. Stressing the positive and dropping hints, that was Kofi Annan's style. He would praise countries that did positive things and he would use vague, non-judgmental words in speaking of US actions.

The trouble was the Americans never seemed to get it.

The UN entourage left Jowhar and started for Balidogle airport, a small military facility near Mogadishu where a small plane would fly them to Nairobi. The Mogadishu air terminal was closed because so many battles had been fought there. They stopped at a crossroads and approached a Red Crescent Hospital tent to ask directions. The nurse came out to the jeep and asked Pilar if she could tour the hospital. "It would mean a lot to our patients," the nurse said.

Pilar agreed. Alex turned off the jeep and he and Asha followed Pilar and the nurse toward the hospital.

"Wait for me," Quan said, as he scrambled out of the jeep. "I have to be informed." Yusuf and the others stayed in the SUV.

Smells of soiled bandages and disinfectant mingled with smells of diarrhea and vomit. Pilar walked down the rows of beds, nodding to the patients, stopping especially to smile at the children. Near the end she came upon a woman who sat on a chair in an examining area. She held a child on each knee. Pilar stopped – there was something familiar about her. She squatted down and looked at the woman's face. *Oh my God*, she thought, it *was the woman from the picture*. Pilar gazed at her face. She assumed the picture was only a few weeks old, but already the woman had aged. In the picture the woman's eyes begged for help – but now she just looked tired and hopeless.

The woman had a big shawl over each child. Pilar lifted the shawl and smiled at the first child. A little girl lifted her head and looked at Pilar, but didn't smile. "You are beautiful," Pilar said, "What is your name?"

Asha translated, but the girl continued to stare. She did not respond. Pilar placed the shawl back around the girl and turned her attention to the other child. This child also was a girl, but Pilar could not tell the age. The girl's eyes were only open a slit and they stared down at the floor without moving. Her face was an ashen color. Pilar felt her hand – cold. Pilar pressed her fingers on the girl's veins above the wrist – nothing.

"Nurse, oh God, nurse," Pilar shouted to the woman who was talking to another staff person. The nurse hurried over and desperately looked for vital signs. The mother came out of her stupor, moved the other child off her lap and began to cry and wail in Somali to the nurse. She held the dead child tightly in her arms.

Pilar reached out to touch the woman on the arm, to show she sympathized, but the woman turned away and cried out in Somali.

"What is she saying?" Pilar whispered to Asha.

Asha didn't answer. The woman cried out again. Pilar saw that Asha was crying and couldn't talk.

Finally Asha said, "She is praying to Allah. She says the girl helped her in the fields."

"We have to go," whispered Quan from behind her.

Pilar turned around quickly. "Will you shut up?" she spat at him.

The nurse struggled to take the dead child from the mother, but the woman fought her. Tears flooded Pilar's eyes as she watched. Just a few weeks ago when the picture was taken the girl was alive and now she was dead. She had failed this one child; she must not fail the other.

Pilar saw that Asha's face was streaked with tears. She hugged Asha and then the two of them tried one more time to comfort the mother. But the woman just clutched the dead child and cried out its name, "Malika, Malika, Malika."

Pilar turned toward the exit of the tent. "Come on, Asha." She strode forward, her jaw set. "We're going back to New York and get some help for this woman."

Chapter 8

Appointment Schedule for the Secretary-General
Monday, October 9

11:00 AM– Mr. Roumen Chervenyakov, Ambassador from
            Bulgaria
12:00 PM – Presentation of special award and Luncheon with
            the New York Philharmonic Orchestra
 1:00 PM – Presentation of Credentials – Amb. Mr. Augusto
            Berardi, Republic of San Marino
 2:00 PM – Visit from Social Studies Class of Riverside High
            School, Durham, North Carolina
 3:00 PM – Mr. Rajwinder Singh Pahra, Chief Minister of Punjab
            State, India.

At 8:30 A.M. on the following Monday, Pilar stared at a week
and a half's worth of work on her desk. But next to the pile, leaning
against her monitor, right where she'd left it, was the picture of the
Somali woman with the two children. One child was dead. What
was she going to do to help the other?

There was a Security Council meeting tomorrow, her best chance
to get some concrete help moving toward Somalia. But she had to
have Brennan on her side. Russia, China, Britain, France – they
would all be willing. But what about Brennan?

She started through the pile on her desk, hoping a strategy would come to her.

On top was a note from the environment minister reporting an alarming rise in the world's average temperature. Then a staff report describing refugee problems in the Balkans. A report about human rights abuses in China. A staff document which described inadequate health care in the Congo. A news item about children working in Thailand. A communiqué from the US Congress stating why they were *not* paying their assessment. An internal memo reporting that two top aides in the Geneva office were about to be arrested for shifting money from UN refugee programs into their own Swiss bank accounts. A private note from the senior official in charge of the General Assembly that a member of his staff was procuring prostitutes for UN representatives.

She put all the papers back on the pile. An idea was forming. She placed a call to the US State Department and asked for the Somali desk. Had they ever heard of a man named Yusuf? No. Did the Department plan any emergency aid for Somalia this year? Yes. How much was budgeted? Thirty million for food and water, but there was a hold on the funds. Who put the hold on? The official wasn't at liberty to say.

She thanked the man and hung up. She called Brennan's office to see if he was in. Yes, but he had a 10:15AM appointment. Pilar told the secretary that she would cross the street to his office, rather than Brennan coming to her office. The US delegation was right across United Nations Plaza from UN Headquarters.

The secretary sounded flustered. "You're coming over here?"

"Don't worry," Pilar reassured her. What did office etiquette matter if it meant getting help for Somalia?

"9:45, would that be all right, Madame?"

"Fine," Pilar said.

She next called Asha in the translation office. Asha had said she might be able to find out about the connection between Brennan and Quan. She had a friend who often translated for Quan.

"Can you come up to my office?" Pilar asked when she reached her. "I need that information we talked about ASAP."

Asha agreed.

Then Pilar called Alex to accompany her across the street.

"I've been checking into the company Brennan owned," Alex said. "I'll tell you when I get to your office."

Pilar thanked him and hung up. Alex was amazing – he knew something about everything. And what he didn't know, he had the ability to find out. In Mogadishu he mastered the complex tribal structure and on the trip back he talked about everything from the Nairobi stock exchange to the wing span of the Boeing 747 they were on.

Ten minutes after she called him, he was in her office. "Brennan's former company has established an office in the north of Somalia, in Berbera, and they've sent over oil and mining experts."

"Interesting," Pilar said.

A few minutes later, Asha arrived and gave her report. "Just before we went to Somalia my colleague translator accompanied Quan to a meeting of the IMF. While she was translating for him, a messenger arrived from Brennan with an envelope for Quan. He pocketed the envelope, but my friend accidentally walked in on him when she was looking for a mop to clean up a spill. He was in a closet in the staff lounge, counting the money. She said there were a lot of fifties and hundreds in there."

"So we know why Quan stayed with us," Pilar said. "Thank you, Asha."

Asha turned to Alex. "Do you know about the IMF?"

Alex shrugged. "Sure. The International Monetary Fund."

"Yes, but do you know the background?"

Pilar smiled to herself. This was Asha, trying to educate Alex. Or maybe Asha's lectures were aimed at her and she used Alex as the occasion. In any case she lectured him about how the rich nations of the West had set aside the monetary agencies called for by the original UN. Instead, they established the IMF, the World Bank and, later, the WTO. "These organizations operate outside the UN," Asha said, "and they are dominated by the rich Western nations. Their values and their concerns are not those of the poor."

Alex listened attentively, but Pilar suspected he already knew what she was telling him.

Pilar picked up a few papers from her desk. Alex had a lot more lectures coming. Pilar had seen Asha's dog-eared copy of *For a Strong and Democratic United Nations: A South Perspective on UN Reform.*

"Alex is going to accompany me across the street," Pilar said to Asha. "Thank you for your help."

"My pleasure, Madame."

Asha left and a few minutes later she and Alex took the elevator to the ground floor.

As they stepped outside the UN, Pilar breathed the cool fall air. She smelled the air of the ocean and the scent immediately transported her to her native Vancouver, even though Pacific air was moister. How often she and her mother had breathed that air as they walked in Stanley Park. Never again. If only she could talk to her mother again.

Pilar stopped suddenly. She knew in her heart what her mother would tell her at this very moment. She could almost hear the words: *Go back inside the building, Pilar. Security is there.*

"Madame?" Alex asked.

"Nothing," Pilar responded. "Let's go."

As she and Alex waited for the light to cross United Nations Plaza, a family approached them. The woman wore the long robes and head covering of one of the Muslim countries. The man pointed to Pilar and she heard him say to his children, "She is the sheik of the whole world."

What a responsibility, Pilar thought. To win a second term she had to listen to the United States; but to be sheik of the whole world, she had to listen to every nation. This was not just a job she had won – she was a world leader. She knew how to weave her way through the jungles of office politics, but how did one become a world leader?

Alex had been staring up and down the street, his eye on every passing car. The light changed and they started across the street. He seemed on high alert and he began to talk, almost nervously. "You know, Madame, Asha's right about the IMF, the World Bank and the WTO."

"Un-huh," Pilar responded.

"They're not very democratic. The United States gets to name the head of the World Bank. Watch the curb there, Madame. And the WTO operates on consensus of the rich nations. In effect the rich nations have a veto over trade policies."

A few more steps and they were in the US mission – and Alex's speech stopped as suddenly as it had started. He looked at ease now as they took the elevator up to Brennan's office. *When he's tense, he talks*, Pilar guessed and dismissed the matter.

Alex and Pilar waited in Brennan's outer office. 9:40, 9:50, 10 AM. Pilar's secretary had called ahead to verify the 9:45 appointment time.

As they sat there, Pilar caught sight of Yusuf in the corridor with two characters who looked as if they were extras in a Mafia movie. She tapped Alex on the knee and nodded toward the corridor, but Alex was already looking. "What's he up to?" she asked.

Alex shook his head. "Brennan's spy," was all he said.

She knew every government had spies – every government but the UN.

At a few minutes after 10 AM Brennan's secretary told her to go in. She had waited more than twenty minutes. Brennan practiced the old school of business – make the petitioner wait in order to enhance your own position.

Brennan was on the phone and motioned her to sit down. A half dozen old leather chairs made the area in front of his desk feel heavy. Pilar noted that, though this room was larger than her office, no casual coffee table/chair arrangement allowed for open communication.

"No. No. I won't allow it," Brennan said emphatically to the person on the phone. "This is a matter for the Security Council, not —" He listened again and then said, "I won't hear of it. The General Assembly will chew this thing forever."

Here was confirmation of another complaint that the small, poor nations made – that the big powers shifted matters to the Security

Council where they had the veto. Pilar thought of Madeline Albright's comment that the UN was just a tool of American diplomacy. Pilar lectured herself not to get angry at Brennan – or at Madeline Albright.

On his desk was a business card holder, a small metal figure of a cowboy twirling his lasso. The base of the statue was a horseshoe.

He saw her looking at it and faced it toward her. He motioned for her to take a card.

His facial expression changed to frustration with his caller. "You just have to get a better slant on it. It's not good enough." He banged the phone back into its holder. "State department bureaucrats," he muttered, "they make more than me, but they're dumb as a bum on the run."

He reached over and picked up the cowboy. "Ain't that somethin'? Made by a Texas rancher."

He pointed to a small desk clock on the opposite side of his desk. The clock was framed and supported again by horseshoes and it had a small silver spur near the base. "Given to me by a little lady – she was a rodeo rider. She could wrestle a bull to the ground in no time flat. She said I should be president of these United States."

God help us, Pilar thought.

"What can I do for you, Madame Secretary?" Brennan asked in a bright tone.

"Tom, I'd like to proceed with your suggestion for aid to Somalia. It seems your approach was the best one."

"My approach?"

"Yes, keeping things out of the limelight. I've prepared a brief report." She took a single sheet from her brief case and handed it to him.

He scanned it and looked up. "Yes, yes, I see – the Red Crescent, the Red Cross, Doctors Without Borders and CARE. Give UN funds to them and let them buy the food and water."

He put the paper down and looked across the desk at her. Pilar had the feeling she was going to get a father-to-naïve daughter talk.

"Talked to my staff about this. You have to understand the Somali people. They need a strong leader to run the country. Siad Barre ran the country for twenty-two years. You and I might like democratic structures but we have to be realistic with these people. They're all involved with clan and tribe – stuff we don't know much about. Pilar, I honestly believe the American approach is best – support a strong leader who is friendly to the West, not a despot but a decent human being. I really think we're doing the right thing. We just need a little more time to get everything in place for him."

"I hear you, Tom, but a lot of people are dying while you get ready. And with all due respect, your plan places one tribe ahead of all the others. This may lead to future wars. The UN plan is to educate and strengthen *all* the clans and get them to cooperate with one another."

"We're speaking frankly. That idea is a little too *UN*, if you know what I mean."

"I disagree, Tom. I think it's realistic and humanitarian. But forget our differences on political structure. We've got to provide some immediate help for people who are in trouble."

Brennan picked up her paper again. "Well, it's an interesting idea, but the amount is way too high. Can we cut it down – way down?"

She had expected this and had already inflated her needs. "I suppose we could cut a little if you feel strongly about it. What percent cut would you suggest?"

Brennan studied the page. "Twenty percent?"

"How about fifteen?" She had figured the request with a twenty-five percent inflation.

He dropped the paper and pushed it toward her across the glistening surface of his desk. "No, I tell you, Madame, on second thought I don't like the whole thing. Like I said, the time isn't right. You did a great turn for those Somalis going over there. You got some good press. Called the world's attention to the problems. That's enough."

"Thank you, Tom. Publicity helps, but you can't drink it or eat it."

"I don't need to tell you, Pilar, it's the US that pays most of the bills."

"And it's US suppliers that receive most of the money, you know that, Tom."

He looked exasperated and shifted position in his chair. "You met Hassan in Mogadishu, didn't you?" Brennan asked. "At least….I heard you did."

"Yes, I did. And I'm not surprised you heard. I saw Yusuf outside your office. It turns out he doesn't work for the State Department as you told me, but for the CIA."

"My mistake. Sorry."

"And my deputy Secretary-General, Mr. Quan. He came along. You know, Tom, it's a side issue now, but I'd like your advice sometime on whether the pay is adequate for that post. We don't want any corruption in the UN, do we?"

Brennan sat up straight. "Do you suspect him?" She heard the nervousness in his voice.

"Do you?"

Brennan waved his hand to dismiss this topic of conversation. "Let's get back to Hassan. He's our hope for Somalia. When the circumstances are right, we'll round up lots of food and water for him."

"And weapons?" she asked.

Brennan became defensive. "Hassan needs strength to establish law and order. That country is a mess. Why don't we just forget about this for now? You've done enough, Madame."

He handed her proposal back. "Now if you'll excuse me…" He looked at his watch.

Pilar didn't move. "ABC News is interviewing me this afternoon about my trip to Somalia. I'd like to tell them that Ambassador Thomas Brennan has found a way to help the agencies in Somalia. The press usually ask a lot of tough questions, for example who put the hold on the thirty million dollars in the State Department's budget? And why is the money being held when a half million people have died? And why has the company you started opened an office in Somalia? And—"

"Hold on. I have no connection with the company anymore."

"I know that, Tom. But you know how the press are. They're a nasty bunch. They'll ask me what I think about you becoming Secretary of State and, of course, I'd like to tell them that you'll make a great one because you're worried about Somali children dying."

"Fair enough, little lady. Let's see what tomorrow brings."

He stared at her for a moment, his mean eyes taking her measure, his face stuck in that sickening diplomatic smile.

"Will you back me," she continued, "in the Security Council?"

He stood up. "I can't do that, Madame. And you'll have to talk to ABC news as the professional you are. We can have our differences, but we can't be accusing each other of things that can't be proved."

"Tom, this really doesn't affect your plan for Somalia. This is UN money and it's for an immediate humanitarian project. If I can convince the other council members, let me at least get your promise that you won't veto it. You can abstain, if you want."

"Fair enough, little lady. Let's see what tomorrow brings."

Chapter 9

Appointment Schedule for the Secretary-General
Tuesday, October 10

8:30 AM– Prayer Breakfast with the Ecumenical Society of
    New York
9:30 AM – Ms. Valencia Folguera, President of the European
    Parliament
10:30 AM – Meeting of the Fifth Committee
1:30 PM – Security Council Meeting

On her way to the prayer breakfast, Pilar reached the Chilean
ambassador on her cell phone. Alex sat opposite her in the jump
seat of the limo.

"Ambassador, I need your vote this afternoon. I'm bringing
forward an emergency request for food and water for the Somali
crisis."

She listened to his response and then pleaded again. "Please,
Ambassador, contact your government. Half a million people have
already died. It's a true emergency."

She snapped the phone shut. "Trouble," she said to Alex.
"Brennan's been lobbying the other way."

This morning Alex looked strong and tough in his navy business
suit and sunglasses, like a secret service man or a Clint Eastwood
character. Security men had often accompanied UN missions she'd

been part of, but she'd never had her own bodyguard. In her experience protection people were competent, but very ordinary. Alex was out of the ordinary.

"I checked further for you last night, Madame," Alex said. "Brennan's former company has placed a large order with the Dimico Corporation. They're out of Ontario, a big producer of small arms."

Pilar shook her head and muttered, "Damn fellow Canadians."

Alex took off his glasses. With his eyes showing, he looked very compassionate. "Back to the vote, Madame, what's the count?"

"I need nine of the fifteen, eight if Brennan abstains. I've got France, Britain, Russia, China, Argentina and Pakistan, six in all. I was on the phone last night with Gabon and Namibia. Brennan's been talking to them, promising big US projects in their countries. Same with Chile. But those three countries are my only hope. He's got five countries solid for him and his own makes six. We each have six and we're vying for Gabon, Namibia and Chile."

"Very tight."

"Yes, Alex."

Pilar fell silent as the limo worked its way through the early morning traffic. Manhattan was coming alive, cabs weaving in and out, couriers on bicycles racing headlong into traffic, people hurrying to work.

Pilar envied them. They were heading off to work, but she was on her way to disaster. Unless she was sure of the outcome, she should have never introduced the Somali proposal.

As she looked out the window, she evaluated her first few weeks as Secretary-General. They had not gone well. She was reacting to situations, rather than being pro-active. She was no better than a city councilman or a ward politician. She had probably alienated a key player – *the* key player, Brennan – if she wanted to win a second term. If she failed, it would be a long time before another woman served as Secretary-General.

If her motion this afternoon was defeated, it would be a public relations nightmare from which she would never recover. The press would write her off as ineffective.

Could she change her style if she lost? Could she revert to the methods she used to rise in the bureaucracy? Many previous Secretaries-General survived by just going along and smoothing things out. Where had she come up with this idea that leadership was important? Only Dag Hammarskjöld before her had been a true leader. He did not sit back and let situations get out of hand. He was the first to employ an emergency force – a UN army to protect the peace between opposing nations. No *statement-maker* was he – in fact he died in a plane crash in the jungle on his way to arrange a cease-fire in the Congo.

But the hard truth was that she had failed to be a Dag Hammarskjöld.

What about the Somali woman in the photograph? If she changed her style and stopped worrying about Somalia, what would happen to the woman and her remaining daughter?

*   *   *

She said a few words at the prayer breakfast, even though her mind was still on the upcoming vote and then she hurried back to her office to meet the President of the European Parliament, Valencia Folguera. The two discussed the Balkan situation and the Middle East. At 10:30 she attended the meeting of the Fifth Committee, the one concerned with the UN's budget. The Fifth Committee met until 12:45, giving her just forty-five minutes for lunch. She used the time to attempt to reach the ambassadors from Gabon, Namibia and Chile, but without success. Asha came up to her office to report that she had failed to sway her fellow African countries. "Very attractive aid packages from the US," Asha said.

When Asha left, Pilar made a cup of tea and tried to get herself under control. This is what her mother did when she was under pressure – make a cup of tea. But her mother seemed to live life without crisis, every day the same as the last, everything under control. Most often, tea was a drink of friendship and relaxation – seldom one of crisis.

Pilar knew she was like her mother – at least she had been when she was a department head. She handled department crises firmly, immediately and calmly. Tea was a soothing drink and not a response to crisis.

What was wrong with her now?

A few minutes later Pilar sat in her designated seat at the Security Council. As she read through her notes for the afternoon's agenda, the British ambassador approached her. Charles Kent-Ashley was an old friend, his time in the British Foreign Office matched hers at the UN. They had helped each other many times in the past. Technically, he and the United Kingdom had introduced the Somali resolution because the Secretary-General could not introduce resolutions by herself.

"Madame, just a word. We might be wise to drop our Somali resolution. It's Brennan, you know. Chile is against it. A big US project for water purification. Probably others. The US mission has been very busy. If the motion looks like it will win, well…" he shrugged "… I wonder if they will veto it?"

She wanted to reach out and touch him to thank him for his support, but she stopped herself. A part of her mind noted how often in recent times she had felt a need for human, physical contact.

"Let's wait until the recess, Charles," she said as the chair for that month called the meeting to order and started with the agenda.

While the council discussed the refugee situation in the Balkans, Pilar considered what she should do. The United States had its own plan for Somalia and they didn't want the UN interfering. This was nothing new. In Kosovo the US depended, not on the UN, but on NATO. The problem was *when* would they help Somalia. How many people would die first? When would Brennan arrange his big shipment to Hassan?

What if the woman in the picture was not part of Hassan's tribe or clan?

At 3:30 when the Council recessed, she made straight for Brennan. She intended to let her anger out. By actively campaigning against her, she felt he had gone back on his word of yesterday.

Brennan looked up and saw her coming and immediately turned and headed for the men's room.

He came out only after the call to resume.

She glared at him as the meeting resumed, but then she tried to control her anger. After all, she reminded herself, every country operated on self interest and America was no different. She was Secretary-General and spoke for every country, including America.

Should she pull the resolution? Practical wisdom said not to suffer a public defeat, but maybe she still had a chance to convince others. If she could get a majority on the council, then the US would have to veto the resolution with others in favor. They would not want to do that – especially on a resolution to help people dying of hunger and thirst.

4:30 – the resolution finally came up. Pilar stood, itself a departure from Security Council procedure where all speeches were delivered sitting down. The paper shuffling stopped. All eyes turned toward her.

Ambassadors, Presidents, honorable members, guests, The United Kingdom and I have before you a resolution I think you should reject.

The members stared at her. She could read their minds. A resolution they should reject? She continued.

It's too weak. It tries to help the dying people of Somalia by giving money to NGOs, and then letting them aid Somalia. Further it only calls for a million, not nearly enough to save the lives of the people. I hope you will amend this resolution and make the UN responsible. Let's start with UN funds – two and a half million dollars – and let the UN distribute the aid. This is a world problem and we need a world solution.

She went on to describe the suffering of the people and told of her visit to Mogadishu. She called on all the countries of the UN to be generous. She told how the United States had generously budgeted thirty million for the Somalis. And she reassured the members that this time the aid would go to the people and not to the warlords. She related how she had personally met with the key warlords. Yes, they would need some peacekeepers, but not many if the cooperation of the warlords held.

I come before you with this change of plans because I think what the UN needs is strong leadership. The time has passed for the Secretary-General to flit around the diplomatic circle and deliver carefully phrased, subtle diplomatic messages. It's time for action. It's time to help the Somalis.

Pilar sat down. She saw responsive faces around her. Instead of chatting with staff and passing notes to their assistants, the ambassadors had been listening to her.

Ever loyal, Charles Kent-Ashley offered the necessary amendments and other nations made statements. Pilar listened as country by country gave their reaction, all favorable. Gabon and Namibia said they had been strongly lobbied to oppose the resolution, but they would vote for it with the changes.

She called a brief recess for countries to contact their governments. She had created a bandwagon effect and she figured that everyone would like to be part of a winning resolution.

When the session resumed, Pilar listened carefully as the ambassador from Chile spoke. She knew enough Spanish to understand most of what the woman said. The ambassador indicated that Chile was originally against this project. Chile badly needed help to clean up some of its domestic water supply. "All we ever have money for," the ambassador said, "is to pay interest to North American and European countries. But we do have water, even if it's not clean water, while the people of Somali have none. We have been lobbied fiercely and even threatened that funds for our water purification program will be cut. But Chile is standing up for what is right. We are voting for this resolution."

Pilar smiled. All ten non-permanent nations were in agreement. Then came the five permanent members – the ones who had the veto. One-by-one Britain, China, France and Russia supported the motion. Only the United States remained.

Good, Pilar thought, *I've got it. Brennan won't oppose all the others on a humanitarian motion.*

Brennan was conferring with an aide and the Council waited for him to speak. After a few minutes, he began:

Honorable members, the United States is the only country here with practical experience of helping the Somalis. In 1993 we sent our troops there when – I speak frankly– when UN forces fell down on the job. We wanted to see people fed, just like the UN did. But there was no law and order in Somalia and I regret to say there still isn't. We lost eighteen of our finest soldiers trying to control the warlords. President Clinton pulled the troops out. Warlords still rule Somalia and if we send aid, the same thing will happen – only those loyal to one warlord or another will receive aid.

The United States hopes someday democracy and a legitimate government will come to Somalia, a government with the power to enforce the law. When that happens I hope all countries will help.

Madame Secretary has worked hard and has called attention to the problems there. She has risked a lot to go there and see conditions for herself. We owe her a debt of gratitude. But until such time as we see law and order in Somalia, we cannot waste our money sending food and water that will just go to warlords. The United States calls for a study to be made and for now, it vetoes this resolution.

Chapter 10

Appointment Schedule for the Secretary-General
Wednesday, October 11

10:00 AM – Meeting and Photos with UN Guides
12:30 PM – Presentation of Credentials: Amb. Mr. Mathabiso
Moleleki of LesotoAmb. Ms. Marie Ajodhia of
Suriname
1:30 PM – Address and Presentation of a UN scholarship award
to Dini Abdallah Waiss of Djibouti
3:00 PM – Mr. Toomas Pärnoja, President of Estonia
4:00 PM – Mr. Anatole Zoungrana, President of Burkina Faso

Pilar looked at the headlines on her desk. *Secretary-General suffers defeat. US vetoes aid for Somalia.* Far worse, however, was the commentary piece: *The Peter Principle – Has the Secretary-General Risen to the Point of her Incompetence?*

Incompetence? She closed the paper and slammed it on her desk without reading the whole article. She knew the words that would there – *realities of the situation, woman, political skills, gentler sex.* Sometimes the cliché-ridden press made her sick.

She stood and strode to the window. Was she incompetent? Absolutely not. Her rise to power showed that. But what then? The article had a point – she had responded to a situation instead of carefully planning her every move. Previously she had moved up

through the bureaucracy like a stony chess player, but now she had
reacted emotionally, a woman trying to get some water for another
woman. She had been an Anne Sullivan helping a Helen Keller.

"That's not how you play the game of Secretary-General," she
said out loud as she gazed down at a sunny New York. She had to be
a Margaret Thatcher.

"Follow the path of your predecessors," her mother reminded
her at least five times in the short two weeks between her election
and her mother's untimely death. "They were very careful
diplomats."

There was need for reform, but reform was a matter for a second
term. Reform raised hackles and redistributed power. Study after
study had laid out the changes needed in the UN. First of all, the
veto had to go. It poisoned the very heart of the organization. And
the UN needed a big dose of democracy, control by all the members
of the UN and not just by the rich nations. Further, the world brushed
the UN aside as a debating society, not as a real government with
power. US presidents used it only when it served their convenience.

She glanced at her watch. In fifteen minutes she had to get her
picture taken with the UN guides. Photographs were positive. A
young aide would probably show off her picture with *Madame
Secretary*. This was the way her predecessors had built their good
names – a thousand photographs of a thousand handshakes. Why
had she been so foolish to venture into the quagmire of Somalia?

Perhaps a quick walk in the UN gardens would revive her spirits
before meeting the aides. She took her elevator down and stepped
outside to the beautiful day. The sun shone on October roses in the
gardens. She listened to the languages of people walking through
the gardens – German, Spanish, Japanese, an Indian language,
possibly Punjabi, and English. Yes, the UN was a western invention,
arising from western concepts, but it was a wonderful idea. It
provided a forum for people to talk and it did practical things like
the Farjano Water project.

As most people said, "It's got its faults, but what else is there?"

She just had to calm down and take her place on the great mandela, the wheel of life. She was not a world leader, she was just another Secretary-General.

After meeting with the guides, she returned to her office and had her secretary set up several trips for the next several days. She chose locations that would give her plenty of photo opportunities: a visit to Washington with many political hands to shake and a trip to Los Angeles and Hollywood, where a reception would honor celebrity UN supporters.

Handshakes and photo ops ignored the charge of incompetence. The person who shook famous hands would be famous themselves.

* * *

At ten minutes to four, as she waited for her last appointment, she reflected on her day. Despite yesterday's defeat, interesting people enlivened her spirits. The president of Estonia knew twice as much about the UN as Brennan did. The new Ambassador from Suriname was a young woman, filled with ideas about how the UN should be reformed. She complimented Pilar on her actions for Somalia. "I want to work with you, Madame Secretary," she said. "My country thinks the UN needs reform, but you must lead us, show us the way."

Nothing *incompetent* about that statement.

The only negative in the day had been the appearance of a Raging Granny at the 1:30 PM scholarship presentation. Pilar had seen the woman at other UN events. She wore an outlandish hat with fake grapes, apples and bananas on it. Her skirt was a quilt and she had flung a granny shawl over her frilly blouse. Apparently she had passed security, hat and all.

"This scholarship is funded by the World Bank," the woman shouted right after the ceremony, pointing her umbrella at Pilar. Pilar knew the grannies usually traveled in groups and sang, but this woman worked alone and yelled instead of singing. "The World Bank and the International Monetary Fund keep poor people poor."

As security guards muscled her out of the room, she called out, "I'm Elizabeth Cady Stanton and I'm watching you, Pilar Marti.

You didn't help the poor people of Somalia. You're a dupe of the United States."

How infuriating. To be accused of *not helping*. And how insensitive the woman was to the young man from Djibouti who won the scholarship. His parents stood right there. Indeed, there was nothing *poor* about this young man. His father was a doctor, his mother, a lawyer. And a dupe of the US? That accusation was precisely what she had fought against – and lost. That's what Brennan wanted her to be – a dupe. That's what his action at the Council yesterday was supposed to teach her, that if she wanted to succeed at the UN, she had to do what the US wanted.

And the woman's name was suspicious. Elizabeth Cady Stanton was a nineteenth century suffragette, a colleague of Susan B. Anthony. Who was this Raging Granny and what was her business?

As the woman was hustled out, Pilar caught sight of Yusuf just outside the room. He stood there, his face as impassive as ever, his arms folded as if he were waiting for some future apocalypse. Why was he stalking her? Hadn't he and Brennan won? Was there a need to embarrass her further?

Her secretary ended these reflections by announcing that her next appointment was here –   President Anatole Zoungrana of Burkina Faso. She knew Anatole personally. He was one of the most charismatic people she'd ever met.

Seven years ago she was sent to Burkina Faso as a special UN envoy to find solutions to a tribal fight that threatened to break into a full civil war. Anatole was the mayor of the village where the fighting centered. It was he who got the warring sides to sit down together. "I have a plan," he said to both sides. "I have figured it all out. There is enough water for both tribes, if we are careful. Here, come and look. I have put it on paper. Let's talk about it."

All she did was back his plan up with western conservation and recycling techniques, but it was Anatole who listened for hours to tales of how the Lobi stole water from the Mossi, and the Lobi claimed it was their water, but the Mossi said no, it was their water. Anatole got everyone to agree to joint tribal management and inspection by all sides.

When the media did a feature story on the peace agreement, Anatole gave Pilar a lot of the credit. At the time she was competing with three men for a senior leadership position in the UN bureaucracy. The Burkina Faso publicity won her the position.

On her last day there, Anatole took her to the airport and waited with her an extra four hours because of a delayed flight. They had lunch. In her experience diplomats and politicians were full of themselves, but not this man. They talked, not about him and his great accomplishments, but about her. He steered the conversation to her life at the UN and her life in general. Under his gentle persuasion she talked about herself more than she had in years – her parents, her early life, her desire for advancement at the UN and even the years she spent with Stuart. All the way back to New York, she thought about Anatole, even fantasized about him.

Two years after Pilar worked with him, Anatole's wife stepped on a land mine while she and Anatole were out walking. His wife was killed and he was severely injured. The explosion completely blinded him, marred his face with an ugly scar, blew off his right ear and damaged his legs so badly that he had to use two canes to walk.

Despite this tragedy he had risen to power in Burkina Faso. Pilar had followed his career in the papers. Without portfolio, without even the approval of the weak government in his country, he went to the European Union and convinced them to invest in the future of Burkina Faso. Then he returned home and worked tirelessly to get the government to agree to the European Union's conditions. He went to Australia, Canada and the United States and asked for grants. Again, he was successful. He became a symbol of hope to the people and he brought them together. He was elected president by a landslide.

This wrecked human being had accomplished what powerful military men had not been able to do – he unified the country.

Pilar learned this information from friends in Burkina Faso and from news reports. She had not seen him herself in seven years.

Quickly she glanced through the fact book about his country. Twelve million people in western Africa, almost half a million living with HIV/AIDS. Like Somalia, the country had faced drought, poor crops and tribal fighting. But there was no immediate crisis in the country.

She stepped into her restroom and checked her appearance in the mirror. She smoothed a wandering strand of hair, powdered a too-shiny nose, and then smiled at her action – Anatole was completely blind. She held her left hand up in front of her face and spread her fingers out. For once there was no need to hide her missing little finger.

Instead of buzzing her secretary, she went out herself to bring him into her office. Somehow he sensed her presence and stood. "Pilar, is that you?

He allowed her no time for shock at his appearance. "Y-y-yes," she said.

He stood slowly with his two canes and stepped toward her. He shifted his left cane to his right hand and reached for her as if to hug her. She took his arm and placed it on her shoulder. His head touched hers and she felt a sudden thrill, but she excused it as not having seen him in such a long time. He smelled fresh, like the cool air that descended on Vancouver after a hot summer day when she was growing up.

"Anatole," she said warmly, "it's so good to see you." His frizzy hair was whiter now, but his calm, steady face still emanated strength.

"Pilar…no … Madame Secretary," he said, the scar on his face crinkling with his smile. "Congratulations on your election."

Obviously he did not want her to go on about his injuries. "Come in," she said, gently nudging him in the right direction.

Slowly he hobbled into her office. She had read that he always refused a wheelchair, even though his progress on canes was very slow.

She led him to one of the leather chairs and then sat opposite him. What did he want, she wondered.

He settled in and rested his canes against the arm of the chair. She looked at his deep ebony features and mentally traced the ugly scar that ran from the corner of his mouth to the top of his nose. He was about her age, maybe a few years younger. He spoke perfect

English, having studied for six years at the University of Washington in Seattle.

They chatted about their time together in Burkina Faso, but she noted how different she felt with him. With anyone else she would have been on guard, waiting for the request for money, trying to think three steps ahead of her petitioner. With Anatole she could relax. If he had a request to make, she knew he would have already anticipated how it would affect her. Perhaps this ability to understand things from another's point of view was the reason for his phenomenal success in his country.

He was indeed a cool breeze after her defeat yesterday.

There was a break in the conversation and then he said quietly, "You did the right thing in regard to Somalia."

"A *losing* right thing," she replied. "Politicians judge things by success. In their eyes, my efforts were a failure."

"On the contrary. You showed the people of Africa that you were willing to stand up to the United States."

"Confrontation is not a good strategy."

He said nothing in response. His sightless eyes blinked a minute and then he took his canes and pulled himself up. "Let's walk to your window."

She led him to her big window. Red reflections bounced into her window from the sun in the west sparkling off the glittering surface of New York skyscrapers. "When I was coming here," he said, "I felt the sun shining on me. This is such a wonderful country, Pilar, this America." He reached his hand toward her. "Of course, Canada is great, too. But what I mean is that the sun shines so brightly on America. God must love it very much."

Most Arabs she knew, and many Africans, did not have pleasant words to say about America. This man was certainly an exception.

He stood in silence for a moment. "Let's go back and sit down," he said finally.

She guided him back and they sat. Gently she asked, "What can I do for you, Anatole?"

"What do I want?" He gestured toward the window. "I want this great country to live up to its promise, to bring freedom and a good life to the rest of the world. The United States started the United Nations in the closing days of World War II — well, there were others — but the United States was the key. What has gone wrong?"

Pilar knew he was in what she called, 'his speech mode.' Back in Africa he would rehearse his speeches out loud, improving them as he went.

"The world is not fair now, Pilar. It is not right that Somalia and my country do not have enough food, while Westerners have too much. We in Africa despair of the situation ever righting itself. Despair is the curse of Somalia and it was the curse of my country. I have tried so hard to give hope to my people. I talk to the people every day on the radio. I tell them that small things are happening, that last month fewer trees died from overgrazing, that the Israelis are coming to show us how they made the desert bloom."

He paused and put his hand out to her. She hesitated for a second, then reassured herself that it was okay to touch Anatole's hand. Since he had no sight, that was one way he communicated – by touch.

She took his hand and noticed how rough and callused it felt, like he himself had been out planting or laying pipe for an irrigation system. "You did right in Somalia," he continued, "even if it was only a little request. Never mind that you lost. We in Africa know you will fight for us. We know you will try to help us. We know you are not going to allow other countries to take our natural resources. You give us hope and that is the most important thing in the world."

She smiled openly at his compliments and let go of his hand. Funny, there was no need to mask one's face around him and it was not just that he was blind. She could be her natural self. He was complimenting her for Secretary-General-type actions. Helping suffering people is what a Secretary-General was supposed to do. She was living up to the expectations of her office.

The political part of her brain called up a saying, "Champions of the downtrodden don't get re-elected." But then she recalled the case of Franklin Delano Roosevelt, the champion of the forgotten men, who won four terms as President of the United States.

"But what does your country need today, Anatole?" she asked quietly.

"I came for what I said, to thank you for trying to help Africa. It is not just me, but several African leaders feel the same way. When they heard I was in the United States raising money, they asked me to represent them. But I speak for me as well."

"Thank you, Anatole."

"In my country we have a custom – we offer a visitor a cup of water as soon as they enter our home. Water is very precious in Africa. You have offered us a cup of water. You have done the courteous thing. Now we are ready to get down to business."

"Anatole, don't speak in riddles. What is the business?"

"To give hope to Africa. To fight off despair."

She was about to ask *how* when he interrupted her. "No, I misspoke. You must give hope to the whole world. You are Secretary-General of the United Nations."

"How?"

"Right the wrongs."

"Anatole, we know each other. That is too simple."

He held out his hand to her and she grasped it again. "The answer is in the problem. What I mean is the hope for the UN is *in* its biggest problem, America. The government in Washington has drifted away from the ideals of the people and away from their own heritage. Go talk to the people of the land – they support the UN. They approve of the idea.

"Study America. It's a true democracy. The UN must be a democracy. The veto must go. The power of the Security Council must be limited. The people of the United States believe in fairness. The world must become fair, just as Americans try to be fair. Resources must be shared.

"Go to the American people. Tell them about a UN that is *like them*. Look at the great country these ideals have produced. Put democracy and fairness in the UN, and we will have a *great* world."

He let go of her hand and sat back, as if he was resting after his dramatic speech. She sat back, too, and together they enjoyed the quiet.

"How is your country?" she asked at last.

"As the rest of Africa. I am sure you know that Africa is getting poorer, not richer. But I must go now." He struggled to his feet using his canes. "You have much to do, Madame Secretary."

After he left, she sat at her desk and stared at the picture of the Somali woman with the two children. She had begun her day feeling incompetent. Her strategy then was to shake hands for the next five years. Now Anatole had reminded her that incompetence was in the eye of the beholder and that her strategy should be to find the answer to the UN inside its biggest problem, the United States of America.

Chapter 11

Appointment Schedule for the Secretary-General
Wednesday, October 25

1:00 PM – Arrival from Los Angeles
2:30 PM – Meeting of the General Assembly

Honorable members,…" the Egyptian delegate began as Pilar slipped into her seat, "…and also you, Madame Secretary, I want to nominate the great river Nile…" he spread his arms wide, as if to indicate how long the river was "… as our choice for *Year of the River.*"

Pilar acknowledged his greeting with a nod. The debate about the river would continue, the real issue being which country would get the million dollars for promotion. She stole a glance at the page her secretary had prepared for her, the summary of important correspondence that had come to her office while she was away.

There were letters from India and Pakistan accusing each other of incursion into the other's territory in Kashmir. The delegate from Tanzania charged that a restaurant in New York was racist. The summary also mentioned communiqués about human rights abuses, children working, land mines and an official letter from the City of New York demanding money for police services.

She looked up from the paper, trying to pay attention. "The Nile flows 6,677 kilometers to the sea and…"

Pilar suppressed a yawn. Up since 4 AM, an early flight back from the West Coast. She felt drained, a vacuum inside her. However, it had been a great trip, first Washington, D.C. and then Los Angeles.

In Washington, she met with senators and representatives. Stuart still had good contacts with White House staff and he got her in to see influential Democrats. But Pilar broadened her perspective and met with several key Republicans as well. She found individual senators and representatives to be reasonable, intelligent people. Whether Democrat or Republican, they seemed supportive of the UN's work. One senator knew the history of the UN and how the United States backed it fully after World War II. Another senator appreciated the regulatory work of the world body and said that without it, the world would have disintegrated into chaos.

Where, then, did the strong anti-UN sentiment come from? The only answer was the leadership – the leadership of the country in the person of the current incumbent of the White House and the leadership of the party in control of the Congress.

Leadership was key, in Washington as it was in UN headquarters.

In Hollywood she was a celebrity. Fierce competition went on behind the scenes for her to appear at various homes for parties. She could almost hear the discussions, "Well, that's nothing. The Secretary-General was here for a party and…"

Several Hollywood personalities seemed genuinely interested in her efforts in Somalia and a promoter offered to arrange a fund-raising concert. She suggested that he had a good idea and should work with an agency like Doctors Without Borders or the Red Crescent.

She spent a day meeting ordinary Americans in a visit to a factory, a school and a shopping mall. She was amazed at the level of support for the UN and the concern people had for the poorer nations. Good leadership had a lot to build on in America.

The whole trip confirmed Anatole's words about the greatness of America, their love of democracy and freedom, their concern for the poor. Brennan was *not* typical of the American people.

The high-pitched voice of a translator jarred her out of her reflection. "It all depends on how you measure the length of a river," the translator squeaked out the words of the Brazilian delegate. She knew Carlos, the Brazilian, a mountain of a man, who wrestled in his youth. The chirping translator did not fit him. The voice screeched on. "Everyone knows the *Amazon* is the longest – and the greatest – river in the world – and it drains a far larger area than the Nile."

Pilar suppressed another yawn and glanced at the second page of her summary correspondence. It was a note from Brennan. In reality, it was her own letter returned to her with several red marks on it. She had sent out a list of nominees for her cabinet to every nation that had a name on the list. She meant it as a courtesy and, of course, as a way of double-checking her candidates. Her letter indicated, however, that the decision was hers to make. The Chinese may have imposed Quan on her as her deputy, but she was determined to name the rest of her staff, her legal counsel, her economic advisers and the third highest official, the Chef de Cabinet.

Brennan's note was an insult. Not only had he crossed off her American nominee, but he had also put a line through all her key advisers. The only names untouched were the humanitarian cabinet positions, such as UNICEF and the World Food Programme. Most of Brennan's substitutions were Americans and only those of a conservative frame of mind. At the bottom of the page Brennan had penned a note: *The names I have indicated will show your willingness to work with the United States Government and will help you persuade a reluctant Congress to fund this organization.*

"A tidal bore sweeps up the Amazon at 65 kilometers an hour. The bore travels up the river 650 kilometers. Sometimes the waves are five meters high." The trilling bird translated the story of the mighty tidal bore. "The tributaries of the Amazon are…"

Pilar felt like standing up and ripping Brennan's letter to pieces in front of the General Assembly. For a minute she considered nominating *no* Americans, but that would be acknowledging Brennan's power over her. She had tried working with the man. What was the diplomatic answer?

She felt her face flush as her anger rose. She bent down and covered her forehead with her hand. The hell with Brennan. She would send a noncommittal note to him, thanking him for his input and then appoint every damn name on the list. No other country had said anything. Without a staff she couldn't function. Brennan be damned.

The Chinese delegate began to speak. "China's Yangzi River has to be included in any discussion of...."

She needed a plan. *The Washington Post* defined her problem as *crisis lurch* – lurching from crisis to crisis. *The Dallas Morning News* insulted her in an editorial, claiming she ran the UN like most women went shopping – bouncing from store to store. *Mission creep*, the paper called it.

Perhaps a strategy session would help – Anatole and Stuart, maybe Alex and Asha. But only after she got some sleep.

"I think we should delay this matter to another day," the President of the General Assembly said. "It's approaching 4 PM and several members have evening functions to attend."

Pilar knew the President referred to a banquet sponsored by the US Chamber of Commerce. The meeting had lasted an hour and a half and nothing had been resolved. If the General Assembly was going to have more power, it had to work harder.

After adjournment, she started for the back of the General Assembly hall where she liked to spend a few minutes in reflection after a meeting. Kao Shu-ling, an unofficial negotiator from Taiwan, stopped her. "Madame, my government wants to send you an invitation to come to Taiwan. We thought it best to approach you first informally."

"Thank you. I'll consider it," she responded.

He departed and she walked toward the back of the hall. What a diplomatic nightmare that would be. China considered Taiwan nothing more than a renegade province. And, of course, China had the veto. But why shouldn't Taiwan be recognized as a country? They wanted representation. Was she going to let the big nations of the world bully the little nations?

As she approached the visitors' seats in the back, she recognized Stuart coming in her direction.

Oh my God, she thought, *I can't take him today. All talk, no help. Criticize, criticize, criticize.*

"Madame. Nice to see you. How was your trip?"

"Good, Stuart, but I'm pretty tired. Jet lag and all. What can I do for you?"

As usual he wore a white shirt and a bow tie. And the fabric of his shirt pocket strained to hold in many pieces of paper.

"I need to talk to you. I have a plan you may find interesting."

Despite his cynicism, the man did have some creative ideas. She pointed to the last seats. "Can we go up there and sit in the back? After a meeting I like to look at the big symbol of the world in the front of the hall. It reminds me of what we're all about."

He walked with her. "They don't need a world up there on the wall, they need a big river – the longest river. What a bore."

She decided to misunderstand him. "Yes, that's really something, isn't it? A tidal bore 400 miles back up the Amazon."

That silenced him and she welcomed the quiet.

Stuart's easy stride next to her reminded her of Anatole's agonizing struggle with his two canes.

Even though he was back in Africa, Anatole had been on her mind a lot in the last two weeks. Once, while attending a party at a home overlooking the ocean in California, she stepped out to a verandah and gazed at a star in the western sky. It put her in mind of him – steady, bright, soothing, definite, clear.

When they reached the back, Pilar said, "Let's sit quietly for a moment." She really wanted sleep, but knew she must be courteous.

Pilar stared at the large painting of the world, viewed from space looking down on the North Pole and bracketed by the two olive branches. It was good to get away from words.

She closed her eyes and drifted. A blue color spread over the earth starting at the North Pole. Peace covered the earth. She was a successful Secretary-General. Suddenly the color changed to a warlike red. Flashes occurred all over the globe. She was a failure.

She shook her head awake.

"Sleeping, huh?" Stuart mocked.

"Just resting my eyes. What can I do for you?"

"I have developed some new ideas about Somalia, a new approach."

Somalia again.

For two weeks she'd been meeting people and shaking hands. It was hard to get back into issues. The Somali problem felt heavy, like an armful of books.

"What did you think of the General Assembly meeting today, Stuart? Were you here for most of it?"

As soon as she asked the question, she knew it was a mistake.

"What an organization," Stuart said. "Talk, talk, talk."

Down the aisle Pilar noticed Asha talking to Alex. Alex pointed to where she was and Asha started up the aisle toward her. Asha would be a pleasant balance to Stuart. Asha was a soft pillow; Stuart was a starched sheet.

Pilar got up and hugged her. She appreciated Asha's fiery nature and her commitment to Somalia. "I've missed you. I think you should leave the translation section and come work for me."

Asha smiled. "I'm ready. Are you serious?"

"Yes. I will get back to you. But I'm glad you're here now. My friend, Stuart, was just about to suggest a new plan for Somalia. He's a former White House aide."

Asha and Stuart exchanged greetings and then Stuart took a sheet of paper from his shirt pocket and handed it to Pilar. "This is a list of unused funds in the UN budget and my comment on each item."

Pilar examined the paper:

- $500,000 for a conference on water resources for the third world. *Hell. Use it for real water.*
- $200,000 for unfilled development positions – *let's develop some food.*
- $175,000. Unused de-colonization funds – *help Somalis solve their own food and water problems. Handouts are re-colonization.*
- $25,000 planning for outer space exploration conference – *concentrate on Planet Earth*

- $600,000 unspent refugee relief fund – *if we don't help Somalia soon, we'll have more refugees*
- $50,000 conference planning for information technology. *People have to eat first.*

Pilar added the numbers in her mind. It was $1,550,000.

At the bottom of the page Stuart had listed some expenses. First there was the purchase of fresh water, shipping it by barge to Somalia, distribution by tanker truck from there and then emergency food, mainly rice, the total coming to well over two million.

Stuart pointed to the bottom of the page. "Expenses don't equal resources yet. I'm working on it."

Pilar handed the paper to Asha. She knew what the young woman's reaction would be: *Do it. Release the funds. Help the people.* If she asked Asha to help, she would. As for Stuart, his commitment only went as far as drafting the idea.

Asha finished the paper, looked up and stared at her. Her eyes were wide, hopeful. But with Quan and Yusuf watching her every move, Pilar knew she could do little. She'd already gone to the Security Council and been turned down.

"The situation is getting worse," Asha said. "More Somalis are dying."

"Brennan wants more people to die," Stuart said. "That way his man, Hassan, looks like a bigger hero when he brings in the food and water along with the guns."

Pilar's head began to hurt. "Stop, Stuart," she said, putting up her hand. "Too cynical." As soon as she said it, she reprimanded herself. *Too harsh.* But Stuart bounced right back.

"Well, feed a man who is a *little* hungry and you make him strong for revolution. Feed a man who is on the verge of death and he's too weak for anything but gratitude."

Pilar nodded. "True enough."

"So, will you help, Pilar, I mean Madame?" Asha asked.

Pilar smiled. It was nice to be called *Pilar* by this fiery young woman. But she had to disappoint her. "You know I can't, Asha. I'm sorry."

"You can help if you want to," Stuart came back at her.

Oh, this man, pushing her toward action she knew would cause her grief. "They turned me down already, Stuart."

"So? Do it anyway. US presidents do it all the time. Fudge the budgets. It's easier to get forgiveness than permission. You've got to move this crowd off dead center. Leadership." He gestured to the General Assembly in front of him. "The whole damn thing needs leadership. Not since Dag Hammarskjöld have you had a leader here. This is a fat, lazy organization and you have to push it to the limit. No wonder the popularity of the UN reached its apex in 1945 when it was founded. It's been going downhill ever since. It needs a leader."

Meaning *her*, meaning she wasn't doing a good job, meaning she wasn't a leader. "And what does a leader do, Stuart?"

"She creates the future."

"What's the future, Stuart, as if you knew?"

"Well, it sure isn't what I saw this afternoon – delegates reading the paper while others talked. And it was just talk. They didn't *do* anything. *Year of the River.* Give me a break."

"The UN feeds people, takes care of their health, worries about their education and sends troops to ensure peace and you dismiss all that with a wave of your hand."

As she sat looking forward, arguing with Stuart, she noticed someone coming up the aisle. It was Yusuf. Alex sat several rows in front of her and he jumped up to confront Yusuf. She watched a heated exchange and then the flashing of badges from both men, with Alex finally letting him pass.

What in God's name is this man up to? She was almost positive she had seen him in Hollywood just outside the door at a reception for her. "What can I do for you, Yusuf?" she said, keeping her voice cold.

He bowed politely, still standing in the aisle. "I fear I have interrupted a séance."

Pilar stared at him, kept her face inscrutable, and ignored his attempt at humor. Every time he came near, she felt the presence of something evil, like a vampire from the horror movies of her youth.

What was Yusuf doing in New York? The CIA and the State Department were in Washington.

"I just stopped by to give Asha a greeting from her grandmother. She wishes you well." He stepped behind their seats and pointed forward to the UN emblem. "Wonderful symbol."

Asha turned to him. "What? My grandmother?" She turned to Pilar to explain. "She lives in Atlanta with my brother."

"How the hell do you know my grandmother?" she fired at Yusuf, "And why were you talking to her – and where?"

"I ran into her."

"Out of millions of people?"

"Here. I wrote her name down." Yusuf pulled a card from his pocket, but dropped it. He picked it up and showed it to Asha.

"That's her name. When did you see her?"

"Oh, ah… just a few days ago. Anyway she wishes you well. I'm sorry, I didn't mean to disturb your conversation. Goodbye now."

Yusuf came from behind their seats and walked down the aisle. Pilar shivered. American intelligence reached deep into families.

As soon as he was out of hearing range, Asha said, "I talked to my grandmother the night before last. She would have said something. He's lying, Pilar. And he's spying on you – and on me."

Pilar watched Yusuf walk past Alex and leave. If it wasn't for Alex, she would fear for her life.

"He's a real CIA type," Stuart said, "but let me get back to giving you a picture of what I think the UN should look like."

"I'm tired, Stuart," Pilar said. "Can't it wait?"

"It'll just take a minute. I've been thinking a lot about the UN since you became Secretary-General. Now watch."

He walked down the aisle to where the representatives sat. He picked up cards from the desks nearest him. "Here," he said in a loud voice, "Uzbekistan. Vanuatu. Each of them important, as important as Russia or the United States. But Uzbekistan has a lot of people, millions, while Vanuatu can't have more than a couple hundred thousand. One man, one vote. In the end Uzbekistan's millions need to have more say than Vanatu's thousands."

He tossed the cards back on the desks and stared at her, arms folded, as if he had presented irrefutable evidence. Then he glanced around at the empty desks and walked up to one. "Here," he said and held up Rwanda's card. "What if you have another genocide in Rwanda? Last time the UN did nothing. Your great Nobel prize-winning predecessor did nothing. 800,000 killed."

Pilar let out an exasperated sigh.

He stepped up the aisle and stood in front of her and Asha. "You have to take action."

"You don't just *take action*," Pilar said.

He ignored her and kept on. "The UN should be a no-nonsense organization with power to tax, ready to step in and help at a moment's notice and ready to stop the bad guys if that's what's needed. A fair structure, each state important, each with an equal share of power. You'll pardon me, but I think the United States has a great system. You take a certain number of people and they send a person to the House of Representatives. Then two people represent their state in the US Senate. Each state is important, but so is the idea of population. One man, one vote."

He had a point. The General Assembly was hardly representative with Vanuatu having the same vote as China. And with only fifteen members, the Security Council didn't reflect much of anything.

"We could have something like that at the UN," Stuart went on. "Leave the General Assembly the way it is. That would be like the Senate, each state with one vote. And turn the Security Council into some kind of a representative body, say one representative for every sixty million people. North America would have five delegates, Indonesia would have four, India would have seventeen and China would have twenty-one."

Asha nodded her head to many of Stuart's points, but Pilar noticed her folded arms and her serious mien. When Asha liked somebody *and* their ideas, she was all enthusiasm.

"Yes, yes," Pilar said. The man *did* have imaginative ideas, but she saw the problems right away. "You know, don't you, that the US could be outvoted?"

"So?"

"They are hardly going to vote for something they can't control."

Before he could respond, Asha looked at her watch and spoke up. "I have to go, but sign me up for your UN, Stuart. I like it. Madame, I hope you can help Somalia."

As Asha left, Stuart said, "I'd better go, too."

"Can I count on your help?" Pilar asked.

"Somalia? The UN can do it. Through your agencies."

"Stuart, you know I can't win on this issue, don't you?"

"Go over their heads, go right to the people."

"Get real, Stuart."

"You get real. You're too timid, like all Secretary-Generals."

"I'm an administrator, Stuart."

"You're a leader. Act like one."

How had she ever loved him, she wondered.

Stuart went to pick up his raincoat from the back of his chair, but it slid to the floor. He stepped around to the back of his seat and bent down. "Oh, oh, trouble," he said, picking something off the floor. A finger over his lips, he showed it to Pilar. She saw that it was a listening device.

Yusuf. Pilar felt her anger rise. Even here in the UN General Assembly she wasn't safe. She couldn't talk to anyone freely. She remembered the Americans and the British had done this in the Second Gulf War, spying on Kofi Annan and other members of the Security Council.

This had to stop.

Pilar motioned for Alex. She warned him to be silent and then showed him the bug. He shook his head and then raised his eyes upward toward her office. She nodded in agreement and Alex departed.

She motioned goodbye to Stuart, slapped her chair with her papers and went for the nearest phone to demand that Brennan appear in *her* office *now*.

Chapter 12

Appointment Schedule for the Secretary-General
Thursday, October 26

10:00 AM – Honorable Thomas Brennan (Ambassador to the UN,
United States of America)
11:00 AM – Honorable Sufian Abdella (Ambassador to the UN,
Ethiopia)
11:30 AM – Honorable Marha Musyoka (Ambassador to the UN,
Kenya)
12:00 PM – Luncheon and speech to The Internet Engineering
Task Force
2:00 PM – Honorable Akban Goita Farah (Ambassador to the
UN, Djibouti)
2:30 PM – Ahmad Ibrahim Mustafa (Secretary-General of the
Arab League)

When Pilar's secretary announced that Ambassador Brennan
had arrived at 10, she glanced out at New York's cold rain and opened
a staff report about Somalia. The situation there was even worse
than Asha had told her yesterday. Her staff had studied weather
patterns, crop reports and conflicts in neighboring agricultural areas.
Three hundred thousand more people would die unless there was
immediate relief. The report concluded with a hope that the
Americans would soon release the foreign aid they had budgeted.

To further research the problem, she had scheduled meetings that day with all of Somalia's neighbors and with the Arab League.

When the secretary rang again after ten minutes, Pilar told him she was involved with critical negotiations and it would be just a moment more. She had tried to deal with Brennan in an intelligent fashion. Confrontation was not a good strategy, but sometimes it was necessary to establish boundaries.

She returned to her report and finally, at 10:20, buzzed Brennan in.

"What's the big wait all about, Little Lady?" he asked as he strode into her office and headed for the comfortable chairs.

Pilar stood behind her desk and motioned to the chairs in front of her. "Over here, Ambassador," she announced in a clipped tone.

"Please sit down," she said in the same tone when he stood in front of her desk. He sat, but she remained standing. She opened a small plastic bag and spilled six listening devices on her desk in front of him. Most were nondescript small metal cylinders, but one looked like an inexpensive pen. "Can you please tell me what these are all about – listening devices, in my office, my secretary's office, in the General Assembly. Your man, Yusuf, placed one of these in a chair behind me yesterday. Is this what you call diplomacy? How would this look in the press – *Secretary of State bugs the UN?*"

She saw fear in his eyes for a moment, but he assumed an angry face. "That's a ridiculous charge. The pressure's gettin' to you, Ma'am."

Still standing, she tried to convert the hot anger in her heart to an ice cold exterior. "Mr. Brennan, one more incident and I go to the press."

He sat quietly for a moment. Then he stood and walked to a window in her office. After a moment more, he turned to her. "You got it all wrong, Madame. President George W. Bush, a great president from a great state, showed what this UN was all about. The UN wouldn't support his war on Iraq so he and the Brits did it on their own. The US of A doesn't need the UN. It's the other way around. Without our tax dollars you wouldn't exist. We pay 25% of your budget. I needn't remind you, Madame, that we supported you for Secretary-General. Of course, if you don't see things our way, well then..... I guess you won't be Secretary-General very long."

She smiled to herself at his speech, almost word for word what she had predicted in her notes last night – except for the bit about George W. Bush, though her interpretation was far different than Brennan's – the UN's rejection of Bush's war on Iraq was a sign of the health of the UN.

She gathered up the listening devices and put them back in the bag. Arguing with the man would do little good. The only thing he understood was the big stick. "I'm saving these for the media," she said. "And now..." she picked up his red-inked copy of her letter and held it so he could see it. "Did you write this?"

"I wrote the notes in red. You have to show the Congress you're willing to work with them. Like that famous Texan, Sam Rayburn, said, "If you want to get along, go along.""

"I note that you have replaced the nominees from ten countries with Americans. Is that correct?"

"They're the best qualified."

"And you have rejected nominees from Russia, Britain, France, China, Japan, Germany, Italy, India, South Korea and Turkey. That's an amazing list of America's strongest allies."

"So?"

"So, I'm going to send a copy of this letter of yours to all those countries and explain how you wish to veto their nationals. I wonder what they will say about you when your name is bandied about as US Secretary of State."

"You wouldn't."

"I would."

Brennan smiled easily. "Now, now, Lit ... Madame..., don't go getting a burr under your saddle. I was just making some suggestions. I'm sure we can work things out. If you need a little money for them folks in Somalia, we'll look around. There's no need to get upset. Of course, you have the right to name your own staff; I was just trying to save you from all those left wing intellectuals."

"They're not left wing. They are qualified lawyers and economists and..."

"Okay, okay." His brows knit and a few beads of sweat appeared on his forehead. She had made her points, but she knew victory was only fleeting.

"And I don't want to ever see that Yusuf person again."

"That's not me, Little Lady, that's the State Department."

"Yusuf is CIA and my title is *Madame Secretary,* not *Little Lady.*"

He folded his hands and put them up to his mouth as if in prayer.

"That's all, Mr. Ambassador," she said. "Please close the door on your way out."

Pilar sat down and read the report on her desk until she heard the door close.

*   *   *

In morning and afternoon meetings she talked with the ambassadors from each of Somalia's neighbors, Ethiopia, Kenya and Djibouti. They all wanted her to take action so refugees would not be showing up at their borders. Ethiopia denied blocking the rivers that led into Somalia. The Arab League reminded her that she represented the entire world, not just the western democracies. Kenya and the Arab League pledged a hundred thousand each to aid Somalia.

But how could she help without the UN funds which Brennan had vetoed? His promise to *look for a little money* would be just that, little and hard to find.

What could she do?

*   *   *

At the end of the day she called her secretary in and dictated the press release announcing her cabinet – all her original nominees, including the American, totally ignoring Brennan's recommendations. Then she got Alex to drive her home to her lonely mansion on Sutton Place.

She ate dinner by herself, reading *The New York Times* and *the Washington Post*. Even though she had logged on earlier and read some news, she still liked to read the print papers in the evening. For years when she worked at the UN this had been her pattern – return to her apartment on Roosevelt Island after a hectic day at the UN, read the news during dinner and then read scholarly journals and books until the late TV news. Her quiet evenings restored her.

But the old formula wasn't working. The events of the day welled up inside her like an annoying radio station she couldn't shut off. She wanted to talk to someone. The housekeeper came in to serve her herbal tea. She knew the woman's name was Charanjit and she was from Punjab in India, but she had never really talked to her.

"Sit down, Charanjit."

Charanjit hesitated, but finally did.

"How do you like your job?" Pilar asked.

The woman looked worried. "Something is wrong?"

Pilar laughed. She put out her hand to touch the woman and reassure her, but she stopped before she touched her. She chided herself over this. *You won't even touch another woman to ease her worry. What's the matter with you?*

"No, no, don't worry, Charanjit. I just wanted to talk. I think you told me you're taking English classes. How's that going?"

Charanjit relaxed a little. "The class is well, Madame. The teacher is good. He said everyone to tell where they worked and I told at the Secretary-General's house and he say, "Great. She is wonderful woman. She help poor people.""

Pilar almost cried. This simple woman – and her teacher – counted more than all the Brennans in the world. She reached over and touched Charanjit on the arm. "Thank you," she said.

A little later, as she sat reading in the library, Alex came in to check the next day's schedule, she asked him to sit for a minute. He sat down and she detected the scent of gunpowder on him. "Where were you?"

"I grabbed a bite and then shot a few rounds with the NYPD. Have to keep in shape."

"I'm grateful," Pilar said.

She said nothing for a long minute, then rubbed her forehead with her hand.

"What's wrong, Madame?"

"Nothing," Pilar said. "No, actually, Somalia." Pilar felt relief that she could speak openly with Alex. "The crisis is worse than I thought."

"I know," Alex said quietly. "I've seen the long-term weather reports. They are predicting eight hundred thousand people in danger now."

The image of the Somali woman in the photograph came to her mind. What must it be like to starve to death? Worse – what was it like to watch your children die of starvation? "I don't know what to do, Alex. I'm stymied."

Alex scratched his head and stretched his long legs out. "I was just talking to a detective at the shooting range," he began, his voice easy, quiet, almost relaxed. "This detective was closing in on a big crime lord, but his boss in the police department wouldn't give him the staff he needed. So he created several sub-crimes associated with his case, robbery, drug smuggling, break and enter, jury tampering, that sort of thing. That way he involved other bureaus in the police department. Anyway, by going at the problem from a different angle, he got the help he needed and was able to make a case against the gangster."

What a wise person Alex was. And how clever. His advice always used the side door, not the front door. He never held up his opinion as *the* truth. Often he told a story instead of answering a question. What he was saying was – find other ways to help Somalia.

"Thank you, Alex," she said quietly.

When they had reviewed the next day's schedule, he left.

* * *

Late at night her mother visited her again in her dreams. Pilar was working with her father in the garage wood shop when her mother came in. "Pilar, you're spending too much time here with your father. You tell me you have a lot of homework and yet you're here. You know what happens when you get tired and you work around these power saws."

Even in sleep her missing finger hurt. "Mother, I...I ..."

"Go do your homework, Pilar."

"Yes, Mother, but I have something to ask you. What should I do about Somalia?"

"It's very simple, dear. The Nile should be the river of the year."

*   *   *

Pilar spent the next morning at her computer and on the phone. She discovered that a month ago the UN Refugee Agency had routinely contracted for two ships to carry water and food for refugees in Mozambique. This shipment would replace warehouse supplies that had already been used. The ships were loaded in Cairo and right now they were exiting the Suez Canal.

She tried to reach her key staff person in Somalia, but it was already evening there. She finally found him at a restaurant outside Mogadishu and she suggested that he file an emergency request for food and water with the UN's World Food Programme. Next she invited the acting head of that agency to her office. He agreed that the situation in Somalia was a crisis and he would honor the call from UN staff there.

She next turned her attention to politics. She needed to find a Texas oil man who supported the current president, a man with influence in Washington, but one who might stand up to Brennan. Maybe Brennan had some competitors back in his oil days.

Her search took until well after lunch, but finally she found a man named Conrad Schmansky who had contributed heavily to the president and his party. He was the CEO of a rival company to Brennan's former oil firm. In fact, five years before he and Brennan sued each other over an oil lease. Brennan won the suit after a key player changed his testimony to support him. Schmansky appealed and the case was still in the courts.

Here was a man who had the president's ear and yet had a score to settle with Brennan. He was perfect. She called him and asked if he would accept an appointment to oversee emergency food supplies in Somalia and – his second task – to investigate oil and mineral resources there.

She explained the background, including Brennan's opposition, but the magic word was *oil*. He was interested. He said he'd consider it and would let her know in a week or so. She explained that the mission had to be undertaken at once.

"I'll call you back, Madame," he said and he did an hour later. "I'm your man," was his reply.

Maybe she couldn't get around Brennan, but she could certainly create some stiff competition for him in Somalia.

* * *

A day later the head of the UN mission in Mogadishu called her. "Madame, Hassan has learned that the ships are being diverted here and he's preparing to take both of them."

"I have appointed a special representative who's on his way. Can you hire some troops?"

"I tried. No one will stand up to Hassan. They say he's too well armed."

"He's not. The American Congress hasn't approved Brennan's arms shipment."

"Madame, I'm sorry. The rumor of arms is as powerful as the arms. The ships arrive in two days."

"I'll have to get back to you," Pilar said.

She hung up and called the man in her cabinet in charge of Peace Keeping Operations. Could he arrange a small force to protect a shipment of food and water? "No way, Madame. It will take two or three months."

She hung up. What a terrible state of affairs. The Americans refused to let the UN develop an emergency force and yet they were the first to blame the UN if a situation got out of hand.

Could she hire mercenaries in a hurry? Probably, but with what result? If they attacked Hassan she would have a repetition of 1993, a blood bath.

Who could she send to this dangerous and sensitive place? *Ah, Anatole.*

She reached him late in the evening in Africa. Waking him, she explained the situation, all the while picturing him scratching his head, rubbing his eyes. Did sightless people rub their eyes, she wondered.

At the end she asked, "Can you go and get the food and water to the people?"

He paused for a long moment. "Pilar, the food and water *will* reach the Somali people no matter what happens. The question is *which* Somali people will get the food, Hassan's brigands or those who look to the UN? Your staff on site needs you to back them up. As for myself, I am just about to begin a week long program on A.I.D.S. You know the extent of our problem here."

"Yes, I know. But can't you get away for twenty-four hours?"

"My part in this conference is not educational or medical. Rather it's to keep the different tribes happy and to keep them all here, learning and being treated. As you can imagine, that is no easy task."

"I know. But I have no one else."

"It doesn't help, but in a few weeks I will be more flexible. In fact I'm coming to America to raise money."

"This famine is getting out of hand. I have to do something."

"Pilar, once I had a meeting with a tribal chief. I met him near Kaya where he was pasturing his family's goats. He was very reluctant to stop his personal war with the Mossi, the leading tribe in our country. We talked for an hour, but he was adamant. Then one of his goats wandered off down a dry riverbed and he followed the goat, leaving me without saying anything.   I was left with the rest of his goats. I stayed there for the whole afternoon and into the night. When he came back he was very surprised that I was still there. 'I see that you care about what is mine,' he said. 'So I will trust the peace you propose with the Mossi. I know that you will look after me and mine.'

"Like the story, Pilar, I think you should go. Your staff will know they can count on you and you can show the warlords that you are personally involved. But I will respect your decision. It is not a simple matter."

Not a simple matter, indeed, she thought when she got off the phone. Africa might see her action as concerned and caring and her staff might appreciate it, but the western world would see her as overly concerned with one country. And, of course, Quan would say she had gone against the decisions of the Security Council.

Her new special representative, Mr. Schmansky, might be able to counter Brennan's influence in Washington.

A year ago, three months ago, she would have finessed the issue, kept it quiet. It was only two ships and who cared if the warlords got them?

But the Secretary-General of the UN could not let such a thing happen, even if she had to face down Somali warlords.

She called Alex and told him to arrange another trip to Somalia.

Chapter 13

Appointment Schedule for the Secretary-General
October 30 to November 3:
Canceled due to an emergency trip to Somalia

As Pilar stepped out of the UN jeep, she gazed ahead at the Port of Mogadishu. She had expected a breath of fresh air from the Indian Ocean; instead, oppressive, humid Somali air surrounded her. Her three companions, Alex, Asha and Conrad Schmansky, got out of the jeep.

"Damn hot, worse than Texas," Schmansky said.

"The water looks refreshing," Asha said, "but it's loaded with sharks."

"Not hard to see why water's important," Alex added.

The sun glinted off the harbor's stone barrier and off the low, white buildings huddled on the drive-on pier. Alex pointed to the two ships that were delivering food and water. He handed his binoculars to Pilar. "See, Hassan has a water tanker and other trucks to unload the ships. Stevedores are carrying bags of rice and boxes of bottled water."

Asha stood next to Alex, shielding her eyes against the burning sun. "You see, Alex, what happens. America does not share its wealth. People become needy and then they steal. I'm angry with Hassan, but I understand."

For a moment Alex did not respond. Then he said quietly, "You mean the American government. Americans as a people are very generous."

"Yes, of course, that's what I meant."

"I knew you did."

Asha laughed and put her hand on Alex's arm. "You're such a wise one."

Alex smiled and gazed out at the port.

Pilar kept her eyes squinted and her mouth solemn, but she enjoyed this interchange. Alex and Asha had developed a routine where Asha would lash out at Alex with her anti-American feelings. Alex stood by calmly and absorbed the hits. He seldom responded, but if he did, it was with a short phrase that went right to the heart of the issue.

The two were almost stereotypes, Pilar thought – Alex with his whitening hair was age and wisdom, while Asha with her fiery eyes was youth and idealism. But on further reflection she pictured them as a loving father-daughter duo.

Conrad Schmansky, Pilar's special representative, pointed beyond the port, out into the ocean. "A pipeline could go out there to an offshore loading platform."

"Yes, but first we have to establish order here in Somalia," Pilar said. "For now, let's be sure these supplies stay in UN hands."

They got back into the jeep and headed toward the drive-on dock. Behind them a line of UN trucks followed.

"What's your strategy?" Alex asked as they neared the dock.

Pilar snickered a little. "Faith in God."

With a hint of a smile, Alex drove onto the pier and the UN trucks followed.

Pilar saw Hassan ahead, on the left by one of the ships, next to a large unloading crane. A dozen men with machine guns surrounded him. He was pointing instructions to the crane operator and to the drivers of the trucks.

Alex drove onto the dock. When he reached the jetty where Hassan was working, Pilar asked him to stop. She closed her eyes for a second to compose herself and calm her fear, then she got out of the jeep and walked toward the knot of men. *Right foot forward, left foot forward,* she told her shaking legs. Ahead of her, she saw Hassan's men take their weapons off their shoulders and aim them at her. They seemed nervous, glancing at Hassan for direction. She noticed a man slinking away from the group. Something about the man's walk was familiar. Yusuf? Brennan's spy? She couldn't be sure.

She walked forward, trying to look brave and in control. She turned her head slightly to see how far she was from Alex. He was right behind her, and Asha was with him. Schmansky was behind the two of them.

Pilar wanted to take a deep breath to calm herself, but the air reeked of fumes. The oppressive heat trapped the exhaust from the trucks, the smoke from the ship and the discharge from a large dock generator. It was smog times three.

She stepped up to Hassan, reminding herself to keep her voice steady. "I'm glad you've come to help me load these trucks."

A white turban covered his head and his shirt was white, while his slacks were navy. He had the look of a leader about him, just as the last time when she visited him in his Mogadishu dwelling.

"You joke, Madame. Now please get your trucks off this pier."

Asha stepped forward and addressed Hassan in rapid-fire Somali. Pilar watched her expression and her angry gestures. She did not need an interpreter to know what was said.

Hassan ignored Asha and spoke to Pilar. "How unfortunate that you surround yourself with hotheads. Who is this new person?" He pointed to Schmansky.

"He is an oil man from Texas. I've asked him to take charge of food distribution and to advise me on oil production in Somalia. I'm sure you'll want to talk to him – he's got the ear of the US president. You know what they say – the wise man makes friends at the top."

"I see that Madame is full of proverbs. We Somalis love proverbs. Here is one for you: *Do not walk into a snake pit with your eyes open.*" Hassan nodded toward Schmansky. "I am interested to talk to you, sir." He turned back to Pilar. "You, Madame, must leave."

"No, I won't," Pilar said. "We will have law in Somalia." She took a bold step forward, through the knot of armed men, toward the men who were loading Hassan's trucks. She stopped a stevedore carrying a bag of rice on his shoulder, took him by the arm and led him back, through Hassan's mercenaries, to a UN truck. Asha and Alex did the same thing with the next two stevedores while Schmansky stayed back to talk with Hassan.

From the UN truck Pilar led the stevedore back toward the skids of rice bags, again approaching Hassan and his men. This time he blocked her way. "We have another saying, Madame. *Strike the whip next to a fool; if he doesn't get the hint, strike him on the head.*"

Alex came up beside her and scratched his head, as if he were trying to remember something. "Doesn't the Koran say, *Indeed, We have honored the children of Adam; provided them with transport on land and sea; given them for sustenance things good and pure, and conferred on them special favors, above a great part of Our Creation.* With all due respect, Mr. Hassan, the food and water should go to the children of Adam. If you steal this food, it will no longer be *good and pure.*"

Pilar was astonished. How in the world did this man come up with quotes from the Koran?

Rather than get angry, Hassan smiled and put his hand on Alex's arm. "But wait, my friend, we have another saying, *Doowlad xun, waxeey...*"

Pilar didn't wait to hear the translation; she pulled the stevedore's arm. She saw Hassan's eagerness for verbal battle with Alex, confirming everything she had read about Somalis' love for semantic jousting. The two might be at it for a while. However, the stevedore she was pulling, refused to move as did the one Asha was leading. Pilar motioned to Asha to join her and the two of them stepped over to the skids of rice without the stevedores.

Had Alex defused the situation? Were the men surrounding Hassan watching her, their hands on their triggers? She didn't know.

Pilar tried to lift a bag of rice, but couldn't. "Give me a hand," she said to Asha. The two of them lifted it and started to carry it awkwardly toward the UN truck. As they passed Hassan, Pilar felt his eyes on her. She heard Alex trying to persuade him, but she didn't look up from her carrying job.

As Pilar and Asha struggled a few steps further, the bag slipped from their grasp. Pilar squinted, her eyes almost shut in anticipation of a bullet whizzing by. But none came. Alex bent over and hefted the bag onto his shoulder. "Mr. Hassan, sir," he called back, "law and order must come to Somalia. This woman represents order and the rule of law. We must stop talking and act."

With that he carried the bag of rice to the UN truck.

Pilar and Asha started back to the rice skids, but this time three of Hassan's men shoved them against a truck and stuck weapons in their stomachs. Pilar saw that Alex had been pushed to the ground near the truck and Schmansky was knocked down at Hassan's feet, a dozen steps away. Loud arguing came from the group around Hassan.

"What are they discussing?" Pilar asked Asha.

"Whether to kill us."

Pilar could not suppress a twisted smile. "I hope they decide in our favor."

The man in front of her shoved his gun harder into her stomach and growled. This was the end – she had pushed things too far.

What was she going to do? Let Hassan take the ships? No. She felt the sudden presence of Anatole. He spoke no words, but he gave her strength and belief in her job. After all, she was Secretary-General of the United Nations.

Pilar took a deep breath and stepped forward, pushing aside the weapons near her. Safeties clicked off. She saw one man look to Hassan for direction. Her heart beat rapidly. She struggled to keep her voice calm. "Come on, Asha," she said.

Hassan stood directly in their way.

Pilar bent down, grabbed hold of Schmansky's arm and pulled him up, shoving aside the man who held an AK-47 on Schmansky's neck. "Get up, Conrad," she said.

She faced Hassan directly. "Please tell your men to free Alex, over there by the truck. He is a man of great wisdom."

"He's your bodyguard."

"He's more my soul-guard, but please, Hassan…" She spoke softly, "I need your help. I do not have an adequate security force to guard these trucks on their way to the UN distribution points. I know you are a man of wisdom and a man of God. I need your help to bring these supplies to the people in a fair and organized way. Please assist me. I think this is what your wife and your wonderful daughters would want."

For a long moment he stood still, staring at her. "Madame," he said finally, "Somalia is a failed state. You do not solve such a big problem with a few bags of rice and some water. It takes massive help like the Americans are going to give me."

"I agree, Hassan," she answered. "It will take many bags of rice and a lot of water. But we must draw a line in the sand right now and say that from this moment on, Somalia is no longer a failed state. We will have law and order and fairness from here on. Please free Alex and instruct your men to help load the trucks."

He shook his head, as if he had not seen such a strange woman before and then he gave several orders in Somali. Alex was allowed to get up and he joined Pilar. Men picked up bags of rice and loaded them onto the UN trucks. A crane from the ship swung down several loads of bottled water and that, too, as well as the rice, they loaded on the trucks.

A few hours later the first convoy pulled out of the dock area with Pilar's jeep in the lead and Hassan's men interspersed in their weapons-loaded pick-up trucks. As they pulled out, she caught a fleeting sight of Yusuf on top of a building, observing the convoy through binoculars.

*   *   *

By the next day the UN had distributed food and water to some of the major centers of the drought in southern Somalia. Pilar, Asha and Alex left the Araba hotel and drove to the military airport at Balidogle. Schmansky stayed to research the oil situation and to talk to Hassan further. Pilar knew she had planted some competition for Brennan.

From Balidogle their plan was to fly to Nairobi and then to London. In London they planned to rest a day before returning to New York.

When they reached the Balidogle airport an urgent message from Quan waited for Pilar. She assumed that Yusuf had told him everything that had transpired. After a half hour working with the Somali telephone exchange, she finally reached Quan.

"Madame, you must come back immediately. The most terrible thing has happened. The Security Council has discovered your plot to ship food to Somalia."

"Plot?"

"Oh, yes, Madame, that's what everyone is saying."

"It wasn't a plot. People are dying here. And I didn't order the food shipped here. The head of the World Food Programme did."

"The Security Council is holding an emergency meeting on Monday. It's about your….your impeachment."

The word was an electric shock that jolted through her body. *Impeachment.* The end. Disgrace. She struggled for her breath. But wait, was it the reality? Quan had an overdeveloped sense of drama. "Who sponsored it?" she asked, her voice now firm.

"Costa Rica. It's very serious."

Costa Rica meant that Brennan had sponsored it, but didn't want his name associated with it.

"It's very serious," Quan repeated.

And I'm sure you're doing everything in your power to make it more serious, she thought.

"I'll be there, Quan," she said and hung up.

Chapter 14

The Secretary-General is expected back from Somalia on
Sunday, November 5

Appointment Schedule for the Secretary-General
Monday, November 6

10:00 AM – Arunas Balacytis, Foreign Minister of Lithuania
11:00 AM – Toranosuke Kawaguchi, Ambassador from Japan
12:00 PM – Luncheon and Speech at Conference of the
                    International Association for Volunteer Effort
1:30 PM – Security Council Meeting

On Thursday night as Pilar's flight approached the Jomo
Kenyatta International Airport in Nairobi on her return from Somalia,
the word *impeachment* turned over and over in her mind like a large
water wheel gone out of control. It was a shame word, similar to
many other words her mother had planted in her subconscious –
sex, no college, old maid, overweight.

Impeachment – Richard Nixon, Bill Clinton and Professor
Thomas J. Taylor, a colleague of her mother's at the university who
was charged with having sex, not with a student, but with the younger
sister of a student. He lost his job, his family and his self-respect.
He was sentenced to ten years in prison, but killed himself after the
first week.

Impeachment.

Pilar tried to stop the crazy wheel from turning. After all, impeachment was more publicity than reality. How could they impeach her for feeding starving Somalis? The real danger lay in how the media handled it. Would it be sloughed off as a nuisance from a small Central American country or would it be treated as a serious effort to remove a disgraced world leader?

As the plane landed she saw a crowd of reporters standing by the door of the airport. That answered her question about the media. Brennan and the White House had been busy.

Before exiting the plane a flight attendant got permission for her to link to the Internet through a wireless connection. She scanned the headlines, most of them negative. Her staff had responded with all the right phrases – humanitarian mission, routine shipment of food and water to a crisis spot, personal courage to back her staff. But her press assistants were few and the forces Brennan commanded were many. Most stories appeared without a response from her office. *Secretary-General ignores Security Council. A Loose Cannon at the UN. Special Envoy to Somalia Did Time. Food and Water for a Warlord. Will More Americans Die in Mogadishu?*

She unplugged her computer and prepared to face the reporters. Conrad Schmansky had told her he did time *as a juvenile.* He and three friends stole a car and took a joy ride through Texas. When they were arrested, the cops discovered that one of the three had a few marijuana cigarettes on him. Texas, Schmansky said, was no place to get arrested. But since then he had turned his life around— a college degree and a successful career as an oil man.

She shook her head at the power – and immorality – of the government to reach into the past and reveal a supposedly expunged juvenile record. They could destroy her if they wanted. She recalled the amazing, but frightening, ability of President George W. Bush and his staff to convince the American people that fourth-rate Iraq was a world threat, that they had weapons of mass destruction and that Iraq was somehow responsible for 9/11.

She walked across the tarmac toward the reporters. When would they start thinking for themselves instead of using White House handouts? She felt perspiration on her forehead despite the mild evening temperature of this mile-high equatorial city.

The airport officials guided her into the transit lounge inside, where they had set up a few dozen folding chairs and a lectern. The couches around the edges of the room were all taken by sleeping passengers waiting for flights.

Even before Pilar got to the lectern, a reporter raised his voice, "Dan Reilly, Reuters. Are you going to resign?"

"Absolutely not," she responded and then gave the background of her whole trip. As she talked she noted the news agencies present in addition to Reuters – CNN, CBS, Al Jazeera, the BBC and the CBC from her own Canada. It would be interesting to see how each interpreted the news.

"Ted Chombers, CBS News. A White House source suggests you're in collusion with Warlord Hassan."

An annoying fan overhead kept ticking against its screen cage. "Who is your source?" she fired back at Chombers.

"That's not important. The question is…"

"You answer my question, Mr. Chombers, I'll answer yours," Pilar said. "But for heaven's sake, man, use your head. Why did I go to Somalia?"

"I don't know. You cooked up a deal with this Hassan and you went there to make sure he got the supplies and not somebody else."

"Did you call the UN office in Somalia and check on the facts?"

"You're avoiding my question."

"No. I'm trying to tell you how to gather the news."

Chombers sat down, his brow knit, a pout on his lips. She had lectured him, she knew and she cautioned herself to calm down. The news people were just trying to do their jobs.

"Alice Paterson, USA Today. Can I ask how you see your role as Secretary-General? According to news stories you have gone outside the bounds of your job description. You are the executive officer of the Security Council, the person who carries out what *they* decide. You seem to be acting as a leader."

Why was it so warm in this room? Pilar felt heat coming out from every pore of her body. "Ms. Paterson, have you read the UN Charter?" She was doing it again – lecturing.

Paterson continued. "Why won't you answer our questions directly?"

"Article 97 says that I am the chief administrative officer of the whole Organization. It's up to me to see that the various departments of the UN function correctly. The UN office in Mogadishu inquired if there was any emergency help available and the Director of the World Food Programme ordered the diversion of two ships bound for Mozambique. Everything went exactly as it was supposed to. The UN is working correctly and that's my job. When I heard that warlords might capture the ships, I went myself – without a massive peace-keeping force – to ensure that the supplies went to our UN officials."

Other questions followed, then Alex stepped forward and allowed one final question.

Carol McIntyre, CBC. "What are your plans when you reach New York?"

"I will continue to be the best Secretary-General I can." She followed Alex into the VIP room. Thank God she was out of the terrible heat and closeness of that room. And that clattering fan.

She sat down and Alex gave her a glass of cold water. She knew the methods to handle the media, why had she failed to apply them? *Answer the question you want to answer, even if it's not the one they asked. In the first sentence answer the reporter's question in a general way and then reshape the question to suit your purpose.*

She sat in silence and blamed herself. After a few minutes she glanced up at Alex. He stared at her with concern in his eyes. "Come on, Madame," he said, giving her his hand. "I've got a hotel nearby all set. Let's go. You need a good night's sleep."

*   *   *

Thursday evening in Nairobi, Friday in London – but no day to rest – Saturday back to New York by nightfall. On Sunday she galvanized her small press staff into action, putting out news releases and contacting friendly media for interviews. Her forces, however, couldn't match the press barrage coming from the White House and Brennan's office.

On Monday afternoon as she prepared for the 1:30 meeting of the Security Council, she knew she had been defeated. No matter what the Council decided that afternoon, she had lost the public relations war. The media in Nairobi did quote her accurately, but they gave far more space to the charges against her. Alex measured several papers with a ruler – for every inch of newsprint they gave her, there were four inches for Brennan's charges.

*   *   *

"And the last issue on our agenda is a discussion of the Secretary-General's actions in Somalia." The president of the Security Council for the month, the ambassador from Norway, glanced at Pilar. She nodded back to him, marking that he didn't use words like *impeachment* or *removal from office*. It was just a discussion of her actions in Somalia.

One part of her mind moved around the table and analyzed who would say what and with what consequence, but another part just wanted to put her face in her hands and cry. Of course, that's all her enemies would need.

She glanced at Brennan. He sat there, his hands folded as in prayer, his fingers touching his mouth. She saw the smug look in his eyes. Was he trying to scare her into resigning?

Behind him sat Yusuf, his face as rock-like as ever. Quan also sat behind Brennan, frequently whispering to him. Quan was supposed to be *her* staff person, sitting right behind her, ready to help her with a fact or a name, her second-in-command. She watched his face, talking seriously with Brennan, then laughing at some little joke, then smiling here and there, just bubbling with anticipation that soon *he* would be Secretary-General.

Charles Kent-Ashley spoke first. "The United Kingdom feels this is, to use a British expression, *a tempest in a teapot.* Madame

Secretary has been doing the business of the UN. I differ from my friend from the United States in this matter. From what I read in the papers, I say she deserves a medal."

Thank God for him and for Britain. In previous times the British government under Tony Blair had been the lapdog of the US. She knew that Kent-Ashley spoke for his government since no one could act in the Security Council without the approval of their country. That meant that Britain would veto any impeachment motions. She was safe from actual impeachment.

Next Carlos Gomez from Costa Rica gained the floor. He was the one who introduced the resolution in the first place. Pilar knew that the president of Costa Rica shared political philosophies with the new president of the United States and she knew that the United States was considering major grants and loans to his country. Gomez would be Brennan's mouthpiece.

Gomez glanced around dramatically at the Council. He cleared his throat, then scanned the press gallery. Pilar saw the little red camera lights come on. The media knew – sound bites were coming.

Her stomach tightened and she felt warm. She reminded herself that real impeachment was not the issue, but that thought didn't help. The real issue was the media war and she had lost that. This public airing was only going to make things worse.

Soon the cameras would pan over to her, hoping to see a worried, terrified face. Instead she put on a mask that showed boredom and even slight amusement at this *silly* impeachment attempt.

Gomez spoke in passionate English. "Does our council mean nothing? Are we not charged with responsibility for peace and security in the world? Is not the Secretary-General an administrative officer who is to carry out our wishes? It seems to me…" Gomez looked directly at the cameras… "that this is a matter for *impeachment*."

There was the word, the word she hoped wouldn't be said. She watched the press scribble away. The TV cameras focussed on her. This was news, dramatic news, the kind the media loved. No abstract principle here – this was about a woman who had dared to lead instead of follow, who had innovated instead of reacting.

It would be difficult to survive this, she knew. Despite the uninspiring record of some of her predecessors, despite revelations that one Secretary-General may have been involved in wartime atrocities, no one had ever been impeached or even threatened with impeachment.

She was the first.

Gomez continued. "I am also shocked to discover that Madame Secretary included a man with a criminal record on her mission to Somalia. Further, I'm shocked to hear that Madame entertains talk of restructuring our council." Gomez dramatically pointed one-by-one to France, Britain, Russia, China and the United States. "She would deny the veto to the five brave countries that won World War II or at least one of her informal advisers counsels her to do that."

Of course. Yusuf's recording of Stuart's conversation with her in the back of the General Assembly. What a terrible life she'd gotten herself into. She had to think twice about every phone call, every conversation, every place she sat down. She had lived her whole life in relative freedom, moving her way up the UN bureaucracy, going to her apartment at night and relaxing. But now she had to look over her shoulder every moment. And what was more galling was that her own security force did not have the numbers to compete with Yusuf and Brennan.

Kent-Ashley called for a point of order. "Mr. President, I think this whole matter should go to our Committee of Experts on Rules of Procedure where we can determine if this is a matter for the Security Council or the General Assembly. The Secretary-General, as we all know, is appointed by the General Assembly upon the recommendation of the Security Council. But which body should review her performance? This matter needs study."

Pilar smiled to herself. Kent-Ashley had the ability to put questions like this into the limbo of eternal debate.

But Gomez refused to yield. "No point of order, Mr. President. Our direct orders have been disobeyed. We feared the warlords would commandeer the aid just as in 1993. Now it appears that our Secretary-General has even helped one particular warlord. In any case Madame Secretary has seen fit to directly disobey this order."

The representative of Nigeria interrupted in an angry tone. "Was Madame's own cabinet minister for Africa consulted? No."

Pilar thumbed through her file quickly. There was the letter to Chistian Sogbandi from Liberia, her cabinet minister responsible for Africa. She held it up. "You mean this letter?"

The Nigerian representative asked to see the letter. Pilar handed it to an aide, the representative examined it, after which he muttered that Mr. Sogbandi must not have seen it.

Pilar knew the real problem. Sogbandi spent all his time with his New York mistress.

Gomez from Costa Rica spoke up angrily. "I'm sorry, I had the floor." Despite the fact that the Nigerian had just furthered Gomez's issue, Gomez was upset. Once again, Pilar reflected, personal dignity was an important issue at the UN.

Gomez continued, "I'm tired of these interruptions. The Secretary-General has diverted valuable supplies destined for Mozambique and shifted them to a pet project of her own. We have made a mistake in choosing our Secretary-General. A different leader would have approached the situation from a more *rational* point of view and would have made decisions based on *logic* and not on *emotion*."

The old cliché – *Women are too emotional*. Pilar kept a straight face, but scoffed at the man in her mind. Sometimes democracy was painful.

When Gomez finally yielded the floor, Kent-Ashley spoke again, reminding everyone that it was the Director of the World Food Programme who ordered the change. "Madame Secretary has risked her life to guarantee that UN goods be shipped to UN agents. For this the Security Council criticizes her."

Speaking in English, the French delegate almost sneered at his fellows. "We wanted a Secretary-General, she would bring peace to the world. Then she goes out to a dangerous place and she takes care of the needy. What do we do? We condemn her. We know – this Council knows – the root cause of all war is human need, human starvation and human suffering, the very things she was trying to alleviate."

The ambassador from Russia praised her courage to go to Somalia.

Brennan said nothing the whole time. He just watched his fellows speak as if he were at a Ping-Pong match. Pilar struggled to control the hot anger she felt against him. She knew that no matter what the Council did, the word *impeachment* had been spoken and she was seriously wounded.

The Chinese ambassador spoke, praising her concern for third world countries. But then he went on to catalogue China's relationship with every previous Secretary-General.

Pilar's mind drifted. Maybe it was time to think about resigning. Now she believed what successful women always said – that women in business and government were judged on a much higher standard than men. A man would have been universally praised for going to Somalia and confronting the warlords.

There was still life ahead for her if she resigned. Cross-country skiing in her native British Columbia. Volunteer work with children in Africa.

The thought of Africa presented another picture to her. She saw herself sitting at a kitchen table in a new suburban bungalow in Ouagadougou, the capital of Burkina-Faso, a cup of tea in her hand. She had just gotten home from a lecture at the International School. Anatole came in the door and told her all the political news of the day. They talked, they ate dinner and then they sat in the garden and watched the sun set. All right, he couldn't see, but she would hold his hand and tell him the colors and the shape of the clouds. It was good. It was enough.

Kent-Ashley's voice brought her back to the moment. He proposed the whole matter of the Secretary-General go to committee for review, a motion that passed.

She gathered her papers. Politicians were supposed to get a one hundred day honeymoon from the press. She'd been Secretary-General for just fifty-eight days.

The meeting ended. Yusuf, Quan and others buzzed around Brennan. She turned to leave. No one buzzed around her.

Only Alex stood behind her.

Chapter 15

Appointment Schedule for the Secretary-General
Tuesday, November 7

9:00 AM - Breakfast and Speech, Physicians Against Land
              Mines.
10:30 AM - Presentation of Credentials, Andrew Ogio, Papua
              New Guinea
11:00 AM - Presentation of Credentials, Mustafa Karakoyunlu,
              Turkey
12:00 PM - Hsien Loong Yeo, Foreign Minister, Singapore
 1:30 PM - Internal Appointments

The day did not start well. At the breakfast, sponsored by the
Physicians Against Land Mines, Pilar sat next to the husband of the
chairwoman. The man talked endlessly of his adventures on eBay.
"I won the bid for a genuine Chicago Bulls jersey from the 1970s."
She nodded politely, but placed the story outside the cannon of great
drama. Then the man switched to the impeachment subject. "What
kind of a job are you going to get if they impeach you? You're the
first one to be impeached, aren't you?"

She studied the man for a moment and then said, "Maybe I'll
go on eBay and outbid you."

That silenced the impeachment talk.

Later, at her office, the ambassador from New Guinea counseled her to stop "chasing around the world" on sentimental, humanitarian missions. She was in charge of a big bureaucracy, he said, and she had to "whip the troops into line." As Pilar smiled politely, she imagined the ambassador back in time one hundred years and heard him telling his wife to "stop chasing around for a woman's right to vote. Clean the house."

Her next visitor, the new ambassador from Turkey, sympathized and told the story of a Turkish woman who tried to break into government, but was much happier now as a teacher of small children. The message was clear: men for government, women for small children.

Her last visitor of the morning, the foreign minister of Singapore, mentioned how his wife was, "Just like you – always talking about people suffering from flood or famine or fire. I love her dearly, but my job is to look after the interests of Singapore." As if the problems of the people were different from the interests of Singapore.

When the foreign minister left, she opened her mail. There was another personal letter from Habiba Saynab. It was the same as the last letter, an offer to volunteer from a former Somali national who now lived in New Jersey and who had a doctorate in Arab studies. She said she would be in New York today and would try to see Pilar.

An attractive offer, but Pilar did not have the time to make certain it was legitimate.

She checked the time – 1:15 PM. For the afternoon she had planned to meet with her key advisers for a discussion of goals. That was the problem – she was drifting from crisis to crisis. She had to take charge of her future, develop goals and clear strategies to reach them. Say what you want about bureaucracy – goal-setting and implementation were its strengths. She had invited Charles Kent-Ashley, Anatole, Stuart, Alex and Asha to meet with her. Luckily Anatole had agreed to delay his fund raising in the States so he could participate.

Her secretary informed her that reporters waited for her everywhere in the building. Some had even joined UN tours in the hope of breaking away and finding her. No doubt they were eager for impeachment stories.

No. This afternoon was for planning – and not at UN Headquarters. She had asked Alex to arrange something.

She called him into her office.

"We're meeting at Anatole's hotel," Alex said. "It's just a block away. The Millennium UN Plaza." He explained the elaborate plan he'd devised to get her out of the building unnoticed.

"Alex, this is the UN, my building. Why do I have to slink around like a spy to get out of here?"

Alex merely shrugged and gave her a key to an unused storage room on the fifteenth floor. "I'll go down and say I heard you were going to make a statement in the Dag Hammarskjöld Library," he said. "That'll get all the reporters out of this building."

A little while after Alex left, she went out to the reception area of her office. An attractive black woman got up from the couch and approached her. The woman wore a conservative navy business suit and she had lively, intelligent eyes set in a dark African face. Pilar guessed this was the woman who had written to her, but she had no time now.

Pilar turned to her secretary and said she was going to the cafeteria for a salad.

"What kind of salad? I'll get it for you, Madame Secretary," the young man said.

"Thank you anyway. I need to stretch my legs."

"Excuse me, Madame," the black woman said, "I am Habiba Saynab. I've been trying to contact you."

The young secretary apologized. "I told her, Madame, she had to have an appointment."

Habiba Saynab was not to be put off. "Madame, I can save you a lot of pain over this Somali business. I have information that…"

Pilar put up her hand. The woman was very pushy. "Thank you, Ms. Saynab. My secretary will arrange an appointment with one of our undersecretaries. I appreciate your help."

"But…"

Pilar got on the elevator and went to the fifteenth floor, which was being redecorated. She knew that Yusuf or somebody would be on the ground floor watching for her to exit the building. She slipped into the storage room on fifteen and put on a white coat, a dust mask and cap Alex had told her would be there. She had seen several men and women dressed in similar fashion coming and going on the elevators. In the hallway she picked up a five gallon bucket with scraps of wall board in it. She smeared some of the plaster on her hands and waited by the elevator. This was terrible. What if the elevator opened and someone recognized her? She felt the sweat on her forehead.

Another worker approached. "Going down?" he asked.

"Y—y—y es."

"I don't recognize you. You new?"

Thankfully the elevator came and they got on. She noticed a secretary from her own floor on the elevator and turned away.

"Are you new?" the man persisted.

She felt sweat on her back now. "I work for the UN," she said, trying to disguise her voice.

"Hey. What are you doing on this job? This is union."

She muttered through her mask, "Safety on the site."

They arrived on the main floor and she followed the man toward the service entrance. She passed near Yusuf and two other men, all of them carefully watching the elevators.

"Listen," the union man said, "I'm reporting you."

As soon as she exited the building through the service door, she dropped her bucket and walked away. She left the man standing by the door, looking puzzled. Alex joined her as soon as she left the building. She pulled off her white mask and walked rapidly to Anatole's hotel. What a terrible situation that all this subterfuge was necessary – and in her own building.

* * *

"You have to go on the attack," Stuart said, as they all settled into the plush chairs in Anatole's suite on the top floor of the hotel.

"You can't sit back passively, Pilar. This whole business is really about oil and not about helping Somalia. You have to expose Brennan."

All right, that was Stuart, Pilar thought. Attack. But it was a good reminder that she wasn't to blame. Like every other woman she knew, she took the fault on herself. Really it was Brennan who should resign.

"Right, Pilar?" Stuart asked, his tone harsh.

"Yes," she said without conviction.

She glanced around the room. Kent-Ashley brushed at his impeccable trousers as if Stuart's words were an annoying fly that had landed there. Asha stared out the window, her brows knit with a worry Pilar didn't know about. Anatole leaned forward, his scarred face turned so he could hear Stuart with his good ear. Alex sat quietly on a wooden chair near the door. He had leaned back until the chair touched the wall. Arms folded, his countenance seemed to say that no one was going to leave the room until Pilar's problems were solved.

"Direct attack is a poor strategy," Pilar said. "It's far more effective to work behind the scenes."

"With anybody but Brennan," Stuart responded. "The hammer is the only thing he understands. He's going for your jugular and you have to come out swinging. This is a public drama. Brennan has thrown down the gauntlet."

Very male, she thought, but he had a point.

Alex answered a knock on the door. A bell hop wheeled in a tray of hors d'oeuvres and drinks and addressed Anatole, "Excuse me, Mr. President, your order is here." The bell hop opened a cabinet in the suite to reveal glasses and a mini-fridge. He arranged the glasses and left.

Alex checked the wheeled-in table for listening devices while Stuart fixed himself a drink.

Kent-Ashley cleared his throat. "We can't have the Secretary-General attacking the American ambassador. Even Brennan was too smart for that – he did not attack Madame directly. He let Costa

Rico do it. Attacking Brennan only lends credence to his charges. He's a minor irritant. You brush him away."

Again the man whisked imaginary crumbs off his trousers. Pilar wondered if he knew he did that.

Stuart scratched notes on a yellow pad, his pen pressing hard. She knew the sign – he was angry and felt insulted by Kent-Ashley. This meeting wasn't going well, the same old problems with the same old answers. It was as if the dreary November weather had entered the room and driven hope from everyone.

"Asha?" Pilar asked. "Your thoughts?"

Asha shook her head and said very quietly, "No, nothing." This was the first time since she'd met her that Asha didn't have something to say. *Very strange*, Pilar thought.

"One of the thoughts I've had," Pilar said, "is resigning."

Alex's chair hit the floor with a thump. "No," he practically shouted. "You can't let them win."

"That would be terrible," Asha said.

"My effectiveness is ruined. All I hear is *impeachment*."

Kent-Ashley brushed his trousers. "Just temporary."

"I agree," Stuart added.

What would Anatole say? She studied his scarred face, but no emotion showed. He seemed to be deep in thought.

Pilar walked over to the bar for a soda. She popped open a can of diet drink and took a big swallow. It tasted warm and bitter.

Anatole leaned forward on one of his canes and pulled himself to the edge of his seat. He looked around the room like a sighted person. "In 1945 America saw a way to bring permanent peace to the world. World War II had killed millions. The Americans gave money, support and encouragement to this new organization, the UN. No one said it would take away American sovereignty, rather they viewed the UN as a way to bring peace to the world. But gradually over the last half century, the UN has lost prestige. I think this is a wonderful time to call back that amazingly generous spirit of the Americans. I think it's time for…" Anatole paused and moved his head around as if he were looking at everyone in the room "…a constitutional convention to revamp the United Nations."

"A constitutional convention?" Stuart asked. "Did I hear you right?"

"Yes," Anatole responded. There was silence in the room.

Pilar felt the impact of his words as if they were firecrackers. She drew in a sudden breath. *What a concept.* No question it was what the UN needed, but immediately the difficulties hit her. Would the five veto nations be willing to give up their power? Would the developed nations subvert the process as they did in 1945, leaving the poor nations with nothing? Would the countries of the world realize that the age of nations had passed?

Noble idea, Pilar thought. *But not practical.*

How were the others reacting? Kent-Ashley's face stayed neutral. She knew his mind, weighing the pros and cons, dispassionately, considering his own mission, but also looking out for her. He was a good friend.

Excitement flashed in Asha's eyes, the energy of Anatole's idea driving out whatever ghost was worrying her.

Stuart broke the stunned silence. "That's a wonderful idea, Anatole, but Pilar is facing impeachment."

Anatole blinked, but continued calmly. "Impeachment is only a symptom of the problem. The UN needs what America is good at – democracy. The structure needs to be changed so it's more democratic. And the UN needs to take the burden of being the world's policeman off the shoulders of the US. This is very important for America, for history shows that when a nation gets overextended, its empire falls. This was true of the Romans, the Spanish, the Germans, the Japanese and, apologies to Mr. Kent-Ashley, the British."

"Right about that, Sir," Kent-Ashley said, "but a frightful job, revamping the UN. Countries that have the veto aren't going to give it up easily, like my own."

Anatole pointed in the direction of Pilar. "And thus the challenge for Madame Secretary."

"I think it's a great idea," Asha said, her words bursting forth like the sun after a thunderstorm.

Pilar smiled to herself. Brennan wouldn't know what to do, at least initially. The best defense was a good offense. But the big five – seldom in history had people given up power. Maybe Gorbachev with his Glasnost presiding over the end of the Soviet system or Daniel Ortega in Nicaragua stepping down after losing an election – these people had given up control. But would the big five surrender their power? She clicked them off in her mind. China might surrender its veto because any restructuring based on population would leave them with a virtual veto. And maybe, just maybe, the British and the French could be moved by arguments of fairness, but what in the world could persuade the Russians and the Americans?

America would be her biggest problem, but the advantage of Anatole's idea was that instead of blaming the Americans, it called for the best in them.

"Come on, come on, we're way off the track," Stuart said.

"On the contrary, sir," Anatole responded, "*restructuring* is the key issue. In the Security Council the vote in favor of Madame's plan for helping Somalia was 14 yes and 1 veto. Why should one voice overrule fourteen? The issue is not impeachment. That serves to put the blame for the organization's failure onto one person. We need a new UN."

"Frightfully wild," Kent-Ashley said, "but crazy enough to work."

Asha stood up, walked to the bar, but took nothing and returned to her seat. She seemed agitated. "Madame, I just have to tell you what I've been thinking about. This is the greatest idea I've heard in a long time. To be honest, I was on the verge of accepting a job with the US Department of Commerce to help American businessmen develop new markets in Africa. The salary would be double what I make at the UN and it's any multiplier you want over what I would make in Somalia, because if I went back there I would have to work for almost nothing. I was trying to figure out a way to tell you, but if you go forward with Anatole's idea, I want you to know I'll be right there with you."

Pilar worried that Asha was going to be hurt, when she had to say finally that the idea was a grand one, but impractical. Of all those here, except Alex, Asha could be the biggest help. She knew how to get things done. Kent-Ashley had his own work, Anatole was running his country, Stuart could help, but probably wouldn't.

"There's another woman that might help," Stuart said. "A Somali woman from New Jersey, Habiba somebody. She contacted me a few days ago."

Pilar frowned. That woman's intensity was unsettling.

"Habiba Saynab?" Alex asked.

"That's the name," Stuart answered.

Alex got up and whispered to Pilar, "Excuse me, Madame, I'll be back in a few minutes." He left the room quietly.

Stuart went over to the bar and added ice to his drink. "All right, people, let's get real. I like Anatole's idea, but it's science fiction. Pilar needs our help with a practical problem."

"I don't know," Kent-Ashley said. "If Pilar does this, she becomes a player. She calls the shots, like you Americans say."

Stuart put his drink down forcibly. "Aw, come on. She calls for a constitutional convention and they really will impeach her."

"Excuse me, sir," Anatole said, "but she is the leader of the UN. The leader."

Stuart knocked his fist on the bar counter. "The American president is not going to roll over and say, 'Take away our veto.' It's not going to happen."

"I understand," Anatole answered. "She has to go to the people."

Stuart let out a big breath of air. "Oh my God, do you know how much time, effort and money it takes to *go to the people*?"

Strange that Stuart would oppose this plan. She remembered his first conversation with her about the UN. "Get rid of the veto," he said. Was there some kind of dominance thing going on, Stuart against Anatole?

But the idea – a constitutional convention. It was such a great concept. The world reorganizing itself. Trying to get it right this time, the League of Nations, The UN and now this new reality. Going after the old problems in a new way: the rich nations and the poor nations, northern rich countries and poor southern countries, the Israelis sitting down with the Palestinians, the Taiwanese with the Chinese.

Maybe the new UN could get something done, really help the Somali woman in the picture. Maybe her other child didn't have to die.

But Pilar knew the work and the trouble that would be involved. Making speeches, lining up supporters, being attacked and challenged. There would be no time for sitting in the garden and watching the sun set.

"I see by the faces in this room," Stuart said, "that you are all in favor of this. I don't know what you're thinking, Pilar, but count me out. The five countries are going to play hardball now. You better double the guard on yourself." Stuart shook his head and walked back to his seat.

Anatole held up his hand toward the bar, the last place Stuart's voice had come from. "Wait. You must listen. There's no need for conflict. Democracy has worked so well for the United States. You have problems, but you survive them. America is rightly proud of its system. Why not try it in other countries? Why not make the UN just like the US government? The world will be more stable, people will have more money, developed countries like America will benefit greatly from a new world order. Please, Stuart, no conflict."

"Harrumph," Kent-Ashley cleared his throat, "British democracy works quite well, also, thank you." He nodded toward Pilar. "And Canadian democracy."

Alex reentered the room. "Excuse me, everyone. I made a few calls. I think we have to be very realistic about the forces we're up against. Pilar has only shaken the boat a little so far. Just a little help in Somalia, which the United States and Mr. Brennan did not support. But as a result, the CIA has paid a woman named Habiba Saynab to infiltrate Madame's office, and my informant suspects an order went out to isolate Pilar – offer Asha a great job elsewhere and give Burkina Faso a big loan provided Anatole stays home. I'm not sure what they have in mind for you, Stuart, or for me."

"They have no morals," Asha said

"The bastards," Pilar said.

Alex went on. "If that's what they do for a little thing, imagine what they are going to do when they hear about a Constitutional Convention. The boat experienced a few waves before. Get ready for a hurricane."

"Yes," Anatole said, "I turned down that loan yesterday. I knew what was behind it. But a new UN is what the world needs. Yes, we will be opposed, but we will also garner a lot of support. I think we should stress the positive."

No one said anything after that. Pilar was aware that they were all looking at her, waiting for a response. "What Anatole says makes a lot of sense," she said. "But maybe if we repackage it in business terms, it might be easier to sell. We need a constitutional convention because there is a lack of stability in the world right now. Business thrives on stability. Give the Arab countries a voice, give the small countries a voice and vast new markets will open for western business. World democracy is just good business. It worked in America, it'll work on a planet wide basis."

Pilar glanced around the room. She couldn't gauge how her words were being received. "And we all know the world is very small today," she continued. "What happens in one country affects every other country. Japan sneezes and Europe catches cold. The experts all tell us our institutions are not adequate to deal with the world as it is.

"So I agree with Anatole's message, but I don't think that it will sell. It's fifty years ahead of its time. He's right, but it won't work, at least now."

"Oh, Madame, I don't agree with you," Asha said. "It's a wonderful idea. It's what the world needs."

Charles Kent-Ashley brushed his trousers again. "Pardon me, Madame, but forget what the world needs. This is what *you* need. World politicos have you down as a soft-hearted humanitarian who will be concerned but ineffective. They expect you to help out when the next earthquake hits Turkey or wherever, but they don't expect you to shake the UN to its roots. Right now they don't see you as a strong leader. People like Brennan will stand there with their mouths open. I say go for it."

"Absolute foolishness," Stuart said.

"Alex?" Pilar asked.

Alex had been sitting with his arms folded, his chair leaned against the wall. When Pilar called on him, he bounced his chair back to an upright position. "Seems to me," he said, "that for fifty-some years now the leadership of the UN has been playing things pretty safe. The diplomatic game. And over that period of time the UN's prestige has gone down – way down. I agree with Anatole, Madame. It's time to shake things up."

For a long minute no one spoke. Except for Stuart, everyone thought it was the path for her to follow. But Pilar saw mines on the road ahead. Even countries friendly to her ideas might blow up in her face. And Alex was right about the United States – what she had done so far was nothing compared to this radical restructuring.

They were asking her to cross the mountains in the cold, on foot and basically alone.

Maybe if she were younger.

"Thank you, everyone," she said. "You've given me a lot to think about. What you propose is very radical. Of course I see that it's the right course of action, but I'm just not sure it's the right time. I promise to think about this carefully. If there's nothing else, let's break up. Anatole, thank you for the use of your suite."

Stuart left and Asha, Alex and Pilar walked back to the UN.

Meanwhile Yusuf entered the suite they had just vacated and looked for the listening device the waiter had dropped on the floor. He found it, carefully nudged under the TV stand. He paid the waiter and took the tape to Brennan at the US Mission.

Chapter 16

Appointment Schedule for the Secretary-General
Thursday, November 9

10:00 AM	Meeting of the General Assembly
1:00 PM	Presentation of Credentials, Ali Omar Hemed, Ambassador from Djibouti
1:30 PM	Donald K. O'Connell, Minister for Foreign Affairs, Ireland
2:00 PM	Meeting of the General Assembly

At her desk, before her morning meeting, Pilar opened a report concerning southern Somalia from the head of the World Food Programme. It stated that the two ships had taken care of immediate needs, but the long term picture was bleak. Forecasters had predicted that the customary rains from March to June would be disappointing in the coming year. The current month, November, in the middle of the dry season, had set a record for lack of precipitation.

The forecast? More starvation in Somalia.

During the morning session of the General Assembly, while the debate over River of the Year droned on, an aide asked her to step outside for an important phone call. "A young researcher in Washington insists on talking to you, Madame," her secretary said. "When I asked him what about and he told me, I decided to interrupt you."

"Put him through," Pilar said.

"My name is Roger Arnold," the young man said. "I'm a student at Georgetown University, doing my masters' research on the relationship of the UN and the United States Government."

"Yes?"

"I've followed your actions in Somalia and I thought you would like to know that the foreign aid bill that was introduced in the Congress yesterday contains new spending of three hundred million to further democracy and fight terrorism in the Horn of Africa. It doesn't say Somalia. Through a friend in the White House, I learned that this item was not in the budget one day before the budget was printed. It was inserted suddenly and it's hidden in a complex section about the war on terrorism."

"What department is it listed under, State or Defense?"

"The Pentagon. Defense."

Pilar thanked the young man and asked him to keep her informed of any amendments or changes.

The Horn of Africa? That could be Eritrea, Djibouti, Somalia, Ethiopia or Sudan. By a lucky accident one of her noontime appointments was with the new ambassador from Djibouti and she would ask him what he knew. Meantime – the River of the Year. If there was ever a symbol of why the UN needed a total shake-up, it was this endless debate. It was like a church group deciding what kind of flowers to put on the altar, while the city around them convulsed with civil war.

* * *

At 1 PM Ali Omar Hemed from Djibouti presented his credentials. Pilar steered the conversation around to the subject of terrorism and then she asked him if Washington was helping Djibouti.

"We thought they were going to. Our lobbyist in Washington – we send our best people there, Madame – told our foreign office that the American government had budgeted three hundred million for the Horn of Africa. Our man has good contacts in the Pentagon and he discovered that the money is meant for Somalia and, further, that the American ambassador to the UN is to be consulted. This was not part of the budget but was in a private memo to the Pentagon from the White House."

There it was. Brennan was making his play. Ten times the original amount of thirty million. Hassan would soon be the leader of Somalia and Brennan would begin to suck the riches out of the Somali earth.

Instead of food, water and medicine, Brennan would bring in weapons. Why didn't he understand that food, water and medicine won the real fight against terrorism? It was especially galling that three hundred million dollars worth of weapons would be called *furthering democracy*, when, in reality, Hassan would be a dictator.

And Pilar knew there was little she could do about it. Even the little comment that the best people went to Washington, not New York, confirmed her status. The person in charge of the world, the Secretary-General of the United Nations, had no power. Anatole was right. It was time to change things.

* * *

During the afternoon session, while the Assembly settled on the *Amazon* as River of the Year, Pilar wrote a press release. When the session was over she took it down to the press office in person, made copies and gave it to the media. She held up her hand to stop the deluge of questions and left the press room.

On the elevator, on her way back to her office, she hummed to herself one of her favorite Beatles tunes, *Here Comes the Sun*.

Her statement read:

> I am calling for a constitutional convention to restructure the United Nations.
> The world has changed greatly since 1945 when the UN was formed. Over the years this organization has kept the peace in many countries, it has provided

standards and laws for international commerce and it has helped developing nations. But every organization needs renewal, needs to remake itself so that it can better live out its ideals. Thus, a constitutional convention. Everything is on the table. Nothing is sacred, not the veto, not the Security Council, not even my own post.

I will be seeking advice from all the countries of the world as to when and where to hold this Convention.

Chapter 17

Appointment Schedule for the Secretary-General
Monday, November 20

Noon: Luncheon with the National Association of Manufacturers,
Chicago, Sheraton Hotel

Pilar stepped up to the podium in the main ballroom of the
Chicago Sheraton, in front of her a sea of executives. She glanced
from left to right – not an empty table. And there – standing in the
back on the right – Yusuf – and with him a heavy-set businessman.
Yusuf wore a suit, not his usual tight T-shirt and khakis.

She grasped the podium. The strong wooden structure felt good,
as if its solid nature imparted strength to her backbone and her
determination.

"There's been a lot of controversy since I proposed that we hold
a Constitutional Convention." Good, she had worked the shakiness
out of her voice. "While I was waiting for my ride from O'Hare
airport, I overheard a couple of local politicians arguing about the
UN. One man said, 'I never pass up a chance to promote the new
UN. For example, whenever I take a cab, I give the driver a sizable
tip and say, *Vote for the new UN.*'

"The other man, with a differing philosophy said, 'I have a better
scheme, and it doesn't cost me a nickel. I don't give any tip at all.
And when I leave, I also say, *Vote for the new UN.*'"

The audience laughed. It was an old joke, but it worked. Yusuf still stood in the back in intense conversation with the businessman. What was he up to? Everything had gone so well in the ten days since she'd made the announcement. Beyond a doubt she had cut the ground out from under Brennan, but it was a little disconcerting that he had not responded in any way, no statements and no new resolutions in the Security Council. Not a word.

Today was her first attempt to carry the message to the people, starting with business leaders.

"Gentlemen, Ladies, I want to thank you for coming today. The words of Carl Sandburg ring true about your city:

Hog Butcher for the World,
Tool Maker, Stacker of Wheat,
Player with Railroads and the Nation's Freight Handler;
Stormy, husky, brawling,
City of the Big Shoulders.

"I come today to plead with the *city of big shoulders* to take on a new task, to get under the heavy weight of a world laden with national rivalries and to lift that world into a new era of peace. I come to ask you to support a Constitutional Convention for the UN. We need a new UN. A UN not based on some foreign concept of dictatorship, but on the very founding principles of American Democracy."

A standing ovation. Things were going well. She had set the date for the convention, UN day, October 24th of the next year, eleven months away. Twenty-seven countries – among them: Indonesia, India, Brazil, Japan, Argentina, Mexico, South Korea and her own Canada – had already endorsed her idea and she knew that China intended to hold a press conference tomorrow announcing their support. Now only four veto nations to go and four times the number of countries she already had so that she would have a majority of the 191 members of the UN.

Yusuf was seated now, but still whispered to the large man. Pilar steeled herself for what might come.

She smiled at her audience and went on. "*We hold these Truths to be self-evident*, states your Declaration of Independence, *that all Men are created equal, that they are endowed by their Creator with certain unalienable Rights, that among these are Life, Liberty, and the Pursuit of Happiness.* That's all I'm here to talk to you about – giving to the world the wonderful ideals that have made your country so great. And I come to you, not as a starry eyed dreamer, but as a woman with a concern for business. Time and again history has shown that no matter how strong the revolution, how deep the ideals, if business is not put on a solid footing, the revolution does not last.

"Bring peace to the world, give all nations an equal say, and you will enter an era of unimagined business prosperity. I guarantee it – reform the UN, and the tool maker, the wheat stacker, the hog butcher of the world will have more business than those big shoulders can handle."

The large man next to Yusuf stood up. Yusuf handed him a microphone and the two fiddled with it.

Pilar knew trouble was coming, but she kept on talking. "Study the generosity of Americans after World War II. Your Marshall Plan saved Europe and, as part of it, you insisted that the European countries work together. You helped start the European Union. You were multi-lateral before anyone ever heard of that term.

"You must also carefully analyze your current situation. Because of the weakness of the UN system, your generous Federal Government has been drawn into being the world's policeman. Take note – that costs a lot of money. Witness the history of other governments who kept troops all over the world, Rome and Spain and…"

The heavy-set man tapped on the microphone and it came alive. He breathed in deeply, his chest expanded. "Excuse me, Madame Secretary…" His voice was deep, resonant and impressive. "As a true American, I simply cannot let this speech go unchallenged. Yes, a lot of people on the extreme right are opposed to the UN, but I am not one of them. My name is James P. Miller. I own a medium size business here in Chicago. What Madame Secretary is saying is anti-American. She is a one-worlder, and the world she proposes is socialistic, anti-Christian, and anti-God. She wants the end of American freedom."

In the back of the room Pilar saw two uniformed police walk toward Yusuf's table. She raised her hand. "Wait. Let the man have his say. I want everyone to know that the changes I propose take away no one's freedom. Rather, they enhance it. The gentleman fears that his way of life will change if we modify the UN structure. Not so. What has worked in America, will work in the world. Let this planet be governed democratically and other countries will have more stability and a better economy with which to buy American goods. I offer you today what you don't have – stable international markets. China has 1.3 billion people, India has 1 billion people. I don't know your product, sir, but those are very big markets."

"You're a free trader," the man said.

"I suppose I am. But what is your product, sir?"

The wind seemed to leave the man. His chest shrunk, his statue diminished. "Canned vegetables," he muttered into the microphone he held.

"Are they safe? Are they of good quality?" Pilar asked.

The power seemed to come back to the man. He spoke with confidence. "Of course."

"Are they the best in the world?"

"No question."

Pilar glanced at her audience, left, center, right. "How strange is this, that here we have world class canned vegetables and yet in Africa, in Asia, people are dying of hunger. Bring stability, bring economic growth to the world and James P. Miller will not be able to keep up with the demand."

Miller looked confused and sat down, while all around him people stood and began to applaud for her. Soon the whole hall rose.

* * *

A long line of people waited to see her. Some offered financial support, everyone extended congratulations for her speech. As she talked, she noticed one man sitting by himself at a nearby table, reading a report. He sat quietly, only occasionally glancing at the line, as if waiting until everyone had left.

Pilar finished talking to one person and turned to find herself facing Yusuf. "Wonderful speech," he said, his face portraying no emotion.

How should she respond to him? Was he going to become a permanent feature of her campaign trips? If his efforts were similar to this evening, he had done her more good than harm.

"Nice to see you again, Yusuf. I hope I was able to respond to your friend, Mr. Miller."

"My friend? Miller? That man who challenged you?" Suddenly Yusuf had more facial expression than she had ever seen on him. "He was just sitting at my table. I never saw him before. I support your efforts, Madame."

Sure you do, she said in her mind. How typical of the man that he would lie, even when she had noticed him talking to Miller. "Nice to see you, Yusuf," she said and turned to the next person. Yusuf left her and approached the quiet man sitting at the nearby table. Yusuf sat down and talked to him, but left after a few minutes.

When the last person in line departed, the man sitting at the table stood at his place and spoke up, "Madame," he said, "can you sit for a minute?"

She sat down at his table. It felt very good to rest. Making speeches and talking to people took far more energy than sitting in her office and running a bureaucracy.

The man opposite her looked very ordinary. His conservative clothes and downcast glance spoke shyness and withdrawal from the public arena; but his eyes – they were alive. She knew he was evaluating her, just as she was him.

"My name is William Cranfield. My background is commercial law, but really I'm a real-estate developer. I'd like to donate half a billion dollars to your effort."

She couldn't breathe for a moment. It was a cliché that something could take your breath away, but this did. "Five hundred thousand?" she asked, her voice uneven. Maybe he had said 'half a *million*.'

He smiled easily. "Five hundred *million*. I said half a *billion*."

Items on her wish list flashed through her mind: a decent salary for Asha, hiring more staff, TV ads, and coordinators in other countries. This was great news, but it was also terrifying. This man believed in her half a billion strong. Could she live up to that?

"I had planned on giving you something, but the way you respected Mr. Miller told me you truly believe in democracy. Besides, you are one hundred percent right about the expansion of American business. If we want to grow, there must be a new world order. I want you to use these funds to sell your idea. If you need more, call on me. Here's my card. Have someone come to my Chicago office to arrange the details."

"Mr. Cranfield, I don't know what to say. Thank you so much, sir."

"I'm glad to do it, despite the efforts of the gentleman from the State Department."

"CIA," Pilar said.

"He told me you were against democracy, which is laughable in the light of your speech today and of my background research about you."

Alex came to get her. "Madame, come, we have to catch a plane."

She shook Mr. Cranfield's hand and left with Alex. In the limousine on the way to Union Station her cell phone rang. It was Quan. He sounded more upset than she had ever heard him. "Madame, you must return to New York at once. Mr. Brennan wants to see you. He's…" Quan's voice faltered to a reverential whisper, "…he's been to see the President of the United States and he has to see you right away."

"I'm on my way to Denver, Mr. Quan, for a speech. I'd be happy to see Mr. Brennan there. The day after tomorrow. You tell him that, okay?"

"But Madame… Denver?"

"Goodbye, Mr. Quan."

Chapter 18

Appointment Schedule for the Secretary-General
Tuesday, November 21

The Secretary-General will speak at an evening function in
Denver.

Pilar and Alex hurried through O'Hare Airport. United Airlines
had agreed to hold their flight to Denver for fifteen minutes, but ten
of those minutes had already passed.

A husky older man, dressed in jeans and a Chicago Bulls jacket,
stepped right in her way. "Say, aren't you the Secretary-General of
the UN? I recognize you from TV."

"Yes," Pilar said tentatively, unsure of what was coming next.
She smelled cigarettes and alcohol on him, but he did not appear to
be drunk.

Alex stepped in front of her and straightened his shoulders. "Can
I help you?" he asked.

"No, don't be afraid," the man said, looking around Alex. "I'm
all for what you're doing. My son died in a training accident, getting
ready for the war in Afghanistan. Like you say, America can't be
the world's policeman anymore. The UN should do it."

Pilar shook his hand. "Thank you, sir. We could chat more, but
I have to catch a plane."

"Sure, sure." He stepped aside, but then handed her his ticket.
"If you could just sign the ticket jacket."

Alex produced a pen and she did as the man asked.

"Good luck, Madame," he called out as she and Alex raced for the plane. "The people are behind you."

* * *

In Denver Pilar spoke at a luncheon of The Women's Club, visited an elementary school in a depressed area, toured a printing plant and visited the studios of a cable TV station. In the evening Asha had arranged a $250-a-plate fund-raising dinner. As the sold-out dinner got started, she caught sight of Yusuf again, standing at the back talking to three waiters. What new scheme did he have for her this time?

After the meal Pilar approached the microphone. She felt good – her Chicago speech had generated favorable world-wide publicity – and in the afternoon she had visited a beauty parlor and gone shopping for a new outfit, a charcoal-gray suit with a silk blend shell and a red scarf. She liked the scarf but worried it might be too bold for the suit.

The introductory speeches had been lengthy, so she got right to the point.

"*What's in it for me*? is a question we all ask of political events. What's in it for me if they hold a constitutional convention and revamp the UN?

"*What's in it for me?* For one thing, world peace. Everybody says the UN is a great place for the different countries to get together and exchange ideas. But if the structure were different, it would be a great place not just to *talk*, but to take action. If Country A invades Country B, the UN could act. If one tribe in Country C decides to slaughter another tribe, the UN could intervene. If famine strikes Country D, the UN could rush in food and water. Too often in the past the veto and lack of adequate funding have stopped the UN from necessary action."

She saw the three waiters moving from table to table passing out little cards, but she continued her speech. Asha hadn't told her anything about waiters passing out cards so this must be Yusuf's doing. What did the cards say? What was his plan?

"What's in it for me? Look down the road. How many refrigerators, home computers, telephones, pencil sharpeners or vacuum cleaners do you need in Denver? Yes, there's always some need, but local markets are almost saturated. What if the world was open to your manufacturers and retailers? What if your cable and satellite companies could sell to China or India or Indonesia? I do not pretend these are simple questions, but if the world prospers, we prosper. The mile-high city can have a mile-high economy."

One of the waiters approached the front tables and she put her hand out and motioned for him to give her a card. The waiter hesitated and then handed her one.

She read the 4" by 6" card out loud. "Pilar Marti wants to take away the power of the United States. She favors countries like Somalia that kill American soldiers. She even wants to restructure sensible organizations like the World Bank and the World Trade Organization. She backs terrorist countries and radical groups. We don't need a constitutional convention. We need a new Secretary-General."

She paused and let her eyes wander over the audience. After a long moment of silence, she bent down to the microphone and said in a low voice, "Pretty evil, isn't she?"

She stood upright again. "Take away power from the United States? Come now. How could a little Canadian woman do that? As a matter of fact, I want to restore America to the amazing power it had after World War II. America was the victor and the most amazing victor the world has ever seen. It poured money into the very nations that had tried to destroy it. America rebuilt Europe – it helped friend and foe alike. The United States had the high ground in the world and when Washington spoke, the world listened.

"I'm trying to put some democracy into the organization. I'm getting my ideas from *your* constitution. If you think about it, I'm sure everyone here would disapprove of the veto. What if Kansas or Missouri could veto anything the other states wanted? What if you joined a club where five members could nix anything the other 191 members wanted? The Supreme Court of the United States stood up for the idea of *one man – one vote* back in 1962. It declared that State Legislatures had to be apportioned by that principle. Why shouldn't the world body be *one person – one vote*?

"And those other organizations – the World Bank and the International Monetary Fund – they were supposed to be set up under control of the General Assembly, so all nations could have a say in their governance. But the powerful countries took them over, set them up as the Bretton Woods organizations in 1944 before the UN even started. And the same can be said of the World Trade Organization which started later. I ask you, what would Americans say?" She held out her hands to the audience.

Nobody answered.

"What would you say if only certain countries controlled the WTO? What would you say?" she repeated. *Oh my God,* she thought. *No one's going to answer me.*

Suddenly a woman in the middle of the hall stood. "Let them be fair," she shouted. "Let every country have a say."

"Of course. That's what an American would say. That's what I'm trying to do with the UN – put American values back into it."

The audience gave her a generous round of applause. As she waited for the applause to die down, she worried about what she was saying. What if she set up a new UN and it turned out worse than the old one? No, she reprimanded herself, she'd just have to trust democracy.

Then from the back of the hall, over the public address system, a question from a young woman in a fashionable white dress. Pilar wasn't surprised to see Yusuf right next to the woman.

The woman read her statement. "Let the poor nations have power and they'll tax the rich nations."

Pilar saw three uniformed security officers move toward the table. The three looked to be wrestlers or body-builders with their bull necks and wide shoulders.

Pilar held up her hand to stop them. "No," Pilar responded. "Let her be. You're right, the poor nations are going to *try* to tax the rich nations as much as they can, but like everyone else in the world, the destitute peoples will have to compromise. A bankrupt America can't help them. If they want our help, they'll have to deal with us. Look at history – helping poor nations always benefits the helper more than those helped. Did America suffer by rebuilding Europe? No. Did we ruin our prosperity by helping Japan and South Korea and Taiwan? On the contrary, we enjoyed an age of prosperity in the 1950s and '60s. Honesty is the best policy – and so is generosity."

"They'll lower trade barriers and flood our markets with cheap goods. Americans will lose jobs."

"Yes, they probably *will* lower trade barriers. So we'll buy their TV sets and they'll buy our medical technology. We'll purchase their cars and they'll borrow money from us to set up the automotive assembly plant.

"Look at it this way – it's an investment in people. There's always a big return on that. Generosity makes good fiscal sense."

The audience applauded. Was she right? She hoped so. The line about generosity came from Alex. He was reading Barbara Ward, a British economist from the 1960s. Only God knew where Alex got his reading list.

The woman sat down next to Yusuf and an old man on Yusuf's other side struggled to his feet. One of the hefty security guards helped him up. "Turn the card over," the man said in a shaky, decrepit voice. He raised his little card just over his head and pointed to the back.

Pilar turned her card over, took out her glasses and read the small print.

> *A short time ago Pilar Marti diverted two ships bound for the poor people of Mozambique. She sent them to a friend of hers in Somalia, a warlord named Hassan. Her bank records show that one week later a mysterious $200,000 was deposited into her account.*

> *Last year Quan Mai Ngo was slated to become Secretary-General. It was the turn of someone from Asia. But Pilar Marti wanted the job so she accused Mr. Quan of hiring his relatives. The people he*

employed were named Ngo just like Mr. Quan, but that is a very common name in Vietnam. None of the people were Mr. Quan's relatives.

Pilar Marti became Secretary-General by lying and cheating.

A few years ago when Israel was building settlements in East Jerusalem, the UN drafted a condemnation of Israel. The USA vetoed it on a 14 to 1 vote. What did Pilar Marti say at that time? "I support the right of the United States to exercise its veto." Today she says the opposite.

Her financial plans – pouring money into third world countries – are <u>economics for the comics</u>.

Another 4"by 6" card flashed through her memory. Six months ago she had knowledge of a similar card circulating about Quan. What she had done to Quan, was now being done to her.

What should she do? Rip up the card publicly, indicating the accusations were nonsense? No, it was better to answer charges up front and right away.

She looked at her audience, turned slowly and faced each section of the hall. "The food and water in Somalia went to UN agencies, not to Mr. Hassan. The $200,000 was from the sale of my Roosevelt Island apartment. Yes, I did compete vigorously for the job of Secretary-General. The third accusation is that I have changed my mind on the veto. Yes, that's true. I now think the veto is a mistake."

But how could she answer the clever little phrase about economics for the comics? That was a sound bite, something the media would feature.

The three muscular security men still stood by the table and it gave her an idea. "The economics I'm proposing are robust, brawny, even lusty. It's going to take time and money, but the future's going to be a powerhouse. It's not economics for bears or bulls, it's *tiger economics*. The tiger sees its prey, stalks up quietly and all of a sudden, pounces. The world economy will grow silently for awhile, the smaller nations building up their infrastructure and then suddenly the world will leap into an era of worldwide prosperity. Tiger economics. It's just business 101: develop a solid customer base."

Again, applause.

* * *

When she got back to her hotel a little after eleven, she took off her shoes and ordered a pot of tea.

Asha came to her room to discuss their plans for a trip to Europe after Thanksgiving. "But the first thing, Madame – Tiger Economics, I love it and – your scarf – just the right amount of excitement – the US Secretary of State called. He wants you to call him back no matter what the hour."

Pilar dialed the number. "I'm sorry to wake you, Mr. Secretary."

"No, it's not a problem. Thank you for returning my call." The Secretary was of the same political party as Brennan, but he was a far more sophisticated man. "I've asked Mr. Brennan to fly to Denver to meet with you. The President himself is very concerned about your ideas for the UN and I must say, so am I."

"I'm happy to meet with Mr. Brennan," Pilar answered. "I'm spending the Thanksgiving holiday with some friends in California," she continued, "but I can certainly meet him tomorrow."

Fifteen minutes later one of Brennan's aides called and told her that Mr. Brennan would meet with the Secretary-General at 10 in the morning at his hotel, the Embassy Suites Downtown. Pilar responded, pretending to be an aide, "I'm sorry, sir, but Madame only entertains visitors at *her* hotel. But I'm looking at her schedule and ten will be fine. Should I make it definite?"

Brennan's aide grumbled an okay.

Early the next morning, about 8:15, Brennan himself called Pilar. "I'm really sorry, Madame, one of those stupid domestic accidents. I slipped in the shower and twisted my ankle." For once he sounded human. "The hotel called a doctor for me," he continued, "and he wants me to stay off it. Could you – I'm sorry to ask – change your plan and visit me here?"

She agreed. She couldn't do anything else.

*   *   *

At 9:30 Pilar walked through the lobby to meet Alex in a limousine. This morning felt different from other mornings. For the past two weeks she and Asha had met and brainstormed ideas to further the Constitutional Convention. They both were filled with energy and excitement. But this morning was dedicated to Brennan, a depressing, heavy cloud no matter what the weather.

The headline of the morning paper cheered her up a little. "TIGER ECONOMICS," it said in bold letters.

Outside she was surprised to see demonstrators picketing in a circle in front of the hotel. It seemed to be a right wing group with signs saying, *UN out of New York, UNESCO is communism, UN supports abortion* and *UN is Godless*. Three Raging Grannies had their own little circle with signs about globalization.

Globalization was indeed a problem, she thought, but it depended on what a person meant by *globalization*. If the Grannies opposed big nations and their large corporations cheating the poor, so did she. But if the word meant that the world was smaller now, that we were all part of Planet Earth, that the age of nations was past, then she was in favor of that.

She walked down the steps of the hotel toward the sidewalk, but moved to the right in order to circumvent the protestors and get to her limousine. Suddenly a small black car jumped the curb and came right at her. She lurched to her right. The car swerved, too, straight at her. She sidestepped again and the car passed her. It was now right at the edge of the hotel steps where the protestors skittered out of the way. The car screeched to a stop, shot backward then forward, backward then forward, until it was headed at her again. She jumped behind a US mailbox. As the black car smashed the mailbox, she felt herself being jerked out of the way and pulled toward the limousine. The masked driver reversed off the mailbox, then slammed forward over the curb and down the street.

She leaned against the limousine, Alex's strong grip on her arm. "Are you all right?"

"I…I think so." She laughed nervously. On the surface she was in control, calm and rational. But inside she was petrified. Someone had tried to kill her. The car had aimed right at her – again and again. What was going on?

"Let me take you to the hospital."

"No." She gently pulled his strong hand from her arm. "I'm all right, Alex. But find out who did this."

"I will. First I'm calling the Denver police and I'm getting some additional security."

She sat in the limousine and waited for the police, her hands shaking, her stomach upset. More than anything she wanted to go back to her suite and get under the big comforter. But she waited for the police and then she and Alex went to Brennan's hotel, arriving with a police escort, fifteen minutes late.

Brennan sat in an ornate, regal-looking chair in his suite. He wore house slippers, his left leg up on a footstool, a large bandage around his ankle. His perfectly tailored dark blue business suit gave a strange contrast to the slippers. "You're making a habit of being late, Little Lady, I mean, Madame Secretary."

Oh my God, she thought. Did he know about the car? Brennan, the State Department, the CIA, an order to *terminate* her?

But not for a second could she show any fear or weakness to this man. "Heavy traffic," she said. "What did you want to see me about?"

She glanced down at his bandaged ankle.

He noticed her look. "Tripped in the shower. They don't make 'em right up here in Denver. Big ledge. Tripped over it."

Good heavens, if the American government was after her…but that was paranoid.

"What did you want to see me about?"

"Sit down, Little…Madame Secretary."

She sat on the edge of the chair opposite him, keeping her body stiff and formal. She waited and gave him no small talk.

"Shucks, little lady, you just got me on the run." He gave a little laugh, as if she had pulled a fast one on him. "The president wanted me to ride herd on the UN, keep everything nice and quiet and now we got all this wild talk about a Constitutional Convention. The president is plum scared out of his boots about all this."

"Yes?" she replied. Brennan was trying to be real *down home* with her. The more he tried, the colder she got.

"See, the president's trying to stand up for America. He doesn't want some two-bit country soundin' off about America at a Constitutional Convention. So he'd like the whole idea to kinda just fade away. And he's prepared to offer you something in return."

"What?"

"First, I just want you to know how serious he is about all this. I don't mind telling you that I got my ass chewed off by the Secretary of State *and* the President."

"That's a lot of chewing. What's his offer?"

"Let the idea just dry up and blow away and you'll get a second term."

"And if I don't?"

"Come on, now...Madame Secretary."

"My early indications are that the American people are for this and most countries in the world support me. It's not going to lessen America's power. It's only fair, you know. One person, one vote."

"Madame, the president is really serious about this."

"So am I."

"I have to tell you. If you don't go along, he's ordered us to cut off all funds – I repeat – *all* funds to the UN."

Now that was serious. Without the US contribution, the UN wouldn't last a month. She would go down in history – not as the woman who reformed the UN, but as the one who presided over its bankruptcy.

"I'll let you know."

"The president wants to know – now."

"I'll let you know."

She stood up quickly. "I hope your ankle improves, Mr. Brennan."

"Your decision, Madame?"

"Wait. What should…"

She turned and left the room. Alex stood right outside with two of Brennan's guards. Alex put his hand on the doorknob and stopped it from closing all the way. Pilar tilted her head as if to inquire what he was doing. He held up his hand to caution her to wait.

One of Brennan's guards asked, "What's the trouble?"

Alex opened the door fully. The supposedly wounded Brennan stood by the desk talking on the phone.

* * *

Later that evening Alex learned from the local police that they had located the black car, but there was no trace of the driver. However, on the front seat of the car, next to the driver, they did find the front page of the Denver Post with Pilar's picture on it.

Chapter 19

Appointment Schedule for the Secretary-General
Friday, December 22

3:30 PM – Mikhail Sergeyevich Ignatyev, Ambassador to the UN,
Russia

It was two days before Christmas and the trouble was the
Russians.

Pilar gazed out the window of her mansion on Sutton Place. On
some days, when the temperature was just above or below freezing,
snow fell gently with beautiful, large crystals. This morning,
however, a cold wind drove the snow across the lawn until it collided
with the dark stone of the building. The snow then eddied its way to
the ground.

The scene reminded her of a week she'd spent in Moscow on
UN business a few years ago and that brought her back to today's
problem – how to win the Russians.

While promoting her idea in Europe a few weeks before, she
had predicted that four out of the five veto countries would be on
board by year's end. The news media called it a promise, even though
she insisted it was just theory. But now the clock was ticking toward
the new year. An article in yesterday's Times speculated that Russia
would not give up its veto before December 31st and, in fact, would
never do so.

As of today she had two of the five, China and France, and it looked as if Britain would come aboard, too. France and Britain both responded to the common feeling in Europe that the UN, as it existed, was outdated. How could a powerhouse like Germany not be involved? Pilar used the same arguments she had used in the United States – that her ideas were just a reflection of the *New Europe*. "You have shown us the way in Europe. Led by people like Jean Monnet, you have molded warring countries into an economic and administrative unit. I'm simply trying to do the same thing with the UN. What's good for Europe, is good for the UN."

It didn't hurt that England's representative at the UN, Charles Kent-Ashley, was solidly in her favor. She expected to hear from him in the affirmative any day now.

All through Europe Yusuf followed her and harassed her at every speech she made. He implied that she was a lackey for the United States government, that she even slept with a White House staff person who advised the president on international issues.

"I slept with Stuart Kilbane twenty-four years ago," Pilar responded to this charge. "He worked for the mayor of New York then. He would come home and discuss with me the sensitive issues he was working on, such as parking meters near Times Square and even the hot issue of parking meters near the UN."

But Russia was her problem on this snowy morning. The media still played up the New Year's Eve deadline, despite her PR staff's efforts. She couldn't afford a defeat now so she called Stuart and Asha for a 'thinking' lunch before her meeting with the Russian ambassador later in the afternoon. Alex, however, would be missing. Upon returning from Europe, he had gone to Denver to follow up on the attempt on Pilar's life. The Denver police were now calling it a *traffic accident.*

*   *   *

At noon Stuart and Asha came to her office. Asha looked wonderful – vibrant, excited, dressed in a brown pant suit that seemed to lend motion to her svelte figure. The job of organizing, of directing staff, of campaigning, was agreeing with her.

Stuart, on the other hand, wore his perennial bow tie which signaled that he was in the same space he was the last time – and all the past times – distant, uninvolved and bitter. She asked about his plans for Christmas.

"Off to Milwaukee. Spending the holidays with my sister. Her husband left her this year and it'll be her first year alone for Christmas. Her son is in the army, stationed in Korea, and her daughter is teaching English in China."

"I'm working Christmas Eve and Christmas," Asha said. "A lot to do."

Pilar felt a touch of holiday sadness. This would be her first Christmas without her mother. She always went home to Vancouver for the holidays and had a good time, despite maternal hints as to how she should run her life.

"Let's go to the translators' conference room," Asha suggested. "I've still got privileges there and that room will be free of listening devices."

All agreed and Asha led them to a solemn room with gloomy paneling and dark furniture. Indirect lighting dissolved any sharp corners in the room.

"UN 1960s church style," Stuart commented when Asha led them into the somber room.

"Bouse Tizi," Asha muttered.

"What?"

"Never mind. It was Arabic."

"Arabic for what?"

"Kiss my…Never mind."

The three sat down with Pilar at the head of the table and Asha on her right and Stuart on her left. Asha spoke up first with her usual enthusiasm. "I have things arranged for Africa right after Christmas and South America the first week of January. It gets easier the more countries sign up."

"Burkina Faso all set?" Pilar asked.

Asha flashed her a woman-to-woman look, but answered in a normal tone. "All set."

"What's the count now?" Pilar asked.

"China and France of the veto countries and – just got a telegram." Asha held it up. "Britain is with us."

"Wonderful."

"We've already reached a majority of countries. 102 out of 191 as of this morning. Oh, and I hired ten more staff as you suggested."

"Good." Pilar said. "Now start planning the actual conference."

"San Francisco?"

"Yes. I want—"

"I know a way to get the Russians on side," Stuart interrupted.

"What is it?" Pilar asked.

"You're not going to like it, but it'll work."

"What?"

"They're not going to give up their veto easily."

Asha waved her hand impatiently, "The idea, Stuart, the idea."

"All right, all right," Stuart answered. "We threaten to reveal a small fact about President Filippov – we threaten, we do not reveal."

"What fact?" Asha asked.

"I learned this while working in the White House. I must have your word, Asha and Madame, that you will not say where you heard this."

Asha sneered at Stuart. "Pass on the dirt, but not say where we got it?"

"You want to win or you don't want to win?" Stuart shrugged. "Makes no difference to me."

"What are you talking about, Stuart?" Pilar asked.

"I have your word?"

Asha nodded assent and Stuart went ahead without waiting for Pilar. When she worked in the bureaucracy hearing and using *dirt* didn't bother her. Now she didn't even want to hear it.

Stuart's gaze shifted from her to Asha and back to her. He seemed to be enjoying their attention. "Early in his career Mr. Filippov worked for the KGB when that organization still existed. That fact is well known, but what isn't known– and would destroy him totally

– is that for the last year of his time with the KGB, he was also an American double agent."

"How do you know this, Stuart?" Pilar asked.

"Because I came across a folder in the back of a filing cabinet marked *Top Secret*. The paper inside was the report of a person identified only as Agent 698. It was a full report on the inside workings of the KGB, but I had no idea who wrote it."

"So?" Asha asked.

"A year later somebody came to me with a paper also stamped *Top Secret*. It had come into the White House in a file from State. The paper consisted of a list of three and four digit numbers like the 698 I had seen on the KGB report. 698 was on this sheet, too.

"I assumed the paper was a list of Russian agents who turned over valuable information to the American government. I got nowhere. Then I speculated that the list might refer to all double agents, Russian to American and the reverse. I picked one number, 4762, and began to play with it. I made lists of Russian and American spies and there it was – #4762 was John Anthony Walker Jr., a double agent who turned over Navy secrets to the Soviets. 4762 were the number of letters in his name. 698 was Sergey Yuryevich Filippov. I had a list, not of single agents, but of double agents.

"I asked the CIA to confirm my analysis and I gave them a copy of the Top Secret paper. A day later two section chiefs and three CIA goons crowded into my office and demanded the original. And they refused to confirm or deny anything. Confirmation enough. The State Department's reaction was the same.

"I went back to the report on the KGB. Only Filippov could have written it. So there it is."

"Little boy games," Asha said. "I don't think we should use things like that."

Maybe not, Pilar thought, but it was interesting. No doubt the American government would use the same information the other way, to keep Filippov in their camp. She'd have to neutralize that advantage. However, she was back to square one – how to win the Russians.

"Thanks, Stuart. I'll have to think about that one. Maybe if we figure out what they want."

"Respect," Stuart answered. "They're not a super power anymore."

That's the answer Pilar thought would have come from Asha.

"Money," Asha said. "They're trying to build a first rate economy."

And that was the answer she thought Stuart would have given.

* * *

Pilar liked Ambassador Mikhail Ignatyev. At sixty-seven he didn't worry much about what anybody thought of him. He was straightforward and honest. He had worked for the government in Gorbachev's time and had survived the confusing years that followed.

She walked around her desk and greeted him, extending both hands, not even bothering about her missing pinkie. "Greetings, Ambassador. Thank you for coming so close to our holidays."

His hair and moustache were salt-and-pepper and he always had a smile. He reminded her of an uncle on her mother's side, a British Columbia logger, who had a moustache and always put a Canadian fifty in a plain envelope – never a card – for birthdays, Christmas, and special occasions.

When they had settled into her leather chairs, she poured tea for both of them. "I need your support, Ambassador," she said.

"Mikhail," he corrected her.

"I need Russia to support me in redrawing the UN."

He shifted uncomfortably in his seat. "Pilar, in times past there were two players on the world stage, us and the Americans. Now there is only the Americans. Moscow uses the veto to gain concessions it wants from other countries. I don't see how…"

Her young secretary stuck his head in the door. "Excuse me, Madame, but it's an attorney from Vancouver on the phone. Says it's most urgent."

"Thank you," she said. "Excuse me, Mikhail, just for a second. It's my mother's estate."

She took the call at her desk. Her mother's condo had been broken into, but neighbors scared off the burglar and the attorney had sealed the place. The attorney told her she would have to get to Vancouver soon to settle her mother's affairs. She put a note on her desk to talk to Asha about when such a trip might be scheduled. Then she returned to the Ambassador.

"More tea, Ambassador?"

He shook his head.

She decided it would be best to put the information about the Russian president right on the table. "As I was saying, Ambassador, I need your support and I want you to know I would never use certain rumors that are being bandied about concerning Mr. Filippov. I think you know what I mean."

He looked confused for an instant, but she knew he would investigate until he found out what she meant. "That's not my style," she continued. "But I have a proposal today for your government. Initially I designated San Francisco to be the place of the Constitutional Convention. But what if we were to switch it to St. Petersburg? I can't think of a better place. Your country stretches from Europe to Asia and this city is your European gateway."

"Interesting," Mikhail said.

"And it serves to honor the heroic fight of the Russian people in World War II in that city."

"All well and good, Madame. I am sure my government would be honored by such a choice. But we would have to put money into improvements and..."

"That's the second part of my plan. This convention is not going to be a one-week event. I foresee it going on for months. There are a lot of things to be weighed carefully. Perhaps a mistake of 1945 was that we went too fast. So an awful lot of money and a lot of delegates are going to visit St. Petersburg."

"That's a generous offer, Madame, and I will relay it to my government. But I doubt if it will compensate for the loss of the veto. You have to understand the nature of Russians. At least in this one area the world pays attention to us."

"What more respect can there be, that the new constitution will be argued out in one of your cities?"

The ambassador did not respond. He just stared at her with a sad face.

"Mikhail, please – in April of '04 and in May of '93 Russia vetoed resolutions about Cyprus and in December of '94 you vetoed one on Bosnia and Herzegovina. Before that, one in '84, one in '83 and two in 1980. That's seven vetoes since 1980. In that same time the United States has used its veto power fifty-six times. I'm asking you to give up something you can live without, you *have* been living without."

The ambassador stood. "We are a very proud people, Madame. I will relay your feelings to my government."

She was going to lose, she knew that, at least for now. Better not to make it public. "I hope we can talk again, Mikhail, *before* your government makes any announcement."

"I'm sure we can. Good day, Madame."

In the silence Pilar walked to her window and looked out at the still-continuing snowstorm, this Russian winter scene. She had no gift from the Russians to celebrate her lonely Christmas.

The Russian veto. Seven times in twenty-five years. But what about the United States? How was she ever going to sway a country that used the veto fifty-six times in twenty-five years?

Chapter 20

Appointment Schedule for the Secretary-General
Tuesday, December 26 until January 6

The Secretary-General will spend the New Year in Africa.

"Welcome, Madame Secretary," the hotel clerk bowed politely, "welcome to Ouagadougou, the capital of Burkina Faso."

"Ou-ga-doo-goo, is that right?"

"Waga-doo-goo. Waga, for short."

"Waga. I'm happy to be here."

"We are honored to have you here, Madame. We have renovated our best suite for your visit and the whole top floor has been reserved for you and your people. Oh, and I have a fax for you."

Who's Watching the Store? It was a fax of a newspaper article sent by Stuart. The article was an interview with Quan about how he was taking care of the UN while Madame Secretary-General was gallivanting around the world. She shoved the fax into her purse. Six months ago she would have fired off a response – now it seemed like the buzzing of a pesky fly.

Alex picked up her luggage and walked with her to the elevator. "Burkina Faso, Madame, it used to be called Upper Volta." While he was telling her this, his eyes searched the lobby and the area by the elevators. How amazing, Pilar thought, that he could relay interesting facts, while all his attention seemed focused on security.

A dozen or so people speaking French crossed the lobby in front of them. "Burkina Faso means *land of the upright people*," Alex said, his attention turned to the French tourists. He reached the elevator, pressed the button and looked over his shoulder again at the lobby. "Most people speak the Mòoré language," he said, "but the official language is French." The elevator came and it was empty. Alex held the door for her and then stood easily by the floor buttons as the elevator rose to the top floor. He said nothing and looked as if he might be whistling a tune in his head.

Pilar smiled to herself. No security threat, no talk. Trouble, and he was a walking encyclopedia.

Alex carried her bag to the room, the luxury suite. Asha and her assistants shared two rooms and Alex and four security men shared the other two.

While Alex checked the rooms, Pilar examined her suite. The rooms smelled fresh and clean, just like a North American hotel. The first room she entered was a large sitting room with generous windows. A door opposite the entry door led to the bedroom, which had that neat, clean, un-lived-in look so common to modern hotels.

When Alex left, she walked to the window. Below her the water in the hotel's pool glinted in the bright sunlight. Next to the pool, a couple clad in white togs played tennis. Beyond the hotel property, a wide boulevard stretched toward the center of the city. Traffic was light and Pilar saw several couples strolling along in the middle of the street. It wasn't Paris, but it seemed friendly and relaxed. The weather was sunny and the temperature, pleasant. Alex had told her there were even a few nightclubs.

"A perfect place," she said out loud. Her staff had been working very hard and needed a break. She did, too. And they all needed time to plan for the challenges ahead. Anatole had agreed to meet with them for planning sessions.

A knock on the door interrupted her reflections. "Sorry to disturb you, Madame," Alex said. "One of my men saw Yusuf outside the hotel. Just to let you know. We've got everything covered, but please stay away from the windows."

She appreciated the concern in his eyes. "Thank you, Alex," she said, "I'll be all right."

Alex left and she sat on the edge of the bed and stared at the bland green wall. No, the window would relax her so she could sleep. She returned to her seat and gazed at the street below. A few people walking, but no Yusuf. Why did Brennan's forces have to pursue her to Africa? This was not a campaign event – this was a retreat, a renewal of herself and her staff. This was a visit to an old friend.

Would there be another attempt on her life? Was she endangering her staff by coming here?

Her phone rang. Asha said it was the Russian ambassador, Mikhail Ignatyev.

"Madame," he said when he came on the line, "I wanted to get back to you. My government was very impressed with your offer of holding the Constitutional Convention in St. Petersburg, but they worry that there will not be enough hotel rooms. The time is short, but with some extra financing they feel they can speed construction of two hotels that are already started. And…." his voice trailed off … "they think a hundred million should do it – the hotels and getting the city ready."

A hundred million. Ridiculous. Greed again. The Russian leaders trying to squeeze more money out of the UN. She stopped herself from responding sharply to Mikhail. It wasn't him.

"You know our financial situation, Mikhail. I'm struggling with the Americans not to cut off our existing budget. They've threatened to do that. Imagine what their reaction would be if I said I needed a hundred million to help a Russian city steal the convention from San Fransisco. No. It's impossible."

"I'll tell the Kremlin," Mikhail said. He sounded sad. "Goodbye, Madame."

Was it just Russian hardball, seeing how much they could get? Pilar shook her head and went back to the window. The beautiful boulevard with the strolling couples. And right in the middle of the street, another couple – Yusuf and Habiba Saynab, the woman from New Jersey the CIA had hired to infiltrate her office.

A beautiful scene, but hardly relaxing with Yusuf watching her and the Russians demanding more money.

* * *

A call from Anatole woke her. It was Thursday morning. "Let me take you on a tour of the city," he said, his voice full of energy. "We'll stop at the market and then I will cook you a genuine Burkinabe meal at my home."

A perfect plan, Pilar thought. They had all agreed that today would be a *personal* day. Thank God for Anatole.

"Dinner at the presidential palace?" she asked.

"No, no, no. The same house I had when you were here. I live there. I just work at the palace."

"I'd like that."

"Your presence here has caused much excitement."

"Oh?"

"Yes, I understand the president of this place, one Anatole Zoungrana, is going to ask Madame Secretary to dedicate a plaque at the Place des Nations Unies on New Year's Day."

"I accept. I'm honored."

Two hours later a security official, driving an old Chevy, arrived with Anatole who explained that he was going to take her to the government building where he had a covered golf cart they could use to tour the city and go to the market. "My security doesn't like it, but I like to get out in the air."

"A golf cart?" Alex asked. "I can't think of anything more insecure."

"My legs do not allow me to enjoy walking," Anatole said to Alex. "but I appreciate your concern and I agree with you."

Alex nodded. "It's just that the CIA has a few operatives here and...I'm nervous. Let us use our limo."

"It's not a problem," Anatole said. Alex asked the limo driver to get the vehicle and when it arrived, Pilar got in the back seat with Anatole, while Alex sat next to the driver. Two of Alex's men followed behind in another car.

Pilar liked sitting next to Anatole. He had that *man* smell about him, sweaty from work, rough, not masked in any way. She supposed he took a walk in the morning or worked in his garden. She was amazed at how he told her to look to her right or left at various sights. The man was blind.

"How do you do that?" she asked, "I mean, telling me to look at the French embassy or the beautiful European house? How?"

He laughed easily. "When you love a city, you never forget it. But wait." He asked his driver for the time and then instructed him to drive to the Moro-Naba palace. "In a few minutes," he explained, "an actor comes out of the palace. The ceremony will seem strange to western eyes, but it's really a story of how we survived as a people."

At the palace when the ceremony started, an actor walked out, dressed in scarlet robes. He mounted a horse and took up his spear and dagger. Surveying the country around, his face suddenly registered alarm as he gazed in one direction. He returned his spear and dagger to an aide, got off his horse and hurried back into the palace.

"It's called *The False Departure Of The Emperor,*" Anatole said. "It's mostly a survival story."

The opposite of what I'm doing, Pilar thought, picturing herself charging into battle with only a spear and a dagger against Brennan, backed by all the tanks and planes of the world's only superpower. *At least the Emperor was smart enough to get back into the palace.*

Anatole asked his driver to take them to see a Mossi village and then the market with its many stalls. Pilar enjoyed the market, the noise of people haggling over prices, the smells of chickens, merchants hawking their goods, customers bargaining, children running between stalls, a well-dressed woman stopping her and thanking her for caring about Africa.

It was fun to walk through a market with another, a man. Had she not missed a lot in her life? Dedication to the UN was wonderful, but could it supplant the personal?

As Pilar examined some beads at a market stall, a small girl ran into her and grabbed her leg. The girl was crying. Seconds later an older girl, dressed in tattered clothes just like the little girl, ran up to the stall. She shouted angrily at the little girl in Mòoré. The little girl cried and grasped Pilar's leg tighter. Anatole sent the older girl away, talked to the little girl and then led her to a government office in the market, where he left her in the care of a woman.

"A street urchin," Anatole explained. "The older girl accused her of stealing food. We try, but there is much pain in Africa."

Pilar felt a strong sense of longing, a motherly feeling. A little girl had clung to her for help. Her heart went out to both girls.

The incident seemed to summarize her feeling of the day. Why had she denied herself the personal, the joys and agonies of motherhood?

She almost felt the little girl still clutching her as Anatole purchased some vegetables for dinner.

After the shopkeeper had lectured him about local taxes, their driver took them to Anatole's little bungalow.

When Alex and the local man had arranged security around the house, Alex excused himself, telling Pilar privately that they were maintaining a twenty-four hour watch on Yusuf and Habiba Saynab.

"It was a lovely tour," Pilar said to Anatole when they were alone in his house. Security was reassuring, but it was nice to be alone. She could be herself now.

"Here's a cup of water," Anatole said, handing her a carved wooden cup. "It's our tradition to give a cup of water to a visitor." He led her into his living room and then excused himself for a moment to use the bathroom.

She drank the water and looked at the pictures on the wall and those standing on two coffee tables. Anatole and his wife at their wedding; another picture of them in front of this little bungalow. His wife, dead now for five years, had been a beautiful African woman. In the photograph Anatole had that same look about him she remembered from the day her plane was delayed and he had waited with her. She stared at his face in the picture – this was before his accident. His eyes showed interest in others, a certain aliveness that she often found lacking in the tired diplomats at the UN. The sight was gone from his eyes now, but not the concern.

Sight or no sight, she knew, as she had that day, that she could spend a lifetime with him.

Another picture showed Anatole and a group of African leaders meeting with UN officials, herself included. Then a crippled Anatole being installed as president of Burkina Faso. More photos: Anatole and Bill Clinton, Anatole and Vladimir Putin, Anatole and Kofi Annan.

When Anatole came back to the living room, he smiled and said, "I will now give you a genuine African home-cooked meal."

"Let me help," she answered and they entered the small kitchen. He struggled as he cooked – finding the right utensils and walking from the refrigerator to the sink and back. Considering his disabilities, however, he did very well.

"We're having rice and beans. I prepared the beans yesterday. And some special foods from my country."

"That's fine, Anatole," she said.

Somehow he knew the light was fading and he switched on the overhead light. "Come, sit," he said, pointing her to a small round table in a breakfast nook that looked out to the garden.

He sat opposite her, but when she began to talk, he slid his chair to her right. "I can hear you easier," he said and pointed to his good left ear.

"Wine?" he asked.

"Yes."

He reached for a wine bottle and poured her a glass and one for himself without spilling a drop.

"I guess you're not Muslim." She had never asked him his religion.

"No. The French were here for sixty years so I am Roman Catholic as my parents were. I went to university in France and I studied the social philosophy of the Church, what some people call the social gospel." His face crinkled with enthusiasm and he spread his hands apart as if this gospel was very large. "I learned so much, especially from Pope John XXIII. He's the one who called the Second Vatican Council back in the late fifties. I practically memorized his encyclical called *Pacem In Terris*. I don't really do much else with religion today."

"I'm Christian, too," she said. "Anglican, like my mother. But my father was Roman Catholic. He was from Cuba. I thought you went to university in the United States."

"That was post-graduate."

Anatole poured another glass of wine during their meal. They ate a vegetable that Anatole explained was "kapok leaves." "We encourage mothers to feed their children these leaves. They are high in carotene."

Pilar ate the leaves and sympathized with Burkinabe children. But the rest of the meal was wonderful. Anatole served her coffee and had some himself. "I wish to say something," he said, his voice sounding tentative.

"Yes, what?"

"You have changed so wonderfully from when I knew you before. Then you were competent and helpful, but, well, it seemed your loyalty was to your job and not to the people. Now every leader in Africa appreciates what you did in Somalia."

"I remember," Pilar said. "I know what you're talking about. It was a woman's health program. The leader…"

"Mariama."

"That's right. She wanted to include information about abortion and I stopped her. The Americans were pressuring us."

Anatole smiled. "I knew why you did it."

She loved the way his face crinkled when he smiled. The big scar that ran from the top of his nose to the corner of his mouth increased the crinkle factor.

"You're right. I've changed," she said. "I'm a lot older now."

"I know what you look like," he said.

Pilar laughed. "You don't remember."

"You have very smooth skin and a pointy chin. Your hair is thick and black and…"

"Gray."

"That wasn't what I was going to say. The last time I saw you, your hair was cut short. Your eyes are blue, sort of almond shaped."

"With lines around them for every struggle at the UN."

He smiled. "You are about my height and have a very nice figure. You lost your left little finger in a home accident. Your fingers are long and thin, like a piano player's."

She did not reply. It was amazing what a clear picture he had of her. Did he think about her a lot? Or did he just have an exceptional memory?

She knew she wasn't a beautiful woman like Asha. Men stared at Asha, but Pilar knew that Asha wanted them to treat her as a competent organizer and not as some African beauty queen.

It was nice to sit at table with a man who knew her and cared about her.

"I'm worried about you," he said. "Alex told me what happened in Denver and he said this Yusuf fellow is here in Waga. And some CIA woman."

"Anatole, can I ask you … Do you ever think of marrying again?"

My God, she thought. *Where did that come from? What's the matter with me?*

"I've thought about it," he said, giving no indication that the question was out of the ordinary. "I do want a companion, someone to grow old with, someone who understands my life and what I have tried to do. Oh…I am so sorry." He chuckled softly. "This sounds like I'm placing an ad for a wife. What about you?"

"I never really thought about it when I worked in the bureaucracy, but now I do think about the future. It's nice to be with someone."

It would be nice to have a day like this every day, to be with a special someone.

He put his hand on the wine bottle. "More ?" he asked.

"No, thanks," she replied. The wine was already telling too much truth.

"My party wants me to run again," Anatole said, "when my term is over. You remember, five years. I have two more to go, then I would like to serve another term. I have a lot to do. And you?"

She laughed. "I may be out of a job very soon. That is, if the American government has its way. They have fought me every step of the way."

He shifted in his chair as if something had made him uncomfortable. "One thing, Pilar, if I might."

"What, Anatole? Tell me."

"The Americans. You are *their* Secretary-General, too. You have let this Brennan and his minions determine your attitude. You have to take what is good in America and build on it. I like what Ho Chi Minh used to say, that the American people were generous and kind, but it was just their government that oppressed people. The American government pretends it is on a mountaintop, way above the clouds. The leaders look around and see no one else. But the truth is that we are all many countries existing on a vast plain. We are all equal. You have to help Americans see that. In any case, you can't have a negative idea of America."

"Thank you. I know you're right."

"Do you want a second term?"

"Yes. Yes – I do.

"Do your best and leave the rest to God. We have a saying, *Wend sin man, sam ka yay.. If God does it, nothing will go wrong.*"

She played with her empty wine glass, sliding it from one hand to the other. How nice it was to talk, really talk to someone. Without any introduction, she said, "The Russians – they're trying to get more out of me. I need their support. I need them to give up the veto. I've already promised to have the Convention in St. Petersburg, but now they want a hundred million. And the Americans – how will I ever get them?"

Anatole's face crinkled into a smile. "The Russian bear tries to see how far it can go. They test your limits, Pilar. Stay strong."

"And the Americans?"

"I have no easy, quick answer. But America is a true democracy and in the end, in the long run, the people are wise and they will make the right decisions."

She shook her head, "But a lot of people will die while they make up their minds."

"I know," he said. His voice trailed off. "I know."

She slid the wine glass again. And the other thing on her mind? Her aloneness? Should she bring it up again? Seven more years for him as President of Burkina Faso and a possible ten for her as Secretary-General, neither of them eager to end their careers.

A future with Anatole looked very doubtful. Unless, of course, she was suddenly removed from office.Sadness came over her and she soon bid goodbye to Anatole and called for Alex to pick her up. As he drove back to the hotel, she played the whole evening over again in her mind. To spend her days in that little house with that gentle man. To shrink the grand scale of her life and do it well, very well. A house, a husband and the setting sun

It was not to be. She listened to Alex quietly whistling to himself as he drove. She smiled – his lack of conversation meant everything was under control.

Chapter 21

Appointment Schedule for the Secretary-General
New Year Holidays

Madame Secretary-General will conduct staff meetings while in
     Ouagadougou.
Dedication of a plaque in Ouagadougou on New Year's Day.

Pilar's concentration wavered. Anatole was using the example
of Europe to show her staff how it was possible to make amazing
changes in the organization of the world. "Early in the twentieth
century the states of Europe fought two bloody wars against each
other. No one would have predicted they would sit down and give
up power to a pan-European government. But that's exactly what
happened, beginning…"

Anatole wore a white sport shirt with stripes running up and
down. Pilar noticed that near his belt he had missed a buttonhole
and the shirt gaped out. She smiled and sympathized with his lack
of sight.

Pilar glanced around the room. The hotel gave them the use of
a private dining room, recently refurbished into baroque, a style
long gone from major hotels.

Everyone scribbled notes as Anatole talked. They sat around
four tables put together in a square. There were seventeen of them
in all, Asha and her key assistant, Josette, a tall Swiss woman; nine

other public relations people: four men and five women, all young and all earnest; Alex and four of his security men and then herself.

Pilar picked up her pen to look busy. The pen Asha had put at her place was a UN pen, one with a round globe at the top, the UN symbol. *Everywhere I go,* Pilar thought. *I can't escape this thing.*

She twirled the pen in her fingers. Yesterday she tasted the joy of being *with* someone, but today, instead of holding someone's hand, she was fiddling with a UN pen meant for tourists. *God,* she said in her mind, and dropped the pen to the floor.

Alex, sitting next to her, picked it up, handed it to her and smiled at her warmly.

She smiled back.

Anatole continued, "Europe began to realize that the world was too small. Russia is almost at that point today and the United States will not be far behind."

Oh, I wish you were right Anatole, but I don't think you are.

Anatole finished his opening talk and Pilar watched Asha take over. Pilar took in the stunning white pant suit Asha wore and how it emphasized her beautiful black skin. Asha laid out the facts about Russia and opened up a discussion on what to do. She spoke with energy and enthusiasm, her hands and arms telling the story of Russia and laying out their options.

People around the table responded to her. Pilar marveled at how other women related to her without jealousy over her extraordinary beauty.

"We can follow what I call the *Anatole* strategy," Asha said, nodding and smiling toward Anatole. "We can point out to the Russians that they don't want to be the last ones on board and since they don't use the veto anymore, why bother with it? Or we can put the pressure on and hint that giving the convention to San Francisco might convince the Americans to give up the veto."

Asha polled everyone in the room and a lively debate ensued. *The woman's talents are wasted in the translation office,* Pilar thought.

While they debated, Asha seemed as placid as a lake on a summer morning. *I wish I were like that,* Pilar thought. *I used to be like that. Day after day, did my job, nothing bothered me. But now...*

After a period of debate, Asha pulled the best of both sides into a plan that everyone agreed with, a combination of both approaches. Then she suggested a break.

Alex brought Pilar a cup of coffee. He didn't ask her anything, or comment on how quiet she was, he just stood there, smiling, while she drank her coffee.

Alex had the same *man* smell that Anatole had, no cologne, just a little manly sweat. Her father smelled like that on hot days in his workshop.

She herself broke the silence, pointing to Asha. "She's good, isn't she?"

"I read that Fatimah, the prophet's daughter, was given the title of "az-Zahraa" which means *The Resplendent One.* That's Asha. The woman radiates light and wisdom and direction."

"She's also very beautiful."

"Is she? I hadn't noticed."

Pilar turned sharply to Alex. Was he serious? No, he started laughing.

Pilar laughed too. She looked directly into his eyes and saw that his eyes watered when he laughed. She'd noticed this before – like he was crying for joy. But when he noticed her looking at him, he turned away as if he was embarrassed by his emotional nature.

Asha called the group back to work and raised the question of the United States. She said that Anatole's original idea of going to the people had worked well – support for UN reform was up – but it hadn't changed the government's mind. "I want to announce one bit of good news," she continued. "It was Stuart's idea originally. The Political Science Department of the University of Michigan has agreed to hold a Model UN, based on some of the ideas we've been promoting, two legislative houses, one house representing population and another with each country having one vote. They're going to model the body based on population."

Pilar applauded along with everyone else, but immediately asked herself, *What if the model UN turns out like the real UN?*

Asha then asked for strategy suggestions about the United States. Conflicting ideas shot around the room. Go to the people, go to the congress, go to the religious leaders. Build coalitions of interest groups; no, appeal to individual lawmakers. Forget St. Petersburg, go back to San Francisco. No, let cities all around the world bid for the Constitutional Convention just as they bid for the Olympics. Get Israel to back the reform; after all it was Israel the US used its veto for. No, put pressure directly on the US administration.

The strategy agreed on was a little of everyone's idea, not very different from what they'd been doing.

The hour approached noon and all agreed that the next two-and-a-half days would be time off. Asha reminded everyone that the next event would be the New Year's Day dedication of a plaque in the Place des Nations Unies in the center of Ouagadougou.

Asha turned to Pilar. "Anything else, Madame?"

Pilar stood. She'd been too quite during the meeting. "You've all worked hard, very hard," she said. "I've planned a little New Year's Eve party here at the hotel for you."

Pilar called on Anatole to finish the seminar.

"We have a saying in our Moore' language," he said. "*When the creek zigzags, the crocodile has to zigzag.* Maybe that is the way we will solve the difficult problem of the United States. We simply have to show the United States that long ago the world zigzagged into a new era and now that big old *Uncle Sam* crocodile has to zigzag, too."

* * *

On Saturday, the day before New Year's Eve, Pilar did little. Anatole invited her to visit the people of the Gurunsi tribe about three hours south of the city. "The Gurunsi women create beautiful abstract African frescoes," he told her. "And Gurunsi architecture sparked the Swiss architect, Le Corbusier."

Pilar thanked him, but declined. It would be too painful, again imagining a life that couldn't be. Instead she took a walk with Alex and one of his men. She walked fast, ignoring the local custom of *ambling.* She felt a need for intense exercise.

On the morning of New Year's Eve, she sat at her window and wrote down her New Year's resolutions:

1. Get Russia and the United States signed up for the Constitutional Convention.
2. Overcome this personal problem of loneliness. Keep busy. Maybe a pet? Take guitar lessons.

Despite her missing finger, Pilar had always wanted to play guitar. Her father used to strum his guitar and sing her Cuban love songs and tell her, not about Castro and politics, but about ordinary life in Santiago de Cuba.

In the evening at her party, she and the staff danced and sang together around an out-of-tune piano and wished each other success. Asha energized the whole evening, suggesting activities when things slowed down, involving everyone in the fun. At midnight Asha put a CD of Auld Lang Syne in her boom box and Alex asked Pilar to dance.

When she was growing up, her parents stayed at home on New Year's Eve. When she lived with Stuart, he liked to watch the events on TV. This was the first time she had ever danced away the old year and danced in the new one.

"Happy New Year," Alex said at the stroke of midnight. He hugged her tightly and gave her a fleeting kiss on the cheek.

It was a wonderful New Year's.

*   *   *

On Monday, New Year's Day, accompanied by Alex, Asha and all their people, Pilar met Anatole at the Rond Point des Nations Unies, a traffic circle in the center of Ouagadougou. In the middle of the circle was a fenced area with a large UN globe held up by a three-story frame. Around the globe were the characteristic UN blue olive leaves. All the major roads of the city radiated out from here.

Nowhere in the world, not in any city she had visited, did she see the UN so honored as here.

Asha wore the same white pant suit she had on the other day. In the bright sunlight she looked even more stunning. Her deep ebony face seemed to radiate light, as Alex had said. Pilar had made an arrangement with her – for this event they would shift their style of dress – she, the Christian woman, would wear Muslim garb and Asha, the Muslim woman, would wear her western pant suit. Asha had loaned her a reddish brown sari with rich embroidery and a tan scarf to go with it.

Anatole looked rumpled as usual, but he seemed extraordinarily pleased. "This is a first for Burkina Faso," he said when he greeted Pilar. "You are the first world leader to come to our country and to our capital city."

The area around the large globe was filled with fresh flowers. The plaque she was to dedicate had her name on it and the date of her visit as well as her favorite quote, *The age of nations is past.* She reviewed the procedure with Alex and Asha, but Alex seemed preoccupied and kept eyeing the crowd. Local police stopped all traffic around the circle and everyone took their seats on a platform in front of the globe, she and Alex to the left of the podium, Asha and her staff to the right. As they waited for the ceremony to start, Alex kept eyeing the crowd in front of them. "You know, Madame, the American embassy here has a great library named after Martin Luther King."

"Is that right? Ah…what's the matter, Alex?"

"We have Yusuf and Habiba Saynab under surveillance – they're in the last row right over there," he said, making a small motion with his hand. "But I'm still uncomfortable, I'm not sure why."

Pilar noted the two CIA people sitting impassively. She scanned the rest of the crowd – about two hundred people – but saw nothing unusual. Next to her Alex shifted his weight to the edge of his seat and watched the crowd like an eagle looking for a meal.

"You know, Madame, that Ouagadougou has the biggest film festival in Africa every other year. They call it the African Cannes."

Pilar couldn't help smiling – unusual facts, the sure sign of Alex on high alert.

Speaking in French, Anatole stepped to the microphone and called for attention. "Our city has always honored the UN. For years we have called this UN globe the center of our city, but today the UN honors us. Madame Secretary is the first Secretary-General, indeed the first world leader, to visit our city."

Pilar waited as he traced her life story. Next to her Alex still sat on the edge of his chair, his eyes focused on the last row. She looked there – two empty seats. That was trouble. Alex barked an order into the microphone on his shoulder.

Anatole stepped aside from the podium. "I give you the Secretary-General of the United Nations, Madame Pilar Marti."

Pilar walked slowly to the podium. It was a surprise to her how beautiful she felt in these rich Muslim garments. The sari seemed to flow with her.

She adjusted the microphone and put her text in front of her. "*Je suis si heureux d'être ici aujourd'hui et...*"

Alex slammed into her side and she fell to the platform. He lay on top of her, covering her with his body. Loud noises rolled over her – a deafening *whoosh*, the sound of metal crashing into metal and then a thunderous crash. At the same time the rapid fire of a machine gun. She opened her eyes to see wood splinters raining down around her. Screams pierced the air. She heard Anatole's commanding voice, "Get down, everyone."

Then silence. Alex whispered in her ear, "We're going to get you out of here."

"What happened?"

"Somebody tried to kill you. The big globe's been hit. Rocket grenade."

"Did anyone else…"

"Stay down. I'm going to check." Alex called one of his men over to guard Pilar and then he stood. As he did a woman screamed, "Asha. Asha. She's been killed."

Pilar pushed Alex's security man aside, got up and crossed the stage. Behind the stage, the beautiful UN globe lay on the ground, twisted metal and smoking ruins. The top of the podium she had stood at a minute ago was shattered.

Asha had been sitting on the other side of the podium. Now she lay on the platform, the sun shining down on her ebony face and a large crimson stain growing bigger on her lovely white suit.

Pilar knelt down. Asha was struggling to breathe, blood now oozing out from under her body. She turned toward Pilar, smiled faintly and died.

Chapter 22

Appointment Schedule for the Secretary-General

The Secretary-General is in mourning over the death of her
assistant, Asha Amina Hassan

Pilar knelt over Asha's white-clad body. The red stain covered
most of her chest now, but Pilar detected the soft smell of roses.
How could one so dead radiate such beautiful life? Pilar bent further
over and kissed her face. Her tan scarf – the one Asha had lent her
– came to rest on the bloody stain. *Why, why? It was me who asked
you to be here today. Oh Asha, almost daughter to me. You were the
star, the beauty, the organizer, the...*

"Madame, you have to come." It was Alex. "I'm taking you back
to the hotel." He pulled her arm.

Pilar freed herself from his grasp. "Go away. I've had enough.
It stops here."

Alex grabbed her again, more forcefully this time, pulling her
up. "Madame. I insist. Now." His eyes were stern, his lips pressed
tightly together. "You must get out of here, and now." He yanked
her arm.

"Anatole," she called back, as Alex tugged at her, "You must
catch the person that did this. You —"

Alex jerked her toward the UN staff car, but as she passed Josette,
Asha's assistant, she noticed blood on Josette's sleeve.

Pilar stopped, despite the pressure on her arm from Alex. "Josette, are you hurt?"

The woman was crying. "Just a surface wound, Madame. Asha…Asha was a good leader. Why did this happen?"

Before she could answer Pilar found herself yanked forward by Alex until she was off the platform. "Hell with it, hell with it, hell with it," Pilar repeated.

When they reached the car, Pilar got into the back seat. Alex sat next to her and a security man drove. Pilar stared ahead. Asha was dead, but the bullets were meant for her. As the car raced away from the United Nations traffic circle, she gritted her teeth, made a fist and beat the cushion between her and Alex.

Alex put his hand over her fist. "I know," he said gently.

"It's Brennan and Yusuf. The bastards."

"Yes."

"They're murderers. I want revenge."

"Yes, Madame."

"Who else is going to die? You? Anatole? Me?"

"We're doing our best, Madame."

"Oh, the hell with it. Is reform of the UN worth one Asha?"

"She would want you to fight on."

"Yes, yes, but I want her here – alive."

Alex said nothing more, but he kept his hand over hers until they arrived at the hotel. Alex took her to her room and suggested she lie down. He used an electronic detector to check the whole suite for listening devices, then he pulled the drapes in the bedroom. "I'm going back to work with the police," he said. "I want to find out who did this. I'm leaving a man at your door."

Pilar sat on the edge of the bed in the darkened room and cried. She wanted to open the drapes and sit by the window, but, unlike a few nights ago, she was frightened. Somebody was indeed trying to kill her.

She got up and turned on the light.

A half an hour later the security man stuck his head in the door and called to her through the sitting room. Pilar still sat on the edge of the bed. "Asha's staff wants to see you, Madame. Can they come in?"

She muttered, "Tell them to come back later."

"Pardon, Madame?"

They were already here, so she might as well. She knew their message would be, *Asha wants you to continue*, but if she kept on, more of them might die. "Yes," she said. "Show them in."

She knew she should get up and greet them in the bright and pleasant sitting room adjacent, but she just couldn't. The ten of them came through the sitting room into the bedroom, led by Josette. Most, like Josette, were in their late twenties or early thirties. Four were from Europe, four from North America, one from South America and one from China.

Josette had white gauze wrapped around her upper arm. Pilar could see red seeping through.

"Your arm – is it all right?"

"It's okay. Thank you, Madame. We came to show our support for you. We know how Asha felt. She wanted the UN to be reformed and she was passionate about it. We want to press forward in her honor."

"Thank you, but…" her voice trailed off.

Josette sat down on the bed next to Pilar. "Madame, we've talked. Alex told us he's increasing the security around you. We understand the danger, but we really want the UN to be something great. Asha died for a new UN."

Pilar put her hand on Josette's arm. "Thank you for your support. Give me some time. I can't be responsible for any more of you dying. And I don't want to die myself."

Josette stood. Her eyes welled with tears. "Please, Madame. We…" Her voice gave out, she paused a moment. "You're a great leader, Madame, and we…we want you to know we're with you."

The others nodded assent and all of them slowly filed out of the room.

Pilar sat on the edge of the bed and thought. Going forward meant facing death. Stopping now meant return to the comfortable life of diplomacy.

* * *

Two hours later Pilar was lying down in the center of the bed when Alex came back. She got up and sat again on the edge of the bed. Beads of sweat shone on Alex's ebony forehead. "News?" she asked.

"We caught the guy, rather the local police did. A machine gun toting soldier of fortune. All too common in Africa. He says a Somali who spoke perfect English paid him $50,000."

"Yusuf."

"Right."

Alex looked down at the floor. "I failed you, Madame. I'm very sorry."

She reached toward him. "Sit, Alex. It wasn't your fault. It was Yusuf. This soldier you caught – he just confessed this?"

Alex smiled. "Good cop, bad cop. I was the good cop. The local police presented the man with a pretty horrible picture of what would happen to him if he didn't co-operate. The problem, of course, is linking this to Brennan's office."

"Where's Yusuf?"

"Nowhere to be found."

"Alex?"

"Yes, Madame?"

"Alex… Should we go on? Should we…" Her voice cracked and she leaned against him, their shoulders touching. She turned her head to cry on his shoulder, but hesitated. Alex put his arm around her and pulled her closer. She cried long and hard.

Finally she pulled away from him. He handed her his handkerchief, then stood and paced to the window and back to her. "You know, Madame," he said in a quiet voice, "this is not the way it happens in the western movies. The bad guys don't win."

"I know, but—" The outside guard called in through the sitting room. "It's President Zoungrana. Should I let him in?"

Pilar got off the bed. "Of course." And to Alex she said, "Would you guide him in? We'll use the sitting room. And, Alex…" she paused and tentatively touched his elbow, "thank you."

He nodded and left to get Anatole. Pilar stepped into the bathroom and brushed her hair and then entered the sitting room. "Anatole," she said and took his hand. Alex stood right by Anatole.

"Please, everyone, sit." She pointed to the chairs in the room and watched Alex guide Anatole into a chair. "What are the media saying?" she asked Anatole.

"The world media say it was an attack on you by your enemies. The US media says it was an attack on *me* that went astray."

"An attack on *you*?"

Anatole laughed. "During the attack I was way behind you, at the edge of the stage, trying to silence some kids. My aide and I. If the killer was aiming at me, he should have his eyes checked."

Again the security man interrupted them. "Josette?" he asked.

Pilar nodded in the affirmative and a breathless Josette entered. "Madame, I apologize for interrupting but the Russians—"

"What?" Pilar replied.

"They said it was terrible that the Secretary-General came under attack. They wanted everyone to understand they had nothing to do with it. Their hesitation to give up the veto was only a procedural delay and they are in accord with the Secretary-General now. They pointed out what you have said, Madame, that they really don't use the veto anymore."

"Yes, yes," Pilar said. "A small tribute to Asha's death, but, Gentlemen, Josette, I'm not sure it was worth it."

Anatole reached his hand in her direction. "Pilar, you must think seriously about this. Of course, everyone says you must carry on, because that's what Asha would have wanted. But it's deeper than that. A lot of people want you to carry on. People who will die in wars if the world is not governed more fairly, people who will die from disease if medicine is not available, people who will not find work if markets remain closed. Sometimes history places demands on us. A war comes along and a general has to leave his retirement. A drought comes and the technician must go back and re-drill the well. You are a leader, Pilar, and there aren't many of them in the world. I hate to sound authoritarian, but you *must* carry on. History demands it."

"Thank you, Anatole. I know that's the right answer."

"You face your biggest hurdle now," Anatole said. "Your Mr. Brennan."

While Anatole spoke, Alex sat quietly but now he spoke up. "I'm looking carefully at these two attempts on your life, Madame. Politicians are smart and they distance themselves from things, but if we can establish a link between Brennan's office and Yusuf—"

"That's not the way," Anatole countered. "You have to be positive. Put your idea out there. Promote it as best you can and leave the rest to God."

No one said anything for a long minute. Pilar fiddled with the tan scarf Asha had lent her. When she stood to speak at the dedication, it was around her head; now it hung over her shoulders. Thoughts whirled in her head: to go on or to stop, to stir more trouble or fit in, to shake up the UN or leave it alone. She glanced down at the tip of Asha's scarf. A reddish brown substance stained the edge – Asha's blood.

Without warning Pilar stood and announced, "We're going on. For Asha."

Chapter 23

Appointment Schedule for the Secretary-General
Monday, January 29

The Secretary-General will travel to the University of Michigan
for a Model UN

As Pilar's limo turned down the street that led to the auditorium
at the University of Michigan, she saw TV trucks lining both sides
of the street. A crowd of reporters waited at the front door. Pilar and
her staff had agreed to be very low key about this Model UN. They
couldn't really predict the outcome, so they made no special effort
to notify the media. But obviously her opposition had co-opted the
event and planned to turn it into a media disaster.

There was nothing to do but go forward.

Her limo pulled up and she stepped out. Flashbulbs went off.
Reporters waited on the steps, microphones in hand. She identified
a few of the reporters – Conway Kelly, a TV reporter that Alex said
was paid by the White House, Cynthia Wenderoth, who had never
done a positive story on her, and Anne Bowden, the author of the
commentary that said she had risen to the level of her incompetence.

Alex leaned over to her as they started toward the steps of the
auditorium, "All your friends are here."

"Trouble," she whispered back.

She smiled politely to the media as they pushed at the barriers the police had set up. "Hello, Anne," she responded when that reporter stuck a microphone in her face, but she walked on.

Inside Stuart waited for her in the front row. She motioned to her left where all the reporters were taking their seats.

"Got me," he said, shrugging his shoulders. "I don't know where they all came from."

Either Stuart was slipping on his game or he had blabbed to the press. A good planner controlled the media, not the other way around.

"Where's Josette?" Pilar asked.

Stuart pointed backstage. "There. Lining up her troops."

Before Pilar could say anything else, the curtain opened and a young woman walked center stage. Pilar and Stuart sat down.

"Welcome to the University of Michigan and welcome to our Earth Parliament," she said. "My name is Cynthia Reckart." Behind her sat about a hundred empty classroom desks arranged in tiers.

Pilar guessed that Cynthia Reckart had her mind set on a political career. The young woman made eye contact with the audience and spoke in a confident and poised manner. *A lot of charisma in one so young*, Pilar thought.

Stuart leaned toward Pilar. "We're about to see how good your girl Josette is."

"She's not a girl," Pilar whispered back. Why hadn't Stuart already taken the measure of the woman? Josette had stepped into Asha's shoes and had done amazing work in the month since Asha's death. The woman was a born organizer. Pilar had just returned from a very successful tour of South America, a trip planned by Josette. Josette and her staff had raised the number of committed countries from 102 out of 192 to 150 out of 192. In terms of democracy, they certainly had a majority calling for reform.

But without the USA it was a hollow victory.

On stage Cynthia continued, "The one hundred and three desks behind me," she turned and pointed to the desks, "represent the nations of the world. Every sixty million people get one seat. For example, the United States has five representatives, while Canada and Mexico are represented by two delegates. The principle we're using is 'one person, one vote.' This is very similar to the US House of Representatives. It is our belief that this would be one house of a reformed UN. The other house would have 192 delegates, one for each state, similar to the US Senate. This idea and many others have been proposed by Madame Secretary-General Pilar Marti, whom I would like to welcome today."

Pilar smiled and waved when the spotlight shone on her. It was great to be with young people – but the Model UN she was about to watch might be a public relations disaster.

"In honor of our special guest," Cynthia continued, "our parliament is going to take up the issue of Somalia today. The outcome of this debate has not been planned ahead of time."

Somalia. She seemed to be cursed with the country. It kept coming up.

What if the young people threw around vetoes or made alliances that hurt the poor or met dire situations with ho-hum actions? The real UN did all those things on occasion. Pilar pictured the headline in her mind, *Same Old UN.* Or worse, *Model UN Opposes Secretary-General.*

Cynthia pointed to the sides of the large stage. "Now, our delegates." A spotlight played on each side of the stage as the young delegates entered and took their seats. One student accidentally pushed the curtain aside and Pilar caught sight of Yusuf talking intensely with a student. She nudged Stuart.

Under his breath Stuart asked, "Isn't that the guy – a CIA guy – who hired a killer or something in Africa?"

Pilar turned around and motioned to Alex, who sat in the row behind her along with three other security people. Alex looked where she pointed and nodded.

"Didn't he pay to have you killed?" Stuart repeated his question.

Pilar kept her voice low. "A witness said he and Yusuf were driving to the southern savannas at the time of the attack. And the shooter changed his story after a few people visited him in prison. Now he says the guy who paid him was from Nigeria, not Somalia."

The delegates took their seats on the stage, but some still talked in little clusters. Pilar glanced at her program. A chart showed how many delegates each country had.

One delegate: Britain, Iran, Congo, Italy, Egypt, Philippines, Ethiopia, Thailand, France, Turkey, Germany, and Vietnam
Two delegates: Bangladesh, Japan, Nigeria, Pakistan, Canada, and Mexico
Three delegates: Brazil and Russia
Four Delegates: Indonesia
Five delegates: The United States.
Seventeen Delegates: India
Twenty-One Delegates: China

Pilar noted that, judged by population, the center of the world had shifted from west to east.

As she skimmed over several smaller countries, a young black man rose and addressed the chair. He was the representative from the Horn of Africa. "Honorable Chair Person," he bowed slightly to the president of the assembly, Cynthia, who now sat with her back to the audience, facing the tiers of desks.

Here we go, Pilar thought. With Yusuf in the background, there was trouble ahead. On her left a light shone. She turned slightly to see the media salivating for a sound bite.

"One of the countries I represent, Somalia, needs immediate help," the man continued. "People are dying of hunger and thirst. The neighboring country, Ethiopia, has diverted water from the two main rivers. Besides food and water, Somalia needs a military force to bring order and peace. Right now armed warlords rule various sections and we have had twenty-five years of this. Somalia needs immediate help."

All true, all current, but very broad, Pilar thought.

Without waiting for recognition, Ethiopia spoke up. "We did *not* divert the rivers. In fact, we want to help Somalia. If the UN pays for our troops, we would be happy to provide the security force."

Stuart shook his head in disgust. "So now Yusuf's free to do what he wants."

"He has friends in high places," Pilar said.

"In a pig's eye," the young man from the Horn of Africa shouted, jumping to his feet and forgetting his official persona. "Ethiopia wants to take over our country."

During this exchange Pilar watched one of the US delegates leave his seat and go over to a back curtain on the right side of the stage. The curtain opened enough for her to see Yusuf. He spoke with the young man for a moment and then the young man moved among other delegates, stopping here and there to talk. Deal making, Pilar thought. The model UN might deliver the answer she had tried to avoid in the real UN – that the US could explore for oil in Somalia with impunity. That was Brennan's approach.

Where was Josette?

The young man from the Horn of Africa continued, "Today we are not seeking help from this world congress. We are simply letting you know that we have signed a deal with the United States. They have generously offered to bear the cost of oil exploration and to share the profits with our people. They have also offered to bear the full cost of restoring order by sending in the American army. This will be different from the last time the Americans came to Somalia. This time they will be working *with* a local leader, not against one."

Brennan and his oil people send in the army, make Hassan the boss and then exploit the oil. It was the real story, Brennan's story, translated into a Model UN.

Pilar bent her head down and tried to calm her insides. This was terrible. The US was simply going to bypass the UN as it did in real life They were going to take over the country and install their puppet.

Stuart leaned toward her. "Share the profits? I'll bet. 80/20 or more likely 90/10. Where the hell is Josette?"

Pilar shook her head. "I don't know."

The model UN was changing rapidly into the real UN.

Pilar looked around the stage carefully and finally saw Josette just off stage on the left side with several students from the Chinese delegation. They were having an animated discussion. After a few minutes their spokesperson, a young woman, returned to her seat and asked to be recognized. When the Horn of Africa delegate sat down, she took the floor.

This representative of China was, appropriately, Asian. Most of the Chinese delegation were white students, political science majors, Pilar assumed. This short woman had fire in her eyes. "My name is Ying-Che. China does not agree. This is a matter that concerns all of us. America is, in effect, occupying Somalia. And just how much sharing of the wealth is the gentleman from the Horn of Africa talking about? What percentage? China believes the *United Nations* should provide the army to restore order. We believe the army should be made up of Arab and African soldiers. China approves the idea of a foreign country investing in oil exploration, but any oil discovered belongs to the Somali people and that should be reflected in the rate of return."

Pilar heard rustling on her left and one overloud whisper of 'boo.' On the opposite side of the stage the young man who had spoken to Yusuf, a US delegate, took the floor. "My name is John Kalensky."On her left several lights turned on. The media were primed to get their sound bite from Mr. Kalensky.

He continued, "Ying-Che has given us another fairy tale version of reality. Everything good and noble. Everyone happy. We in the US delegation wonder what's wrong with this world body? We offer to pay for everything, but China says 'No, the UN should pay.' This, despite children dying of malnutrition, despite millions of refugees waiting for decent housing, despite an AIDS crisis in Africa."

"Hold on there, cowboy," Ying-Che said. "You can't just do what you want, invade countries, put in your puppet government and then rape their oil."

"Easy with the loaded words, Asian super-woman," Kalensky replied.

Pilar had never heard the real UN get this combative, but it was there all the time, just buried under diplomatic language. In history only Nikita Khrushchev had upset the decorum of the UN by pounding on a table with his shoe.

"I move for censure of the United States," Ying-Che cried out. "They are breaking the UN Charter. Another example of their right-wing, Apache-Helicopter diplomacy."

"Second," shouted many Arab delegates.

"We'll see about this," John Kalensky said. "We're going to talk to several of our friends and remind them of US programs in their countries."

Pilar knew the real US would not announce it was calling in its IOUs, it would just do it.

The US delegates spread out and started talking to other countries. Pilar saw one go toward India, another to the European countries and a third toward Japan.

The media in the audience used the lobbying action to buzz about. A few reporters left the hall, she assumed to call their papers.

Stuart leaned over to her. "Not looking good. This is getting all screwed up."

Pilar gave him a hard look. It was like the actions of the young people were her fault.

The US delegate, John Kalensky, announced in a loud voice, "I'm happy to say that our friends from India have joined our cause as well as those in Japan. This puts our total at 24, already ahead of the single nation of China. We're building a coalition here, people. The bandwagon is rolling."

"Come on, Josie or Janie or whatever your name is," Stuart muttered.

"Go help her," Pilar responded.

Stuart looked as if she had presented a foolish idea. "Not me," he said.

There was more milling on the stage, delegates talking to delegates. How like the real UN, Pilar reflected – everything important going on in private.

John Kalensky spoke again, "Add to that Russia, Brazil, Pakistan, the Horn of Africa, and five delegates from Europe for a total of 38. We just need 52 to win, to defeat this motion of censure. Join us now before it's too late."

An older woman walked onto the stage. She wore a long dress with a big hat topped by a bird's nest. Pilar recognized the Granny she had seen before, the one who called herself Elizabeth Cady Stanton The woman grabbed the microphone from Cynthia at center stage. "The future belongs to you young people. I hope you will take a strong stand on global warming. The WTO is allowing big corporations to kill our planet. The UN, instead of standing up to these giants, goes right along with them."

In the front row of the auditorium ten more Grannies stood and began to sing a song about the environment to the tune of 'Three Blind Mice.'

While the campus police removed the woman from the microphone and the Grannies from the front row, Pilar noticed the Chinese delegation circling around Josette.

Ying-Che was tallying votes on a notepad and then she spoke out. "There are other bandwagons rolling in this hall," she said as she glanced over at Kalensky. "The Chinese delegation is proud to announce that the following countries have joined us in our censure motion of the United States..." she glanced at her notes ..." Indonesia, Nigeria, Bangladesh, The Congo, The Koreas, The Philippines, Thailand, Turkey and Vietnam, giving us a total of 35. We're well on our way to 52."

Slowly the totals built. Most of Africa joined the Chinese side. European countries and most of Latin America lined up with the US. The totals came to a tense 50-50 with three countries left. The delegate from southern Africa joined the US side, but this was countered by Venezuela joining the Chinese side. The final vote was left to a group of Pacific Island Nations, including Papua New Guinea, Fiji, and Micronesia.

Stuart spoke in an undertone to Pilar. "This is terrible. You should have never let this happen. A group of small countries being the final arbiter. I give you a perfectly good idea and you blow it."

Stuart got up, adjusted his natty bow tie and walked out of the auditorium. Pilar stared at him in amazement. What was his problem? Recently he had been full of negative comments, he always refused to help, he judged everyone harshly and he seemed upset with her. She had tried to seek his advice, consult him and honor his experience. But to no avail.

She sighed and directed her attention back to the stage. The Pacific Islands were about to vote and decide whether the US would be censured.

Kalensky, the US delegate, was speaking. "And so I offer a new proposal."

Pilar admired the young man's action – he knew he would lose the Island vote, so he got out before he suffered a defeat.

"I see this body prefers a UN army," he said. "Fine. However, the US generously offers to pay one-half the cost of that army up to ten million dollars in return for the privilege of exploring for oil and other minerals in Somalia. Of course, I'm sure everyone would agree to the overall commander being an American general."

Pilar knew ten million would pay for very little.

"What rate of return will the Somali people get?" Ying-Che asked immediately.

"We will be offering the Somali government a bountiful twenty-five percent of the value of all products found."

Ying-Che laughed out loud. "How generous. Twenty-five percent. The Saudis won't even talk to you for anything under fifty percent. Make it sixty-five percent and we'll talk."

"Forty percent," said Kalensky.

Ying-Che and the others caucused with Josette and then Ying-Che said, "In the spirit of compromise, we agree to a fifty-five percent share. The costs of exploration are great and the result is not guaranteed. And a payment by the Americans of twenty million to restore order to Somalia. The UN will cover the rest of this expense and will send its own troops. And somehow we'll survive without an American general."

Kalensky slapped his forehead. "That's a compromise?"

The president of the assembly, Cynthia, caucused with the Chinese delegation and then announced, "The Chinese are willing to modify the terms of their proposal, assuming the Americans will give fifty-three percent to the Somali people and will pay fifteen million toward the UN's military expenses."

"Take it or leave it," Ying-Che shouted. "Why don't we finish that censure vote?"

Kalensky shook his head in frustration. "All right," he muttered.

The various delegates defeated the motion of censure and endorsed the treaty between Somalia and the United States. Pilar was pleased with the result. While the young people might have been off on their percentages and their numbers, they showed that the US could get what it wanted without use of the undemocratic veto.

Pilar glanced to her left. Several of the reporters appeared moody and silent.

Cynthia called Pilar up for a final word. Pilar congratulated the young people, the political science department and the university. "Since the world began, adults have been questioning the younger generation coming after them. I have seen today that twenty years from now we will be in good hands."

When she finished, Alex came on stage and escorted her off to the side. "I want you out of here before anyone else departs," he said.

As she exited by a stage door, Alex said, "I forgot to tell you, Elizabeth Cady Stanton is a Republican chairwoman in Virginia. Her expenses are paid by the State Department. Her real name is Elizabeth Anderson."

"The Raging Granny?"

"Right."

"A paid protestor. What's this world coming to? Anyway, it was a success today."

"Right," Alex said, "and despite the planning to make it come out differently."

Alex opened the limo door for her and as he did, her phone in the limo rang. He answered it. "It's your lawyer from Vancouver."

She took the call. "Madame, you must come and settle your mother's affairs. Her apartment has been broken into again."

Chapter 24

Appointment Schedule for the Secretary-General
Thursday, February 1

The Secretary-General will be in Vancouver, Canada, to settle her mother's estate.

"Let me go in by myself, Alex," Pilar said as they stood in the misty fog at the back door of her mother's town house.

"Sure, after I check it," Alex responded. "Where are the mountains you're always telling me about?"

"Right behind you." Pilar swept her hand to the fog at their backs. "These condos are on the edge of the city. Beyond here, mountain wilderness – and ski trails. This is typical Vancouver weather for February, rain here, snow in the mountains."

"Just a second," Alex said. He spoke into his shoulder microphone and called another security man from the car. "Jim will stay with you while I check the apartment."

When Jim arrived, Alex entered the unit. Security, her whole life was security. A security man at the boarded-up front door of the condo, Jim here with her and Alex inside. Landing at Vancouver airport used to be a joy. She loved the artistry of the terminal and its celebration of native culture. But today? Security. Alex and the others checking all around, talking, making notes. As they went through customs, Alex chatted away about the aboriginal story of two sisters who were turned into the dual mountains above Vancouver as a permanent sign of peace. She knew the sign – danger. He had seen something.

Alex came out of her mother's condo a few minutes later. "I didn't sweep for bugs, so please don't use the phone. You can check, but the local police don't think anything was taken. They didn't find any prints."

She stepped through the door and into the kitchen. Alex's theory was that the apartment had been broken into so Yusuf and Brennan could look for something to use against her. But she knew that only memories rested here and no one could steal those.

The kitchen – neat, orderly, silverware, plates, cans and boxed supplies. The whole kitchen could go to the estate people. Her purpose today was to take anything she wanted before they disposed of all the contents.

But wait – on the wall by the phone, the family bulletin board. She took the items off one by one. Her university graduation picture with both mother and father, then her doctorate degree from Columbia with only her mother in the picture, a favorite recipe of her mother's, the notice of her dad's death, a dental appointment for her mother, scheduled for two days after her death. This last item Pilar held in her hand for a minute. How like her mother, organized, all her own teeth, never miss an appointment. What a pity that death could take everything away.

Pilar put everything in her purse and went into her mother's bedroom. There she found a closet full of retired-lady-professor clothes: dull jackets, blazers, slacks and dresses. Conservative shoes. Drawers of rich-looking, but conventional tops and sweaters. *Just like my closet*, Pilar recognized in a sudden flash. Safe, always safe. Of course no tutus or wild lingerie, but not even a cutting edge dress or skirt for an older woman.

On the dresser, a jewelry box. Most of the items would go to the estate, but Pilar took a UN pin she had sent her mother, that ubiquitous globe with the olive branches. Pilar suspected her mother only wore it when she was home.

At the bottom of the box were the chain Cuban earrings she had bought for her mother when she visited Cuba on a UN mission years before. They weren't her mother's style, but they were a memento of her father's native country. Though Pilar had never seen her wear the earrings, at least she hadn't thrown them out.

The bedroom furniture and the clothes could be sold or given to the Salvation Army.

The living room next – red cedar wherever she looked – the rocker by the window, the coffee table, the desk, knickknacks on the mantle. How her father loved wood. And yet he, too, had followed the family maxim and opted for the safe job in the accounting department of Lions Gate Hospital as opposed to starting his own yard-furniture company, no doubt influenced by her mother who was the stronger of the two. He kept saying, "When I retire, when I retire." But he died two months after his retirement.

She fingered her father's wood creations on the mantle – a beautiful wooden box and polished wooden candleholders.

She would keep all these things in storage for her retirement.

And the big picture above the fireplace, her father and his parents – her Cuban connection. That she would keep. Next the desk, a beautiful cedar desk, an unusual wood for indoor furniture. Someplace in there her mother kept the letters she had sent her over the years. Those she would keep. Where were they?

Pilar searched the drawers. Not there. She checked the closet in the living room and in the bedroom. No. She would report this to Alex.

But first to finish her inventory. She returned to the living room where the big picture window and the rocker drew her. She sat down, rocked and gazed out. There was nothing but mountain out this window, but today all she could see was fog and mist. On the coffee table next to the chair sat a treasured article from her childhood, a flat piece of red cedar with cutouts for inserts of stars, triangles, octagons, circles, squares and rectangles.

Scenes flashed through her mind. She and her father laughing as he tried to fit the triangle into the square cutout. Her mother impatiently putting the star in the star place.

She fingered the inserts and missed her parents.

Next Pilar picked up her mother's photo album and rested it on her lap. Photographs of her parents' wedding, of her as a baby, of their first apartment, of her going to school for the first time. Pictures of her father's Cuban parents and her mother's Anglo-Vancouver parents. And then a photo of her and her mother and father on a rocky beach. She didn't know who had taken the shot, but they all looked so happy. That was the summer her mother was studying archeology and exploring proof of the theory that Asian people had come by boat along the shores of North America. Her mother looked so alive. None of the tight-mouthed, stiff pictures of the lady professor.

Another shot of her and her father building a sandcastle. Her mother would dig around in caves while she and her father played at the water's edge. Or her mother would be talking to First Nations' people and listening to their stories of the Old Ones.

Another photograph of the three of them writing messages in the hard sand.

Pilar turned the page. Winter of the same year, cross-country skiing on Cypress Mountain. All having fun, all sparkling with life. This was before her mother opted for safety in the Department of Sociology, giving up her passionate quest for proof of migration routes and settling for routine sociology and a steady income.

No, her parents were wrong. Happiness did not lie in safety. Happiness lay in taking chances, in sharing the joys of discovery.

A puff of wind separated the fog and she saw the snow on top of the mountain. Cross-country skiing. That's what she needed. She could finish this inventory later. Were her skis still in the hall closet? She put the album aside and checked the closet. Yes, the skis were in the back. Old fashioned, but still functional. Alex and his two men could rent skis and they would all get some much-needed exercise.

She went out the back door and told him of her plan.

"It's not a good idea. What did you find missing?"

"My letters to my mother."

"What was in them?"

She shrugged her shoulders "You know, letters. Twenty-five years of letters. I guess they were trying to learn about me. It's upsetting. Those were personal letters, my mother's health, my health, my... relationships."

"You're right," Alex responded. "Trying to learn about you."

"Okay, but listen, Alex, let's go skiing. No one expects us to do that."

"True, it's unexpected. Let me talk to the others."

She made some notes for the lawyer and Alex was back a few minutes later. "We're against it. How about working out in a gym?"

"In a sweaty fitness room as compared to a winter wonderland? My mom and I used to go cross-country on Cypress Mountain all the time." Through the patchy fog, Pilar pointed to the snowy wonder world at the top of the mountain.

"It's not safe," Alex said.

Pilar gestured back to the house. "Alex, listen, this hasn't been easy, going over my mother's things. Let me honor her memory one more time this way."

"Well, I'm against it, but if you insist... But we have to stick together."

*   *   *

"I'm impressed," Alex said as he skied next to her on the green-signed, easy trails in the cross-country section of Cypress Mountain. "This is very beautiful. If I lived in Vancouver, I'd be here every day."

Pilar found the shoosh of their skis relaxing, like classical music on low volume. She loved the feeling of sliding along on the trail. Nordic skiing exercised almost every muscle in her body. The weather was a little too warm, but the trails were well groomed and it wasn't crowded. "It feels great," she said.

"Mountain hemlock," he said, pointing to a tree. "And those are yellow cypress. Lots of them. Guess that's why they call it Cypress Mountain."

She grew up here and had never made that connection. Leave it to Alex.

"When was the last time you were here?"

"Not last year. Not the year before... About five years ago."

Too busy. Last year she only spent two days with her mother at Christmas time. She was busy maneuvering herself into the Secretary-General slot. The year before...she couldn't even remember. Too busy, always too busy.

She and Alex stopped. One of the two security men fell. They helped him up and everyone had a good laugh.

It began to snow – heavy, wet crystals that Pilar loved to catch in her mouth.

They skied on until they reached First Lake and Hollyburn Lodge, a rustic snack shop with rough picnic tables inside. They took off their skis, went inside and ordered hot chocolate. Alex and Pilar sat at a table near the back, while the two security men sat by the door.

"We always came here when I was young," Pilar said as they sat at a rough picnic table, Alex across from her. "The in-crowd went to Whistler, but my mother liked it here."

Pilar relaxed. She hadn't felt this good in a long time. The exercise, the mountain air, the safety of Alex and his men. She watched the people coming in, ruddy cheeks, happy, excited, in love with winter and snow.

"What was in those letters?" Alex asked.

"They were just letters to my mother. All the things I was doing. My apartment in New York with Stuart. My first years at the UN in Geneva. Skiing in the Alps. And... well, personal feelings."

"They were taken to get a profile of you. Please, what feelings?"

"My negative feelings about Quan, and..." she pressed her lips tightly together "...this is difficult, Alex."

Alex waited.

"My feelings for Anatole. My mother always wanted me to marry, but you know – career."

Mentioning Anatole made Pilar remember him, how he performed the African ceremony of giving her a cup of water when she went into his house. She saw his face when he laughed, the scar crinkling up in a funny way.

"Somebody's got a good idea of who you are."

"I guess so." She sipped her hot chocolate. "We always used to joke that Mom would meet a handsome skier here at this lodge."

Alex frowned. "You mentioned this lodge in your letters?"

"Yes."

Alex began to size up every one in the lodge. "Let's go," he urged. Pilar felt his nervousness and got up. They all went outside and put their skis back on.

She started forward, beyond the lodge to the intermediate trail.

"Wait," Alex cautioned. "Let's go back."

"It's not long. I've done it before."

She started down the trail, Alex catching up to her, the two other men behind them.

Snow covered the upper branches of the trees and fresh snow fell on them. After the scarce vegetation of Somalia and the near desert of Burkina-Faso, this wet, snowy world filled her with awe.

"I'm reading a new book," Alex said, slightly out of breath trying to keep up with her. "The amazing story of how people formed the European Union in a few short years following World War II."

Alex was worried again.

"Tell me about it," she said.

"1940 – they're killing each other; 1991 – economic and political union – after centuries of fighting."

Pilar was about to respond, but they rounded a curve and a sharp downhill lay ahead. She bent her knees and swooshed down the hill, staying upright. On the way down the hill, her ski pole suddenly split in two. She still clutched the top half in her hand, but the bottom lay on the trail behind her. Something whizzed by her and part of a branch of a tree fluttered to the trail. Heavy snow on the branch plopped to the ground as well. Something else hissed past her and then Alex yelled, "Shots." He was right behind her now. "Fast," he shouted, "Next left. Green 17."

On Green trail #17 they were back on the beginner trails with more people. She skied as fast as she could, past a couple and their two children, past a small beginner class. "The parking lot," Alex told her in choppy breaths.

She felt her anger rise. Nowhere was safe from these assassins, not even this mountain, sacred to her and to her mother. How could they violate the winter beauty of this place by trying to spill blood on it?

The parking lot was already a few inches deep with new snow. When they reached the limo, they had to wait for the two security men who were new to cross country skiing.

Finally the two slogged into the parking lot. "Hurry. Let's go," Alex called.

"What about the skis?" one of them asked.

"Leave them," Alex replied.

He placed Pilar in the back seat and put a security man on either side of her. As he started the limo, he said, "This isn't the best car for mountain driving, but at least it's got snow tires."

They drove out of the parking lot and started down the mountain. "Slippery," Alex said. They drove around the first switchback, past a white SUV parked on the edge of the road. Alex slowed to manipulate the sharp, icy corner.

"We got trouble," Alex announced, his eyes on the rear-view mirror.

Pilar turned around. Roaring at them from behind was the white SUV, chains slapping against the fenders, the windshield obscured somehow so she couldn't see the driver.

"Let me tell you about that book, Madame," Alex said as he sped up.

"Now?"

"Yes. Get the license plate, somebody."

As they neared a wooden guardrail over a dizzying cliff, the SUV slammed into the back of the limo with a sickening crunch of metal. Pilar was pushed forward in her seat belt.

"Europe's story is amazing and a lesson for us," Alex said as he fought for control of the limo and struggled to keep from going over the edge.

"After the war, Western European countries united to fight Soviet Communism. No one country could stand up alone against the Soviet juggernaut, so they stuck together and got a sense of unity."

Alex sped up; so did the SUV, but Alex was able to put some distance between them. At the next switchback Alex spun 180 degrees on the slippery road and started back *up* the hill.

"No plates," the security man on Pilar's left said.

"But economics played a big part," Alex continued. "One of the provisions of the United States' Marshall Plan was that European countries had to work together to solve financial problems."

The SUV braked and waited. When Alex neared, the SUV crossed the centerline and smashed into the rear of their car, knocking both vehicles perpendicular to the road. The security man on Pilar's right punched in three numbers on his cell phone.

A car coming up the hill stopped and the driver got out and walked toward them, obviously trying to help. But Alex gunned the motor and spun around the man and started down the hill. "Western Europe developed a sense of unity by being in the middle between the two super powers. They worried that they would be the new battle ground."

Alex maneuvered the next switchback. Pilar saw the steep drop-offs ahead. She turned around – the SUV was right behind them and closing fast.

"After the war..." Alex glanced in the rear-view mirror and stepped on the gas. The limo fishtailed for a moment. "After the war," he continued, "everybody saw what nationalism..."

"Alex, get us out of here."

"Don't worry, Madame. Europeans saw that the world was smaller."

The limo made the next sharp switchback, the SUV almost on its bumper. Pilar knew that as they went lower, the snow would be rain and the pavement would just be wet.

Smash. Another jolt in the rear. The fenders locked and the limo was whiplashed toward the guard rail. Pilar's head shot forward, then back, then sideways. Alex slammed on the brakes and then accelerated to free them. More whiplash. "Multinationals operated across national boundaries," Alex talked on. "The economies of the countries were interdependent. When Germany sneezed, France caught cold."

Another switchback. Only a thin layer of wet snow lay on the road. Both cars raced forward, another curve ahead. "But the authors stress that no one factor alone…"

Alex swerved suddenly into the oncoming lane and jammed on the brakes. The SUV raced past and slammed on its brakes in the curve. It rolled over, through the guard rail and down the embankment.

"It was a really good book," Alex said.

Chapter 25

Appointment Schedule for the Secretary-General
Friday, February 23

The Secretary-General will be in UN headquarters working on administrative matters.

"Madame, I think you'll want to see this," Alex said as he stepped into Pilar's inner office on the 38th floor of the UN building. He held up a thin booklet. "It's something Asha started."

Pilar squinted across her office in the fading light of a February day. "What is it? Let's see."

Alex stepped across the room and handed her the booklet. She put the reports she was reading on an already high stack of papers. In the three weeks since her return from Vancouver she had tried to overcome a backlog of work, but new problems had arisen in the meantime. Argentina and Great Britain wanted her to set up a new Falklands/Malvinas committee, the Israelis and the Palestinians were shooting at each other again and Russia and the United States were confronting each other over oil rights in the Bering Sea.

The booklet, held together by a Duo-Tang, was entitled *Recent Corporate Interest in Somalia.* "It's all about what Brennan's friends are doing in Somalia," Alex said, still standing next to her desk.

"Sit down, Alex," Pilar said, pointing to the chair on the other side of her desk. "No," she said, getting up. "Let's sit over there." She pointed to the casual chairs around her coffee table.

She glanced at the booklet as she walked and Alex continued to explain. "Asha researched the companies. About ten of them, all friends of Brennan's. Through her contacts in the Somali community, she investigated who they had recently hired."

Pilar sat down and Alex sat opposite her. She looked at his face as he continued to explain. He had an open, honest look. Here was a man who told her the truth, a man she could trust. He was a good friend.

"Asha checked to see if they had hired a Somali expert or a geologist knowledgeable about the Horn of Africa. Of the ten companies owned by Brennan's friends, eight had hired Somali experts. Though most kept it quiet, one company set up a *Somali Division*."

Pilar shut the booklet and slapped it down on the coffee table. "My God, he's planning to move. Did Asha do all this?"

"I finished it for her," Alex said. "And it's not just oil." Alex picked up the booklet and opened it. "It's also uranium and iron ore, tin, gypsum, bauxite, copper, salt and natural gas."

Pilar shook her head. "I'll bet the CIA will be involved."

Alex gave a little laugh. "Never mind how, but that's where I got a lot of my information. But wait, Madame, this is more important..." He closed the booklet, put it on the table and handed her a single sheet. "This is a record of all the attempts on your life. The links to Yusuf are clear. But Brennan's the problem. You and I know he's directing Yusuf, but we have no way of proving it."

Again, that sincere look. She loved that look in a man. Was it, she wondered, because she had lived her life among diplomats? Diplomats gave a ten to the person who could dissemble the most.

"Madame?"

"Yes, Alex, right. It's Brennan."

"I've thought of a way, but it involves you – and it increases the risk to you."

Pilar laughed. "I'm already a total prisoner of your security. How could it get any worse? What's your idea?"

"The danger is very real, and there's another problem – my approach is the opposite of what Anatole advised you."

She shook the paper in her right hand. "Yusuf's trying to kill me."

Alex rubbed his forehead. "I don't want to put you in danger."

She reached across the coffee table with her left hand to touch him on the sleeve and reassure him. She stopped just short and marveled at herself for exposing her pinkie-less left hand. "Alex, tell me your idea."

He did. She thought about it for a minute and then agreed.

* * *

"Y'all come on in," Brennan said to Pilar in his waiting room, fifteen minutes after her appointment time. "Miss Wagner, you hold my calls."

Pilar stood up. "I'm sorry, Mr. Brennan, but there have been so many attempts on my life recently that my security guard..." she pointed to Alex, who stood up and extended his hand "... will have to accompany me. His name is Alex Richardson."

Brennan ignored the outstretched hand and looked at Alex as if he had just asked him for spare change. "It's very unusual. You're perfectly safe in my office."

Pilar thought of mentioning the presence of Yusuf at every attempt on her life and how she had seen Yusuf in this very office, but she decided on planting herself right where she was until Brennan agreed to Alex's presence.

"If it's them listening bugs you're worried about, my office is checked every morning."

Pilar didn't move.

"I'll call security and post a guard outside the door."

She stood still.

"Ah, come on, little lady, this is silly."

"If you'd been shot at and had cars almost run you off the road, you wouldn't speak so casually."

"Oh, all right. Let your security boy – man – come with you. I haven't got time for this."

Pilar followed Brennan into the office, imagining how Alex felt being referred to as *boy*.

Everyone sat down, Brennan behind his colossal desk, Pilar feeling small in the massive leather chair in front of the desk and Alex a foot or two to her right in another big chair.

"You sure have me on the run," Brennan said. "Just a few minutes ago I got an angry call from the mayor of New York. 'Why isn't this Consti-tu-tional Convention gonna be in New York?' And then he went on to worry that the new UN might move its headquarters. I tell you, little lady – oh, and the president called me in twice about this idea of yours."

She knew by his grimace that the meetings with the president had not been pleasant.

"Ambassador, I am the Secretary-General of the United Nations. Please don't call me *little lady*."

"Shucks, I *am* sorry. What can I do for you today?"

"I want the backing of the United States. We have a vast majority of countries supporting reform and we have four of the five veto holders. I want to give America a chance to further world peace."

He laughed out loud. "Ah, now, you want us to join the cattle drive toward the ruin of the United Nations. We like the thing just the way it is. The Yew-nited States of America is the leader and the rest of the world follows. You got it all wrong about who follows who."

Without warning, Alex stood up and touched the business card holder on the desk. Pilar had told him about it, a small metal figure of a cowboy twirling his lasso with horseshoes framing the statue. "If this isn't the finest card holder, I ever saw in my life," Alex said.

Brennan looked irritated, but slightly pleased.

"Mind if I take a card?" Alex asked.

"Sure, sure," Brennan responded, waving his hand.

Alex picked up the figure and examined it. "Mighty fine, Sir, mighty fine." He took a card and sat down.

"Where were we?" Brennan asked.

"I came in here today to give you this," Pilar said and handed him a copy of Asha's booklet. She waited while he glanced through it. His facial expression changed from boredom to worry to panic. "Oh, my God," he exclaimed on reading one page.

When he finished, he stared at Pilar, alarm showing in his eyes. "What are you going to do with this?"

Pilar shifted in her chair and pretended to yawn. "Give it to the press."

Brennan stood. "You can't do that. You'll destroy me. This looks like all my campaign contributors are getting ready to move into Somalia and explore for oil."

"Aren't they?"

"You know that's a false presentation of the facts, but it will take me weeks to clarify it and in the meantime the press will kill me."

Pilar stood. "Good luck, Mr. Brennan." She started for the door, Alex right behind her.

"Wait. We can talk. When are you going to release this? You have to give me a chance to respond. Little lady – Madame – wait."

But Pilar and Alex were gone.

* * *

Across the street from the American Consulate to the United Nations, in the front driveway of UN Headquarters, Alex and Pilar walked up to a gray van. The man inside handed Alex a tape. "Got him," the man said. "One minute after you left he called Yusuf and said, "The package has to be delivered. It's extremely urgent.""

"Come on," Alex said to Pilar, "I want to get you back in the building."

"Good work," Pilar said.

"Yes," Alex replied, "that cowboy card-holder had a big lasso and now he's got a big ear."

Chapter 26

Appointment Schedule for the Secretary-General
Monday, February 26

The Secretary-General will meet with the United States Secretary
of State, Mr. Bernard J. Holman in Washington, D.C.

Pilar did not go to the newspapers. Instead she asked for an
appointment with the US Secretary of State who said he could see
her in three days. During those three days Alex was at her side to
make sure that 'the package didn't get delivered,' to use Brennan's
euphemism.

At 10 AM on the morning of the third day Pilar and Alex waited
in the grand office of Bernard J. Holman, US Secretary of State, in
Washington, D.C.

Pilar introduced Alex and let him conduct the meeting.   Alex
handed the Secretary a briefing sheet and began to explain it.

"The first attempt on the Secretary-General's life was in Denver
on the 22nd of November of last year. A small black car drove over
the curb onto the sidewalk to hit her. When the car missed, the driver
backed up and tried again. The local police did not arrest anyone,
but they did find the abandoned car. On the front seat was the Denver
Post with Pilar's picture on the front page. The car was stolen. Their
investigation stopped there. I was told that *higher-ups* told them to
call it *a traffic accident with a stolen car.*

"I went further. Fingerprints on the picture were those of Pavel Wrigley, a small-time Denver hoodlum and former racecar driver. I found him in a local bar, but, of course, he wouldn't talk to me. However, a few hundred dollars to the bartender got me the name of the fence that Wrigley worked with.

"My men and I located the fence and…we *reasoned* with him to tell us the story. It seems Yusuf asked for a hot car and a driver, telling the fence he was with the CIA and it was a matter of national security. The fence got him the car and recommended Pavel Wrigley as the driver."

"How do you know it was Yusuf?" Holman asked.

"Because I showed him a picture of Yusuf and he said, 'That's the one.'"

Hearing the story again sent a shudder through Pilar. Fences, hot cars, contracts to kill, little black cars charging at her. This was the mean world of the streets. This was not the calm, ordinary life she had enjoyed at the UN for twenty-four years. Inside the UN building, it felt like a church. The architects had deliberately buried the sharp corners in darkness, provided generous space for human contact and placed art in key areas to bring forth the great dimensions of human life. She thought the reflective chapel a waste, because the whole building was a chapel.

Perhaps, she thought, *that's the trouble with the UN. It's too isolated from reality.*

Alex continued. "The second attempt happened in Burkina Faso in Ouagadougou, the capital, on New Year's Day of this year. While Madame Secretary was spared, her key aide, Asha, was killed.

"The local police caught the shooter and he talked – after awhile. He said a Somali man hired him. The shooter later changed his story after a visit from some unidentified persons and after a ten thousand dollar deposit to his account."

The Secretary of State interrupted Alex. "How do you know the Somali man was Yusuf?"

"Again, a picture. He said, 'That be the Somali man, he hired me.'"

Alex returned to his paper. "The third attempt was just three weeks ago in Vancouver, Canada. Mr. Secretary, this…this is very upsetting."

Pilar was surprised at Alex's expression. He seemed to be choking on his words. She had come to know that he was a very sophisticated person and very street-wise, despite his act of being a low-level ex-cop. From her conversations with him, she knew he had an almost childlike belief in America. He really was shaken by what had happened in Vancouver.

"Go ahead," the Secretary said.

"Madame Secretary's mother's condominium was broken into twice and her personal letters to her mother were stolen. Nothing else was taken.

"While skiing on a nearby mountain, Madame was shot at several times. Then on the road down the mountain, a white SUV pursued us, trying to drive us over the edge until the SUV itself rolled over and crashed. The RCMP discovered that the purchaser of the vehicle was – I find this hard to say – the United States Government. The operator was listed as Yusuf Ibrahim Abubakar.

"But the worst is yet to come. The driver of the SUV was killed in the accident. His name was Abdul Syed Laleka. After his death the RCMP showed me his bank account. He had deposited fifty thousand US the day before the attempt on Pilar's life. They also found Pilar's letters in his apartment. The RCMP had been watching Mr. Laleka very carefully because – I'm sorry to say this as an American, Mr. Secretary – but Mr. Laleka was a member of Al-Qaeda, the sworn enemy of America.

"What we have here is the CIA hiring a member of Al-Qaeda to kill the Secretary-General of the United Nations."

Alex paused and Pilar guessed he wanted the Secretary to absorb all this information. After a moment Alex nodded for her to pick up the story.

"Three days ago," Pilar began, "Alex and I went to Mr. Brennan with documentary proof – we have a copy for you – that his friends were ready to move into Somalia to exploit oil and other minerals. Immediately after we left the office, Mr. Brennan made a phone call to Yusuf. We have a recording here. You'll hear Mr. Brennan talking to me, me leaving, then a minute later – a phone call."

Alex put a small tape recorder on the desk and switched it on. Brennan's voice came on, tinny, but clearly Brennan. "Wait. We can talk. When are you going to release this? You have to give me a chance to respond. Little lady – Madame – wait."

A door closed and silence. Then a phone call, Brennan's voice again. "The package has to be delivered. It's extremely urgent."

Alex shut the tape recorder off. "If you check phone calls from the US mission to the UN, you will find a call at 10:57 AM to the CIA in Langley to the desk of Yusuf Ibrahim Abubakar."

Pilar handed a copy of the tape and a copy of Asha's booklet to Holman. "He ordered Yusuf to make sure that the package got delivered, in other words that I be killed."

"Yes, yes," Holman said and then grew silent. He gazed out the window, not even looking at them, but Pilar guessed he was weighing his response.

"What do you plan to do with this information?" he asked.

Pilar knew this was a moment of truth. She needed US support for the Constitutional Convention and here was an easy way to get it. All she needed to say was, "You go along with the Convention, and I throw this information away." That's what Alex wanted her to do. He had worked hard to put everything together. Anatole would tell her *not* to use it, to present her case in a positive light.

Holman interrupted her thoughts. "Well, let me tell you this – we've been upset by Mr. Brennan for some time. Frankly, Madame, we're absolutely opposed to what you want, but Brennan has failed in his mission."

"He had a mission?" Pilar snickered at her own sarcasm, but Secretary Holman didn't seem to enjoy it.

"His mission to represent United States interests at the UN. He will be retiring tomorrow from his post as US ambassador to the UN. He will say it's for personal reasons. The CIA will be told to reign in Mr. Yusuf Ibrahim Abubakar."

"He won't be charged?" Alex asked.

Holman ignored the question. "A new ambassador will be appointed, Madame. His name is …."

"Excuse me, Mr. Holman," Alex said, "you didn't answer my question. Will Yusuf be charged? This is a very important question for the Secretary-General. Her life is at stake."

A buzzer sounded on his desk and a polite voice said, "Your next appointment is here, Mr. Secretary."

Holman stood up and looked at his watch. "I'm sorry, I have very little time. The new ambassador is Peter Murphy."

"The former congressman?" Pilar asked.

"The same. He hosts a Texas talk show on AM radio now. He'll be giving that up."

Pilar had heard of him. Right-wing, vocal, anti-UN, obnoxious.

"Mr. Murphy will do the bidding of this office, Madame. He will do everything in his power to defeat your Constitutional Convention and of equal importance to us, he will be instructed to veto a second term for you. We are extremely disappointed with you and we are sorry we backed you in the first place. I hope you will not use the information you shared with me today, but if you do, we will deny it and argue with you about every fact. Further, we will bring charges that you put a wire tap on a government official without a court order. Charges against you both, you and Mr. Richardson."

He paused to strengthen his tie. "Further we will bring forth your record of failure at the UN, plus the lies and deceits you practiced to get to the top. Quan Mai Ngo, your deputy, has given us plenty of information. Good day, Madame."

Holman walked around his desk and motioned for Pilar and Alex to leave. Pilar stood while Alex remained seated. "What about Yusuf?" Alex asked again.

"Good day, Madame. Good day, Sir. Certainly there is no need to call security."

"Come on, Alex," Pilar said. Alex shrugged and followed her to the door, shaking his head.

Chapter 27

Appointment Schedule for the Secretary-General
Wednesday, February 28

10:00 AM –The Secretary-General will meet with her advisers.
The remainder of the day will be spent on administrative matters.

"Damn," Stuart said as he sat down in a leather chair in Pilar's office, "I did so want to see that greedy cowboy roped and branded."

Stuart was the first to arrive for the planning session Pilar had called.

"Yes, yes," Pilar replied, irritated that he was focused on revenge while she faced the problem of what to do about Murphy. "Brennan may be gone," Pilar continued, "but things haven't really changed. The current government is adamantly against us."

"Ah," Stuart said, "but midterm elections are this fall. The Democrats are behind you and they hope to pick up some seats."

"The timing's wrong, Stuart. We've called the Convention for the 24th of October, UN day. The election is early November."

"That doesn't mean it can't be a campaign issue."

Pilar lifted her water bottle and observed him. He looked the same, but he seemed way too buoyant. She had failed to bring the United States on board. Didn't he understand that? A few Democrats weren't going to make a difference. Where were his political instincts?

Alex and Josette came in and disrupted her thoughts. Stuart stood to greet them. "Nice job," he said to Josette. "The model UN thing. Leave it to the Swiss to do a good job."

This also was strange – Stuart giving compliments.

Josette took off her coat and so did Alex. Pilar watched Alex and noticed what he wore: a rumpled gabardine overcoat, an ill-fitting dark blue suit, a clean white shirt that set off his black features and a good quality light blue tie. She smiled to herself – that's what he *was*, a good quality tie, hidden in a rumpled overcoat. "Nice tie," she said.

"Got it at the Salvo," he replied.

"Alex. The Salvation Army?" She laughed out loud. "We have to pay you more." When everyone was seated, Pilar asked, "Who's for coffee?"

Josette said no, but Alex and Stuart accepted. As she poured coffee for Stuart, she noted he wore his usual mild deodorant. Alex, on the other hand, had a rough outdoor smell about him. No doubt he had walked to the UN and absorbed the gale that was coming from the ocean. His face showed the pinch of cold wind as well.

"Enjoy your walk?" she asked.

"Brisk, very brisk," he said.

She saw a colorful brochure on top of his usual beat-up notebook. "What's that?"

"Backpacking in the Canadian Rockies. I'm going as soon as we solve all the world's problems."

He handed her the brochure. A man and a woman hiking along a mountain trail, a brilliant glacier to their right. A couple sitting together on a log in front of a campfire, a mountain lake behind them. *Why have I worked all my life?* she asked herself as she gazed at the pictures. *What's the matter with me?*

She handed the booklet back to him. There was work to be done. Already the new US ambassador to the UN, Peter Murphy, had held a press conference and announced his total opposition to her Constitutional Convention. "We can't let countries that are jealous of our success take away American freedoms."

"Let's get to work," she said. "Stuart was talking about the upcoming mid-term elections. He felt that – "

"The more I think about it," Stuart interrupted, "the more I think we should do nothing. Absolutely nothing. Let the year roll on. Madame continues being Secretary-General. Then, come October, the convention starts and you can be damn sure the Americans will be there like every other nation, trying to make things come out their way."

"What if the American government puts pressure on small countries and they back out?" Josette asked. "I think Madame has to take this Murphy fellow on, debate him."

"Debate a Nazi demagogue like Murphy?" Stuart sneered. "Madame would lower herself."

"No," Josette countered, strong emphasis in her voice and passion in her eyes.

How competent and earnest she looked, Pilar thought. A tailored dark trouser suit, accented by a modest necklace, the young executive on her way up. Just as passionate as Asha had been.

"We can't let Murphy win," Josette continued. "We can't let his view predominate. The American people are smarter than that. Give them the facts and they'll make the right decisions."

"You're right," Pilar said.

"You should study American history," Stuart scoffed. "I mean about those right decisions."

"This debating idea," Alex said, "I just don't know. Murphy's status is increased if he's on the same platform as you. It implies you're equals. You're the Secretary-General. He's just an ambassador. And Murphy is a tough, experienced TV and radio showman. I'm not sure it's a good idea."

"I'm not afraid of him," Pilar said. "Josette is right – we have to get our ideas to the American people."

"Wait," Josette said, "I almost forgot. Good news, great news." She reached into her briefcase and handed Pilar an envelope. "Your friend from Chicago, William Cranfield. We needed more money for newspaper advertisements, so I called his office. I mean, he's already given half a billion. All of a sudden I was talking to the man himself. He asked me what I wanted and I said ten million dollars. He was silent for a minute, then he said, 'That woman...' he meant you ... 'is doing more for world peace than ten preachers and ten presidents. Ten million – no problem.'"

Pilar was about to sip her coffee, but she put it down. "That's wonderful news, Josette." She clapped her hands. "Good work."

"Nice going, Josette," Alex said.

Stuart didn't say anything this time. Pilar wondered why.

"And the other piece of good news – I think. Have any of you heard of the island of Gozo?"

Pilar smiled to herself. *I'll bet Alex has.*

"It's part of Malta," Alex answered. "In the Mediterranean. Nice place. Quiet. Many think it was the island Homer wrote about, the island where the nymph Calypso held Odysseus captive as her companion for seven years."

"Captive?" Josette asked.

"Actually, she promised him immortality if he stayed with her forever," Alex answered. "But Zeus came along and demanded his release. Anyway, I think he wanted to return home."

"So, so?" Stuart said. "What's this got to do with us? Greek gods? Nymphs? Who cares?"

"I do," Josette said. "The point is, they want to give us the whole island as UN Headquarters. They refer to the time the US denied a visa to Yassir Arafat to speak at the UN. And they note the opposition of the United States to our plans for reform. The whole island – it's nine miles long by four and a half miles wide – would become international territory."

"Hardly big enough for an airport," Stuart said.

"Interesting idea," Pilar added. "But let's stay focused for now. Josette, can you draft a personal thank you to Mr. Cranfield? Back to politics and the upcoming US mid-term elections Stuart and I were discussing before you two arrived."

"In my opinion," Alex said, "the trick is to get *both* parties to endorse the Constitutional Convention. Polling results show that Madame's efforts to communicate with the American public have been successful. Seventy-two percent support the Convention. Fifty-nine percent agree the veto isn't fair. We want to contact people in both parties to make this a non-issue."

"That's not a good idea," Stuart said. "The administration controls the Republican Party now and they won't like it."

"I don't agree," Alex said. Pilar enjoyed the way he could say that and make it sound like, "Lovely day, isn't it?"

"Well, I worked in the White House and I know," Stuart countered. "The administration controls the party. Butt in, contact Republicans, and you're dead for sure."

"The Republican Party represents an important segment of America," Alex said. "We owe it to them to present our views. Pilar, it's your call."

Pilar nodded her agreement. "I'll contact them."

"But," Alex said, "What about Yusuf? As far as we know, he's still on the loose. The current administration in Washington has said they're going to fight this to the death. Unfortunately, I think there are some in Washington who interpret that to mean Madame's death."

"Can you hire more security?" Josette asked.

"I will, but we still have to be careful," Alex responded

Josette shifted to the edge of her chair. "Assuming Alex can keep you safe, Madame, I hope you will continue to go to the people and present your views. This is what Anatole advised us. My staff will work very hard to set things up."

"Thank you, Josette. I intend to. I'll debate Mr. Murphy or at least challenge him to a debate." Pilar then turned to Stuart, "Stuart, we need the United States. America is the most powerful country on the earth right now, but, just to remind you, in order to call a Constitutional Convention, we need a UN resolution. The United States can veto that resolution."

"Yes, yes, of course, I knew that," Stuart said.

In the thirty years she had known him, this was the very first time he had ever made an error about something in the political arena. It was political science 101 – get both parties to endorse your idea, and it becomes a non-issue. And why would he be against her contacting the Republicans? Getting both parties on board was just good politics.

How very strange.

Chapter 28

Appointment Schedule for the Secretary-General
Thursday, May 17

The Secretary-General will debate the US ambassador to the
United Nations, Mr. Peter Murphy, on network television.

"This is the end of American freedom." Peter Murphy breathed
deeply of the studio air and stood tall, his big chest expanded. "This
is the end of the John Wayne country, the end of a land of heroes,
the end – I say *the end* – of the land of the free and the home of the
brave."

Pilar gazed forward into the blackness of the New York television
studio, the little red light on a camera aimed at her opponent. She
listened as he described the upcoming Constitutional Convention.
His voice resonated with rich tones. His eyes made love to the camera
and he spread his arms and leaned forward to embrace Mom and
Dad Citizen in front of their TV. How could she compete with such
a man? He had experience in Congress and on his own radio show.

Pilar glanced at him as he spoke. "The people going to St.
Petersburg have not been elected," he said. "They have been
appointed by some of the worst dictator countries in the world, like
Libya, Cuba, and China."

She had to admit he had TV presence. She had hired a TV coach for herself. "Loosen up," he kept telling her. "Get emotional, folksy, down-to-earth. People are tired of diplomats and politicians."

More helpful than the coach, however, was practicing with Alex. His calm eyes, his graying black hair, his gentle smile opposite her, feeding her question after tough question – that's what made her feel confident now.

Murphy gestured over to her. "Madame here has set up one of these typical UN conferences where small nations come to spout off. They get up and condemn the United States of America and then—" he paused, his eyes twinkled "—then they feel good. They don't really have any power, but God help us if they did."

Murphy gazed at the camera, his big Irish face shifting to a worried look. "Madame's new plan for the UN gives these small countries a bigger say, and you watch, they're gonna take away your freedoms. They'll tell you what kind of car you can drive by their air pollution rules; they'll tell you what jobs you can have by imposing import duties; they'll even tell you how many children to have and what to do with an unwanted pregnancy. The United States of America must veto the upcoming resolution to hold this convention."

That was his opening statement. Now hers. Pilar took a deep breath. Alex's words resonated in her ears, "Don't debate the guy. You're the Secretary-General of the United Nations. Put your case out there and trust in God, like Anatole would say."

She started to speak, her voice tentative. "In the Magic Kingdom of Walt Disney World, there's a wonderful boat ride called *It's A Small World*. Hundreds of international dolls sing and dance to the famous *It's A Small World* medley. Every time I go on that ride, it takes me days to get the song out of my head. *It's a small world after all; a small, small world.*"

While she didn't sing this last, she came close. This was Alex's idea, a subliminal message in music that the world had changed, gotten smaller and needed new structures to deal with it.

She knew her audience was with her now and she relaxed.

The Internet, instant news, world trade, travel, the spread of disease – she mentioned all the ways the world was getting smaller. "Nobody is taking away anything, she said. "We're just trying to set standards so everyone in the world can enjoy good things.

"Did the people of North Dakota, Colorado or Maine lose their freedoms by becoming part of the United States of America? No." Pilar paused dramatically and pointed over to Murphy. "Did the people of Ireland – Mr. Murphy's native country – lose their freedom when they joined the European Union? Just the opposite. They entered a new era of prosperity.

"Take one small example – water. One morning there's a knock on your door. Your neighbor stands at your doorstep. His lips are cracked from thirst. He holds out an empty glass. Would you give him a glass of water? Of course you would. Then how about this situation?" Pilar held up to the camera the picture of the Somali woman and her two children. "This woman is from Somalia. She needs clean water. Look how she tries to shield her children from the sun. Look at how lifeless the children are. Look at the despair in the woman's face. " Pilar paused again and took the picture down. "I'm sad to report that one of the children has already died. What if this woman stood at your doorstep? Yes, you would help her. And in today's world, she literally *does* stand at your doorstep."

Then it was Murphy's turn. "Madame doesn't talk about votes or vetoes or the principles the UN should be based on. She talks about one woman in Somalia whose warlord wasn't smart enough or tough enough to get her water. Madame has shown you that picture to play on your sympathy, knowing that Americans have always been generous to help and always will be. But she has yet to explain how taking the veto away will help the child that starves in Somalia."

"The veto– America's veto – stopped me from helping that child, Mr. Murphy. And warlords? I'm sure you believe in the rule of law. You don't want any country run by warlords, do you?"

The moderator, a network newscaster, interrupted. "Madame, I'm sorry, that was against the rules."

"Hrumph," Murphy continued, his face coloring with anger as if someone had just slapped him in the face. "The United States doesn't condone warlords. That's why we need a strong United States, to...to...keep the world safe."

Pilar jumped in again. "The world community needs a strong United States to be a *partner*. Not a – "

"Please, Madame," the moderator said. "Mr. Murphy has a minute more in his rebuttal and then you have three minutes for yours. After that – open discussion. That's what you both agreed on."

"As I was saying," Murphy continued, glancing at Pilar with an annoyed look, "the UN's been working fine for years, providing a forum for countries to meet and talk things over. It's been a safety valve on international tensions."

Murphy went on, filling his minute. "Your rebuttal, Madame?" the moderator asked.

Pilar held up the picture of the woman and her two children again. "Forum? Talk? Does this woman need talk? No, she needs decisions, she needs action, she needs water."

Pilar continued her rebuttal, using as her text the Latin phrase found on American money, *E Pluribus Unum, One Out of the Many.* "I propose nothing different for the UN. People from Louisiana can still enjoy Cajun food while people from Kentucky can take pleasure from their horses and their fine Kentucky bourbon. Yet it's one country. Nobody's taking away the things that people love. Koreans will still cook barbecue, while people from India will sprinkle lots of curry on their food.

"The wonderful thing about America is that all the states are equal. Everybody has the same rights. And the states help each other. If a tornado hits Kansas, other states come to the rescue. No state has the veto over any other state.

"It is for this reason that I have called for a Constitutional Convention. To revamp the UN. To make it fairer."

"Now we'll have open debate," the moderator said.

Murphy looked directly at the camera and threw his arms open wide. "What Madame proposes is the end of America."

"No, it's not, Mr. Murphy."

"Do you plan to deny the USA the veto?"

Alex had reminded her: "Only answer the questions you want to answer. Listen to politicians. They do it all the time. They repeat the reporter's question then wander off into an area they want to talk about."

She directed her response to the camera. "Mr. Murphy has raised an important question about the veto. My whole principle in rebuilding the United Nations is to base it on the American system. Other countries sometimes object to that, but I believe in the American system." Pilar paused to emphasize her words. "A representative body based on population – the US House of Representatives – and another body where each of the fifty states gets two seats. That's the US Senate. A strong executive and an independent judiciary. Where's the veto in that system? Can California veto what the other states want? Absolutely not. Why shouldn't we structure the UN the same way?"

Pilar watched Murphy pause and give the camera a shark-eating grin. *Here comes the surprise*, Pilar thought. "How come you're going to move UN Headquarters to a little island in the Mediterranean, the island of Gozo? That's going to hurt New York City."

Stuart. It all made sense now. Last week Josette told her that her rich Chicago supporter, William Cranfield, had called. "The government cancelled a big contract of mine," he reported. "And the IRS is giving me grief. I won't be able to help you for awhile."

Why had the government gone after Cranfield? She hadn't released a report on her funding yet. No one knew about that money except Alex, Josette and Stuart.

Why had Stuart talked to the government? A lonely, bitter man. Instead of anger, she felt sorry for him. But she should have seen it coming.

She swallowed her irritation with herself and gazed at the camera, instead of Murphy. "The country of Malta sent us a very generous offer to make the island of Gozo international territory for UN headquarters. I wrote back and thanked them and said I would refer the matter to the proper committees, but that I was opposed to the idea because of the expense of rebuilding and because of fifty plus years of generous hospitality by the City of New York. My letter is public record. I find it unfortunate that Mr. Murphy accuses me of things without checking the facts."

Back and forth they debated, Murphy accusing her, Pilar talking to the camera. Murphy said the US paid most of the bills of the UN; Pilar reminded him of how big their arrears were. "No taxation without representation – that's a founding principle of America," she reminded him. "But the reverse is also true – that there should be no representation without taxation."

The debate ranged over many issues, abortion and impoverished nations' attempts to control births, the designation of world historic sites and what that meant for local zoning, and the establishment of a mobile international police force to move into crisis situations.

The moderator called for closing statements, Murphy first

"The United States of America with its allies won World War II. We stopped communist aggression in Korea and in 1991 we defeated communism totally. We have made the world safe for democracy. Madame Secretary-General wants us to give up that successful system and go into a new UN where we are just one country among many. I urge you to support your government when we veto the resolution setting up this convention."

Pilar began her statement in a soft voice. "Mr. Murphy objected to my bringing up the situation of the Somali woman who lost a child to hunger and thirst. However, I think that's the whole essence of the UN. If this woman doesn't have clean water, then all this talk and all these fancy resolutions and programs are just so much paper. I'm sorry, Mr. Murphy, but the issue really *is* this one Somali woman.

"The structure of the UN no longer fits the reality. This is not 1944. The world is a very small place today and we're all in this together. We need institutions that everyone can have confidence in. If we don't have those institutions, those structures, we end up with war. The structure must fit the reality. That's why I have called a Constitutional Convention for October 24th and that's why I hope the United States will support the upcoming UN resolution ."

"America has many slogans. One of my favorites is the state motto of Kentucky. It tells us the situation in the world today. *United We Stand, Divided We Fall.*

"Thank you."

Chapter 29

Appointment Schedule for the Secretary-General
Friday, May 18

The Secretary General plans an early evening after a day of internal meetings.

What was that noise? Pilar awoke, sat up, and the *New York Times* plunged to the floor. When she fell asleep, she had been reading an article headlined: *Solid Performance by the Secretary-General.*

The noise – there it was again, in the back of the building. But the mansion was old and creaky and the night was windy. Besides, Alex was downstairs. He and his men had established two-man shifts.

She turned off her reading light and pulled the quilt over her. Was the *Times* right? It was too early to tell. In a few days the polls would indicate what the American people thought.

A door slammed down the hall. Maybe it was Alex. She got up and put one foot onto the cold wood floor of the hallway. She looked up and down. No one.

What was going on? She knew that often the door on the empty bedroom down the hall slammed when the window was open. But how did the window get open? It was three floors up.

She closed her door, locked it and turned on the light. There must be an explanation. Checking her front windows, she saw not one, but two NYC police cars, one at the entrance to her circled drive, the other at the exit.

Alex would explain it. She picked up the phone. Dead.

Oh, my God. Now what? Locked in her bedroom on the third floor, no phone. She reached into her robe on the chair for her cell phone, then remembered it was downstairs. Her eye caught the paper scattered on the floor by the chair. *Solid Performance by the Secretary-General.* Yes, right, so solid, so effective that now the CIA had put out an order on her.

What could she use as a weapon? The lamp? Against Yusuf and his automatic weapon? Hardly.

The doorknob turned, rattled. She struggled for breath. The closet? No, better to face the enemy than have him surprise her. A noise on the doorknob. Rattle. Rattle. *Snap.* The door flew open. Yusuf and a big man in a leather jacket, neither of them wearing masks, both armed.

No masks – clearly they intended to kill her.

An aggressive stance, that's what she would do. "Alex is downstairs."

"Yes, " Yusuf sneered, "with three of our men."

She had to play for time. "Why do you want to kill me?"

"You do not know the place of a woman." He spoke slowly, his words clipped and cold. "In Somalia we have a saying, "Naag waa guri ama god ha kaga jirto."

"What does that mean?"

"Your woman should be in the house or in the grave."

"Just because I've been a leader, you want to kill me?"

The big man stepped in front of Yusuf. "Fuck this shit. We've got a contract to kill you."

"From whom?"

"Who do you think? Stupid question. Shut up, bitch."

The police outside. Could she get their attention?

She talked around the big man. "Well, Yusuf, you've won. You had better close the curtains or the police outside will see the flash of your weapons."

Yusuf sneered and glanced at the curtains. This was her chance. On her bed stand – the little glass ball with a globe inside, the UN emblem at its base, the kind you shake and snow falls on the globe. She picked it up and threw it through the window with all her strength. While Yusuf's attention was on the window, she grabbed her robe and threw it at him. He dodged, but now she was almost to the door. A sharp crack filled the air. Pain seared her leg, but she slid through the door somehow.

To her right in the hall she saw Alex coming up the stairs. Blood covered his left arm. With a quick gesture he motioned for her to join him at the top of the stairs. She struggled toward the steps, pain soaring up her leg every time she put her foot down. She reached him.

"Stay behind me," he whispered. He reached behind himself and put his hand on her hip and then he started to back down the stairs quickly with her behind him. One step, two steps, three steps. A bullet sped by their faces and suddenly she felt a terrible pain in her right arm. She looked up and saw Yusuf and the big man in the hallway looking down, guns aimed at them. Alex pulled her down to a crouching position on the inside of the stairs, out of sight of the hallway upstairs. "Are you okay?" he asked softly.

"My leg, my arm – hurt like hell, but I think they're just flesh wounds."

"Wait here," he whispered. "I have a theory about the CIA."

"What?"

"Later."

He edged back up two stairs and fired. Alex's weapon made such a loud noise that her ears rang. Then she heard returning shots, one an explosion like the sound of Alex's weapon, the other a quiet thud when a bullet hit something. Another round of bullets, the loud report of Alex's weapon. Someone upstairs cried out. Alex had hit one of them.

He stepped back down to her and supported her down the third floor stairs. "The CIA always gets it wrong," he said.

Before she could ask what he meant, he helped her down the second floor steps to the main floor. He flattened himself against the wall near the steps and she imitated him. He inched forward until she saw a half dozen New York police in the big dining room cuffing three men. One handcuffed man complained that he was *CIA*.

Pilar heard sirens and then the screech of cars stopping outside. More police came in the front door and Alex motioned to them. "Take care of Madame," he ordered. To Pilar he whispered, "I'll be right back. It's me and Yusuf this time. The CIA – they never get it right."

"What do you mean?"

"Just a minute."

He raced up the stairs. There was silence for a short time, then Pilar heard more gunshots. Before long, Alex came down the stairs nudging Yusuf forward with the point of his gun. Blood spotted Yusuf's shirt and pants.

"This is going to make quite a story, Madame," Alex said. "I wonder what Mr. Yusuf will say when the prosecutor asks him who gave the orders."

"And your theory, Alex? What is it?"

Before he could answer, paramedics arrived and treated her wounds and Alex's. News media crowded around her as well. "We're taking you both to the hospital, Madame," a paramedic said.

"Wait," a TV newscaster said, "let's have a statement first."

"I'm grateful to my security man, Alex Richardson. He saved my life."

"Was it the CIA who tried to kill you?"

"I don't know. You'll have to ask the police. But if so, I'm sure they were rogue members. The United States Government does not approve of terrorist tactics."

A news woman looked at her askance, but most of the media nodded their heads.

The paramedics ended the media session and helped Pilar and Alex into one ambulance. Yusuf and the wounded invaders were transported in other ambulances.

On the way to the hospital, Pilar lay on one cot, Alex across the aisle from her on another. A paramedic sat on a chair at their feet.

Pilar said, "Now, Alex, your theory."

"What theory?"

"About the CIA."

"Oh, yeah. Their job is to gather intelligence. But they're too busy trying to kill people and trying to overthrow governments. They missed the fall of communism. They missed 9/11. And they've been so busy trying to kill you, they've missed the changing world. Nationalism is dying."

Pilar studied the ceiling of the ambulance, then closed her eyes and let the tension escape from her. She was tired, very tired. She wanted to sleep, but first she stretched her left hand out – missing pinkie or no – toward Alex. "Alex?"

"Yes?" It sounded like he was close to sleep as well.

"Alex?"

He looked over at her and took her hand.

"The CIA missed something else – my biggest strength."

"What's that?"

"You."

Chapter 30

Appointment Schedule for the Secretary-General
Tuesday, May 22

10:00 AM – Mr. Bernard J. Holman, the United States Secretary
of State

The next morning, Saturday morning, Pilar received a call from
the US Secretary of State, requesting an emergency meeting with
her.

"A meeting? I'm sorry, Secretary Holman, but I'm really
shaken," Pilar said.

"I understand."

She hesitated a moment. She was about to say, *Another plot to
kill me?* but thought better of it. "A meeting about what?" she asked
finally.

"You've read the papers? Seen the news?"

"Yes." She had indeed seen the headlines. *CIA BLAMED FOR
PLOT; SECRETARY-GENERAL SHOT TWICE, CIA Operatives
Arrested;* and *IMPEACH THE PRESIDENT, Congressman Richter
Calls For Hearings.*

"I think we're ready to settle some of these issues, Madame,"
Holman said. "Can we meet very soon? Tomorrow, Sunday, at ten,
my office in Washington?"

Again, the subtle arrogance. She should race down from New York to Washington and solve his PR problem quickly. "How about Tuesday at 10, Mr. Secretary, here in my office?"

"Can't we make it sooner?"

"I'm afraid not."

Holman agreed reluctantly.

On Tuesday morning, Pilar, her upper arm bandaged and a large dressing on her leg, greeted Secretary Holman into her office. She was surprised to see Ambassador Murphy walk in with him. "The UN's his area of concern," Holman apologized.

Pilar noticed the difference between the two of them as they settled into the leather chairs around her teak coffee table. Holman, the Secretary of State, smiled at her. She had never seen the man smile before. He was always a gentleman, but he never seemed to have time to smile at anybody. There was always something he wanted you to do or not do – there was no time for the personal. So why the smile? Nerves? It didn't seem natural.

Ambassador Murphy's appearance was just the opposite. He was *not* smiling and that, also, was reassuring. Normally the man wore a cynical smile which implied that he alone knew the truth in life and everyone else was a damn fool. She always had the impression that he was just waiting to pounce on some misguided liberal thinker and embarrass the hell out of them.

But not this morning. He looked positively sober and serious.

She served them coffee and sat down. "What can I do for you this morning, gentlemen?"

Holman spoke up. "Madame, as you are well aware, our government is in some trouble."

"Yes," she said. The papers were full of impeachment talk. A New York Times columnist had written a piece that morning entitled *Gangsters in Government.* Cautioning herself not to sound smug, she said, "What is it you want from me?"

"We'd like you to take the edge off the crisis, Madame," Holman said.

"How?"

"You know the United States provides twenty-five percent of the UN's budget."

"You didn't answer my question. How I can help you?"

"I will, Madame. But I want to remind you…" he raised his index finger as if to lecture her, but then scratched his chin "… how important stability is to your budget."

He glared at her and repeated the word, "Stability."

The message was clear – she'd heard it all her life. *Hang on to your job, look after the organization, stability is a paycheck every two weeks.*

No, no more of this, Pilar thought. She spoke up. "Stability?" Her eyes widened and she tapped the edge of her chair for emphasis. "Stability? That's the last thing the UN has gotten from the United States Government. Sometimes you pay your bills, sometimes you don't. Sometimes you work through the UN as in the first Gulf War, and the next time you don't, as when your President George W. Bush invaded Iraq without UN sanction. You'll have to give me a better reason to help you than *stability*."

Secretary Holman put his hand up as if to stop her. "I think we have an offer you're going to like."

"Yes?"

"With just three little conditions, we're going to change our stance and support your constitutional convention."

"That's interesting. What are the conditions?"

Holman turned to Murphy. "Tell her, Ambassador."

She smiled to herself. Holman had brought Murphy along to do the dirty work.

"Well, the first condition," Murphy began expansively, "is that you issue a statement saying you don't hold the government responsible."

Murphy gave her that old cynical smile and crossed his legs. He was enjoying himself. "You say that a few government employees went off the deep end and tried to kill you, but you don't blame the government. In fact, you get along very well with the current government."

Pilar looked sideways at Murphy. "And what do I say when the media asks me who gave the orders to *these few government employees*?"

"You mean Yusuf Ibrahim Abubakar?" Holman said, taking the lead back from Murphy. "Well, interesting thing about him. Turns out he was never released from the military. I didn't even know he was a US soldier. So he will be tried in a military court."

Pilar stared hard at Secretary Holman. "You're saying Yusuf and only Yusuf is responsible?"

"That's right."

"And correct me if I'm wrong, but recent military trials have been done in secret. Will that be the situation here?"

"Don't worry, Madame. You'll get justice. But there are two more conditions. Tell her, Ambassador."

Pilar noted Holman's attempt to smooth over her problems, but the questions still remained in her mind. And by calling on Murphy, she knew more *dirty work* lay ahead.

Ambassador Murphy sat up straight and the smile left his face. "Well, we just can't have a convention in St. Petersburg, when the UN headquarters is here in New York."

As soon as he finished, Pilar spoke up. "Any more discussion of site is totally unacceptable. The convention will be in St. Petersburg. Period."

A doubt occurred to her as she spoke. The veto. Were they willing to give it up? "I'm sorry, gentlemen. I should have asked. Of course by supporting the convention, I assume you're joining everyone else and eliminating the veto."

Holman looked shocked. "Madame, never. We would never give up our UN veto no matter what other countries did."

She laughed out loud, even though she knew that was not proper diplomatic etiquette. "Just for curiosity sake, Secretary Holman, what was the third condition?"

Holman looked to Murphy, but Murphy was silent. After a moment Holman said in a very low voice, "Let's settle this veto question first. We just won't be a part to any organization that we can't... that we don't have a mechanism of disagreement."

She stood up. "Gentlemen, you're wasting my time. Thank you for stopping by. Good day."

"Wait," Holman said, still sitting. "We'll hold the convention in St. Petersburg as you have arranged."

"Good day, Gentlemen," Pilar repeated, pointing to the door.

Holman stood, and Murphy got up as well. "Madame, be reasonable," Holman said. "We're making concessions. We're giving up on St. Petersburg. You have no idea what a big concession that is. New York City will be very upset."

"I appreciate that, gentlemen. But we're wasting our time here. The convention will proceed without you. Your government is not ready for a new order of things. Call me if you change your mind. Good day, now."

Murphy looked up at her with his cynical smile. "Playing hardball, aren't you, Madame?"

"And are you?" she responded, smiling sweetly.

"You have to meet us half way, Madame," Holman said.

"I think I have. I've campaigned in America for a new UN. I've explained it to people and a lot of Americans support my ideas. So I've made your political job a lot easier."

"We're talking about power here, Madame," Holman said.

"So am I. Perhaps we have a different idea of where power comes from."

Murphy looked exasperated. "This is going nowhere. Without the US and its money, the UN won't last a day."

Pilar started toward the door. "Perhaps, Mr. Murphy, perhaps. But we're going to try." She opened her office door.

"All right, all right, Madame," Holman said, gently closing the door. "Let's sit down again."

This time Pilar went to her desk and the two men sat in front of it.

"As I said earlier, Madame, our government is in a crisis and only you can help us. We'll make concessions on the veto if you'll issue a statement."

"Un huh," Pilar said, "and the third condition?"

Holman looked down at the floor and muttered to his colleague, "You handle this, Ambassador."

Murphy was not so diffident. "The third condition is that you withdraw your own name from consideration as Secretary-General of the new organization."

Pilar laughed again.

"It's not funny, Madame," Holman said. "These are the terms of our president. He feels that you have done your work by calling this convention, now others can bring it to fruition."

"No," Pilar said, "simply, no."

Nobody said anything for a long moment. Then Pilar stood and picked up the top newspaper from the stack on her desk. The headline read, *IMPEACH THE PRESIDENT.* She pointed to the paper and said, "You'll have to excuse me, gentlemen, I have a lot of reading to do."

Holman remained seated. "All right, all right, Madame. You'll be a candidate for the Secretary-General of the new organization. Now can we get a statement?"

"Certainly," Pilar said. "I'm not interested in the past. I want to build the future."

Holman stood, stepped around the desk and offered his hand. "Let's shake on it."

Pilar smiled and offered her hand. "Yes, we'll shake on it, then we'll have our lawyers draw up a formal agreement which we – and your president – will sign, with copies to the media. Then – and only then – I'll make a statement."

Holman shook her hand. "Yes, that's fine."

"And no country will have a veto, is that right Mr. Holman?"

He spoke quietly, "Yes."

"And anybody who wants to, can run for Secretary-General, correct?"

"Yes," he muttered.

Murphy stood to go. "I get the feeling you're against the United States, Madame."

"On the contrary, sir. What I really want is for the United States to be present in St. Petersburg this October in the same way you were present in San Francisco in 1945. I want the same idealism you showed then – I want you to show us the wonderful democratic institutions that have worked so well for you. I want the United States to be a big part of the future. As much as you need me to ease your governmental crisis, I need you to participate fully in the conference in October."

Chapter 31

Appointment Schedule for the Secretary-General
Wednesday, October 24

The Secretary-General will watch the election returns from her suite at the Nevskij Palace Hotel, St. Petersburg, Russia

UN day came, October 24. The Constitutional Convention opened and the first order of business was the election of a new Secretary-General. The steering committee felt that the Secretary-General, with an election behind him or her, could provide the strong leadership needed to make the convention work. But pundits said that the real issue was who would dominate this convention, the United States in the person of their candidate for Secretary-General, Quan Mai Ngo, assistant Secretary-General, or the world community in the person of Pilar Marti.

Pilar sat in front of a TV set in her suite in the Corinthia Nevskij Palace Hotel on St. Petersburg's famous Nevsky Prospekt Street. She put her head back on the gold brocade couch as she watched. She felt completely drained, like the woman who used to live next to her on Roosevelt Island, a single mom with two pre-schoolers and two neighbor's children to watch.

It had been a very tough race. Quan knew the UN and had a list of which countries might be upset with her. He claimed she would bankrupt the UN with her humanitarian projects. But the biggest factor in his success was the support of the US administration. There had been a sea change over the past months – China, who had previously backed Quan, now supported Pilar. And the US had switched from Pilar to Quan.

As Pilar contacted delegate after delegate, she kept hearing the words America had planted with the delegates: *grant, loan, military hardware, favored nation status, trade deal.*

And now the voting – not the old way, nomination by the General Assembly, selection by the Security Council. This was a new way with each state in the new General Assembly casting one vote.

Pilar folded her hands and put them in front of her mouth as if she were praying. Whatever happened, she felt, the process now was fair and she'd just have to leave the results to God.

> Afghanistan – 1 vote for Quan
> Albania – 1 vote for Pilar Marti

A knock on the door and Alex entered.

"Alex," she said, "come and watch with me." She patted the couch next to her.

"Where's Josette?"

"She's in the hotel ballroom, talking to the media and preparing a victory party."

Alex smiled. "I hope it's a victory."

She smiled, too. "Come on, Alex, sit down." If Josette were here, the younger woman would insist they prepare a speech or phone somebody or go over a position paper. With Alex, she could just relax and watch the election results.

He sat next to her on the couch. "I came to walk with you when you go downstairs," he said.

"Thanks."

> Benin – 1 for Pilar Marti
> Bhutan – 1 for Pilar Marti

That was 12 for her, 8 for Quan. The Bahamas was a surprise, voting for her, and Barbados was an equal surprise, going for Quan.

In this contest she faced the huge resources at Quan's command. All she could do was base her campaign on the strong leadership she had already provided to the UN.

"What are the odds on the street, Alex?"

"Even money."

She laughed. He had a wonderful way to make tense things easy. He placed a pack of literature he was carrying on the coffee table in front of them. She picked the top paper up. It was a handbill in Arabic. "What's this?" she asked.

"It says you're a lesbian."

She smiled. "I'm not."

He pointed to the TV which now displayed a list of countries and how they had voted. "They didn't believe the handbill in Algeria."

"There's Burkina Faso," she exclaimed.

"You knew Anatole would come through for you, didn't you, Madame?"

She turned and faced him. "Alex, do me a favor?"

"Certainly, Madame."

"Call me *Pilar*?"

He stared at the floor for a minute, then raised his head, turned to her, smiled and spoke easily. "Okay," he said. "Sometimes I do, sometimes I don't. I get mixed up."

She laughed. "Me, too."

Canada, Cape Verde, Central African Republic, Chad, Chile and China for her. Costa Rica, Côte d'Ivoire and Croatia for Quan. Cuba, Cyprus and the Czech Republic for her. By the time they reached Egypt there had been 51 votes, 30 for her and 21 for Quan.

She looked through the rest of the papers Alex had brought in. A brown envelope, a few more flyers, one from Anatole urging African countries to vote for her. Another leaflet in several languages, including English, urged support for her. The leaflet came from the people of Taiwan. She had taken a strong stand that Taiwan should be an independent country if they voted for that. Quan had opposed her, siding with China, but China had voted for her.

Sometimes politics made no sense.

The next item in Alex's packet was a section of a doctoral thesis from a student at Yale. *The Interplay of Forces in the New United Nations as Designed by Madame Secretary, Pilar Marti.*

She held up the paper and laughed. "Alex, you continue to amaze me."

He smiled back at her. "It's for when you win, the pressures you will face."

She touched his hand. "Thank you for your confidence in me."

Malawi – for Quan. The one hundredth state. The score, Quan 58 votes, Marti 42. How did that happen? The totals came up again. India and Indonesia had voted for her, populous states. Grenada, Iraq, Japan, Kuwait had voted for Quan. No real surprises.

What was she going to do if she lost? Certainly she would stay in St. Petersburg until a lot more things were settled. The election of the leader was the first – and really the only – thing that had been agreed on. Months of work lay ahead. Privately Canada had offered her the post of ambassador to the UN if she lost this contest.

And Alex? What would he do? The Canadian ambassador would not have the funds to hire a private security guard.

"What will you do if we lose, Alex?" she asked.

He pointed to the bottom brochure in the packet she was holding. She pulled it out. It was the same Rocky Mountain hiking brochure she had seen him reading months ago. The brochure was dog-eared now. Pictures of mountain lakes, a couple by a campfire, people hiking in beautiful mountain scenery.

Josette called on the phone. She was excited. "Russia will go with you, Madame. I just heard."

"Thank you, Josette. Keep up the good work."

She hung up. The numbers looked a little better now. Mexico, Nicaragua, Papua New Guinea for her. Niger and Norway for Quan. The Philippines for her. Qatar for Quan and the vote was 67 each.

She stood and walked to the window. Below her lay Nevsky Prospekt, the main street of Peter the Great's capital. Grand old architecture, a *big* scene in every way, six lanes of traffic and big impressive buildings. There was nothing small about Peter the Great.

Alex had loaned her a book about him. The man was a leader. He modernized the government of Russia, organized the first regular Russian army, and sent Russian students all over Europe for education. He brought artisans, craftspeople, technical advisers and intellectuals to Russia. During his reign Russia rose to great prominence. Even on his deathbed he started the Russian academy of scientists.

No matter what happened with this election, like Peter the Great, she had been a leader. That's all the UN needed, a leader, a person to take the nations of the world into the future. And it had all started with the picture of a woman who couldn't get water for her children. World leaders had to learn to cut through all the *it can't be done*'s and take action.

Pilar returned to the couch and sat next to Alex, who was intent on the election results. Somalia for her. She had developed a great plan for Somalia, but it had to wait for the time when it could be voted on fairly by the nations of the world and not vetoed by the self-interest of one ambassador.

South Africa, Spain for her and on down the list to Zambia for her and Zimbabwe for Quan.

The total? A dramatic pause by the chairman of the assembly and then the results: 107 for her and 84 for Quan.

Time stopped for a second. Then Alex turned to her. "We won."

"Yes, Alex, yes. We won," she replied and hugged him, full and strong.

Alex stood. "We should go downstairs now," he said.

She got up. "Yes," she agreed. "And Alex?"

"Yes?"

She picked up the mountain brochure and smiled. "Next summer make reservations for two, okay?"

He took the brochure from her. "I will."

She saw his mouth break into a gentle smile. "That would be great," he said.

"We *won*, Alex," she repeated.

"Alex pulled the brown envelope from his stack of papers. He opened it to reveal the picture of the Somali woman with the two children. "And she won, too, Madame."

End.

Other books by Ed Griffin

Prisoners of the Williwaw

Three hundred hardened convicts finish their sentences on an abandoned island where, accompanied by their families, they are set free to earn their own way.

Beyond the Vows

A young Catholic priest finds conflict and romance on his journey toward the light.

Available at
www.amazon.com
www.amazon.ca
http://www.trafford.com/

ISBN 142511439-3